The Shot
Copyright © 2018 Joseph W. Bebo
Published by Joseph W. Bebo
(An imprint of JWMBebo Books Publishing)

This is a work of fiction. Names, characters, businesses, places, events and incidents are either the products of the author's imagination or used in a fictitious manner. Any resemblance to actual persons, living or dead, or actual events is purely coincidental.

Joseph W. Bebo
PO Box 762
Hudson, MA, 01749
Email: joewbebobooks@gmail.com
Editor: James Oliveri
Interior and Cover Design: Elyse Zielinski

Library of Congress Cataloging in – Publication Data
Joseph W. Bebo
The Shot /Joseph Bebo – First Edition

ISBN:978-0-9982182-6-7

Historical Fiction

THE SHOT

Joseph W. Bebo

To my cousin, Pat, whose calm strength is an inspiration.

Author's Note

Sometimes great events are caused by small, insignificant acts, like a simple impulse, a coincidence here, a happenchance there. Liberty and freedom are high-sounding words, and rightly so, but sometimes they can spring from the unlikeliest of sources and the lowest of motives, like just plain spite. There are some things that even the best laid plan and most noble principles cannot control, and an unthinking action can sometimes reverberate around the world. It has been said that trivial things have led to wars. This is a story of such an event.

Prologue

Charles Street, Boston, May, 1818

Paul Revere lay in bed alone in his room. He had just seen his many sons and daughters and grandchildren, all come to bid him adieu. He had outlived his two wives, but luckily not his children. It was getting harder to shake off those chills and the drowsiness, more difficult to move his lungs in and out, but he had his good days. Today was one of them. Today he saw all the young people, those who would carry on his name and his memories. He had done and experienced many things in his eighty-three years.

He never got tired of telling his stories about the great war - riding for the militia defense league giving the alarm throughout the land; with the Continental Army during the siege of Boston; the terrible disaster at Penobscot later in the war. They all made good tales, but the story he had been thinking about the most, the story he yearned to recount, was the one that could never be told.

Chapter 1

Acton, Massachusetts, Spring, 1775

Fifteen year old Nathan Daniels had almost walked the whole five miles from his home to school, when he decided to stop and rest beneath the shade of a willow tree by the side of the river,. He was too upset to sit cooped up in a stuffy old school house. His mind was a jumble of conflicting ideas and contrary notions.

It was bad enough that he had such perplexing questions, questions no one could answer. Why had his mother died of fever so soon after he was born? Why was his father killed by Indians in the war a few years later? His grandmother, the only real mother he had ever known, died when we was eight. He hardly knew his older brother, who he looked up to with admiration. His aunt and uncle were raising him, but it was obvious they didn't love him. He didn't belong anywhere. He didn't even know who he was. Now all they talked about was war. Even his own family had become embroiled in the turmoil. As much as he tried to forget, he couldn't get the events of the previous night out of his mind.

His uncle had unexpectedly invited Nate's brother over for dinner. Like everything Jacob Daniels did, he had a purpose. He had heard rumors his brother's oldest boy had been keeping bad company. Even worse, he had been heard spreading dangerous and seditious propaganda. He was going to nip it in the bud and make sure the poison didn't spread to his youngest nephew, the one in his keeping. He couldn't have made a worse miscalculation.

John Daniels, Nathan's older brother by ten years, was in the village militia, which was the best trained and largest company in the colony. Their commander, Colonel Isaac Davis, a local gunsmith, drilled them constantly and made sure they had the best equipment, including the latest firearms, smartest uniforms, and bayonets. Davis was an ardent patriot like Nathan's brother, John, whose hero was the fiery Samuel Adams. Adams and his co-patriot, John Hancock, were not more than ten miles away in Lexington, a fact that caused their uncle, an ardent loyalist, no small concern.

"You have to watch what you do these days, John," advised his uncle. "People might misconstrue your actions. The time is over when anyone can flaunt the laws of the land with impunity."

"You mean the laws of a Parliament 3000 miles away that cares naught for the people of this colony. We didn't ask their leave to carve our lives out of the wilderness. We did it with our own blood and sweat. We owe them nothing. They should stay out of our lives. Do you think they have 1800 regulars in Boston to give them a holiday? I think not. They've come to invade our land and take away our liberties."

"Who, in God's name, have you been listening to, John?" asked his uncle. "These soldiers have come to defend us against a few discontented rabble-rousers, who would deprive *us* of our freedom. Why just the other day, a gang of them had the audacity to tell me that I could not take up my duties as a representative of the crown. I was forced to resign my position in the Mandamus Council. If they think might makes right, your precious patriots are going to learn a lesson."

"It is the British who will learn the lesson if they step outside of Boston. We will be ready for them this time, not like last month."

"I will have no talk of insurrection in my house!" shouted Jacob, standing up. Nathan sat in shock, a piece of half-chewed chicken in his mouth. His aunt tried to smooth things over.

"Please do not argue about politics at dinner," she pleaded. Her words fell on deaf ears.

"Why did you invite me here, Uncle, if you did not want me to speak?"

"I wanted to talk some sense into you, but I can see it is a waste of time. It is a good thing your father is not here to see you now."

"It is a good thing father is not here to see what a cowering toady his brother has become. I hope you are not spreading your Tory ideas to his son. Dad would have been a patriot, not a traitor to his people like you."

"How dare you!" yelled Jacob, standing again from where he had sat after his wife's admonition. "Get out of my house! I will not have you insult me and your aunt, and fill your brother's head with your folly. Your days are numbered, my young rebel, and I will not be able to help you. When the regulars come, and I assure you they will, you and your friends will pay the piper. Out! Get out of my house!"

Nate had never seen his uncle so mad before. He was sure Uncle Jacob was going to grab his sword, which hung on the wall near the hallway, but his brother rose and left the house before he had a chance. Nate's mouth was so dry he had trouble swallowing the still half-eaten piece of chicken. He took a long swig of milk and sat stone still while his uncle paced back and forth across the dining room venting his rage. The episode had a lot to do with his skipping school.

Nate didn't understand what the ruckus was about, or why his brother was so strident, carrying on about God Given Rights and Liberty. Everyone knew we were free. Everyone was his own boss. And who cares if a few people in Boston are arrested or shot if they don't obey the law? At least that's what his uncle would say. Nathan really didn't mind the redcoats, and would have actually liked to see them come marching up the road with their fifes and drums playing. Wouldn't that be a dandy thing, even if it would have driven his teacher, Rev. Smith, through the schoolhouse roof?

He laughed to himself silently at the thought as he dangled his bare feet in the river.

The sun poked through the intervening leaves to dapple the ground where he sat like a spotted blanket of green. The gurgling sound of the rushing water lulled him toward slumber, as the weight of his cares began to lift from him, and he soon drifted off into a drowsy half-sleep.

Suddenly, a harsh voice intruded on his dreams.

"Nathan skipped school. Nathan's a fool."

He opened his eyes to see his nemesis, Jedediah Weekes, taunting him. With him was Rebecca Adams, the prettiest girl in school. They were walking way too close. Jedediah's father was a friend of Nate's uncle, who was the constable of the village. Mr. Weekes had been a colonel in the last war, in the same company as his father, and still thought he could tell everyone what to do.

"I'm telling Reverend Smith you played hooky today, so don't lie and say you had to work. You're going to be in big trouble."

"I don't care. Go jump in the river."

"Why don't you blow away?"

Nathan stood up. Even though he was big for his age, the biggest boy in his class, he didn't know how to fight. In any case, he wasn't violent by nature. Still, his size and brawn would intimate most of the boys in his class. Not Jedediah, who was also big for his age and mean.

"I'm not bothering you. Leave me alone," said Nathan.

"Why don't you go whine to your mama? Oh, I forgot, Nathan doesn't have a mother, nor a father. Nathan's a bastard."

Nathan flared at the word, which made Becky exclaim and put her hand over her mouth in shock.

"I am not. I had a mother and father." He took a step closer to the other boy.

"Your father was shot in the back running away. Your father was a deserter."

"No he's not. Who said so?"

"Everyone knows it. He was shot in the back running away from the Indians."

"No he wasn't."

"Yes he was. And your brother is a rebel."

"He is not," Nathan replied, not liking the term.

"Yes he is, and he's going to hang when the British come."

"No, he's not," said Nathan, hurt and confused, tears welling in his eyes.

Spotting Nate's weakness, Weekes went for the kill. Calling him a cry baby, he punched Nate in the stomach with a hard right, hitting him square. Weekes expected Nate to crumple to the ground crying, but he had underestimated his opponent.

Momentarily stunned, his wind knocked out of him, Nathan stood still in shock. He'd never been hit like that before. It hurt, but even more was the indignation of being struck like that, for no reason, especially in front of Becky Adams, who he was kind of sweet on, though he never would have admitted it.

Without thinking, with no premeditation, he lashed out with his big right fist and hit the other boy square on the jaw. It was a totally reflexive reaction, but it couldn't have been delivered with more power and precision. The other boy went down like his knees had turned to mush, and lay on the ground still as a stone.

"You killed him!" cried Becky. "Why'd you have to hit him so hard?"

Nathan didn't answer, but took off down the road as fast as he could run for home. Before he got halfway to his house, however, he pulled up short.

What was he going to do now? It was bad enough he had skipped school again – the fifth time in as many weeks - now this. Had he killed Jedediah? Where could he go? He certainly couldn't go back home. His uncle was the sheriff and would put him in jail for sure. What if Weekes was only knocked out? Still, he would be in big trouble either way. He weighed his options. He had none.

He wandered in indecision like this in the general direction of his home, a few miles south of the village of Acton. The closer to supper time it became, the nearer he ventured home, until he was peeping out of the woods bordering his uncle's farm. He waited, not sure what to do. He wanted to run away, but he had nowhere to go, unless he could find his brother. In any case, he couldn't leave without his father's musket and some food.

It was growing dark. He hid in the woods near the house trying to decide what to do, when two riders rode up. The speed with which they were moving and the way they abruptly pulled up short of the farm's hitching post, boded ill. They ran to the house and knocked on the door loudly. Nathan could only imagine what they were saying. Soon his uncle was saddling his horse and riding off with them toward town.

Nathan slunk into the house after they were gone.

"Where you been?" asked his aunt when she saw him. "Did you not go to school today? What's all this about a fight?"

"I don't know what you're talking about. Who told you that? What did those men want?" said Nate, feigning innocence.

"They said you hurt that Weekes boy something awful. They had to wire his mouth shut. His jaw is broken."

"That has nothing to do with me. I'm hungry."

"There's some bread and milk, and a couple of pieces of bacon in the kitchen. You sit down and tell me what happened and I'll get it for you. You sure are in a lot of trouble. Jedediah wrote your name down when they asked him who did it. You weren't at school today, were you?"

"I didn't feel good after last night," said Nate. "What else did they say?"

"I don't know. I didn't hear all of it. It really wasn't my business to eavesdrop. It's your uncle's business. He's the sheriff."

Even if Jedediah couldn't talk, Rebecca Adams, who witnessed it, could. Nate wondered what she would tell them, especially if his uncle interrogated her.

"Jacob sure was upset when they mentioned your name," continued his aunt.

"Well, it wasn't me," lied Nathan, adding another sin to his list.

"Why didn't you tell me you weren't feeling well?"

"Because I didn't want you stay here with Uncle Jacob so mad."

"You should have told me. Then you wouldn't be in all this trouble."

"I felt bad after last night and was looking for John. I wanted to talk to him."

"You know what your uncle said. Stay away from John right now. You don't want to be around him when he and those troublemakers are brought to account."

"That's just it, Aunt Margaret, I want to be with him. I want to be just like John."

His aunt didn't know what to say, but prayed out loud that she might be delivered from these earthly calamities.

"Listen to your uncle," she pleaded finally. "He will know what to do."

"No, I can't stay here. I'm leaving."

He got up, grabbed some food and his father's musket, and headed for the door.

"Tell Uncle Jacob I'm not going to take the blame for something I didn't do."

"But where will you go?" asked his aunt as he left the house.

"I don't know," he yelled over his shoulder. "I just don't know."

Chapter 2

Nate ran out of the house and down the road. It was a warm, cloudless night, the almost full moon low in the sky. Not knowing where else to go, he followed the main track back toward town, the same one he walked to school on everyday, but never this late at night. As luck would have it, as he came around a bend, Nate ran into his uncle returning from his errand. He was on Nate before he had time to hide.

"So, there you are, you rascal," he scolded. "What have you been up to? I've told you what happens to idle hands when you skip school. Now look what you've done. Mister Weekes wants to press charges. You will have to pay restitution for the hurt you have done his boy. Where are you going?"

Before Nate was able to stammer out an answer, his uncle went on.

"I should take you into custody tonight. You hurt that boy very badly."

"He hit me first. He called Pa a coward. He had no call to do that. Then he hit me for no reason. I didn't do nothing."

"You broke the poor boy's jaw. They had to wire it shut. He won't be able to eat or talk for a month. His father is a very important man. He says you are a menace and should be in jail. I may not be able to help you in this matter. You've gotten yourself in a lot of trouble. Not only that, you are causing a lot of trouble for your aunt and I. After all we've done to try and help you when Ma died. This is the thanks we get."

"I never asked for your help. I can take care of myself. I don't need you."

"You will have to come with me. It's late, way beyond your bedtime. You can't run away from this. You will have to take your punishment like a man. Perhaps you can show you were only defending yourself. The young lady that was witness to the fight, a Miss Adams, may support your story, although she was reluctant to talk about it, which is no wonder. Still, if it is as you say, perhaps the judge will be lenient with you. In the meantime, I can't have you walking around the countryside carrying a gun."

13

"I told you I didn't do anything! Why is everyone bothering me?"

"Here, give me that gun."

"This is my pa's gun and you can't take it away."

"There are people out there who would shoot you for sure if they see you carrying a firearm. People consider you a menace to society. Do you know what that means, to be outside the law? Anyway, all you care about is that gun. It isn't natural. Give it to me. You have brought shame on your father's name. You don't deserve to have his gun. Give it to me and come home."

"No," yelled Nate, pulling the gun away as his uncle reached for it. Holding the musket close to his chest, Nate spun around and sprinted into the woods by the side of the road before his uncle had time react.

Mounting his horse, Jacob tried to follow, but was soon tangled in tree limbs and unable to see in the darkened woods. Returning to the highway, he headed to his home with haste.

"You can't run away from this!" he yelled as he rode away.

But that's exactly what Nate intended to do. He ran blindly through the trees. Would his uncle get a posse and hunt him down? Nathan didn't know. All he knew was that he had to get away. He needed a place to hide.

Staying in the woods for some time, he came to the road along the river, not far from the school house. That track led east all the way to Lexington and Boston beyond. That seemed like a good direction. He might even see some marching redcoats if he was lucky, and Boston seemed like a good place to disappear in.

As he approached the township of Acton, which the road crossed on its way to Concord, he noticed a commotion not far away near the South End Church. Several men had gathered on the green, which was unusual for this time of night. Nate wasn't sure, but it must have been around midnight. He approached carefully, keeping to the shadows until he could discover what was going on. He wondered if it was a posse out looking for him.

"They've spotted British officers along the road from Boston," said one of the men. "They say they are holding anyone they spot. They must be up to something. They're moving their troops into the country, I tell you. We'll be getting the alarm any time now."

"Ah, you've been saying that ever since the false alarm last month. We ain't heard a word yet, and we ain't going to."

"That may be, but Colonel Davis wants us ready."

"And ready we will be if the British come poking their heads around here."

At least they weren't looking for him, Nate decided, but if the militia was out maybe his brother, John, would be here as well.

"Excuse me," he said, moving out of the shadows to approach the two militiamen, who eyed him warily.

"Yes, what can we do for you?" asked one of the men. "You here to volunteer?"

Nate had seen him around, but the man didn't seem to recognize Nate.

"No," he replied. "I'm looking for my brother."

"You appear to be a stout lad," observed the man, giving Nate a closer look. "And who may your brother be?"

"John Daniels. He's a minuteman."

"John's over by the church," said the man, smiling.

Nate thanked him and soon found his brother talking to two other militiamen.

"What are you doing here?" his brother inquired on spying Nate.

"I came to see you. I wanted to talk to you after last night."

"What is this I hear about you beating up the Weekes boy? They say you hit him so hard you broke his jaw."

"You heard about that already? It only happened a few hours ago."

"It's all around town. You made quite a reputation for yourself beating up that Tory bastard's son. And good for you, I say. But you are in a heap of trouble. Old man Weekes is pressing charges. He wants you arrested."

"I know. I bumped into Uncle Jacob when I left the house. He told me. He wanted to take Pa's gun."

"That will be the day," said Nate's brother.

"That's what I told him. I'm running away."

"Where are you going to go?"

"I don't know, but as far away from there as I can get."

"What do you want me to do? We're being mustered out tonight. You cannot stay with me. I cannot take care of you."

"I'm not asking you to. I don't want nothing. I just have to get away from here, that's all. What's going on, anyway? Why are they calling out you minutemen? Did someone lose a minute?"

"This is not funny, Nathan, and neither is your running away. The British are on the move, we expect the alert any time. They're on their

15

way to Concord to get the powder and cannons we have hidden there, and to arrest Mister Adams and Mister Hancock, the head of the Committee of Safety. I would take you with me if I could, but that is not possible. In any case, it is not a good night to be wandering around, especially not alone. Why don't you just go home until things settle down? It's not a good time right now. I don't even know where I'll be in the morning. There may be fighting. I can't worry about you. I've got my own problems to think about."

"I don't know what you're all so riled up about. I'd kind of like to see the redcoats come marching up the road. That would be a grand sight."

"You better not let anyone around here hear you talk like that. Perhaps it is good that you get away from Uncle Jacob and his Tory ideas."

"I'm not a Tory."

"Well, you sure sound like one."

"I just don't see what all the fuss is about."

"You will see if the redcoats get hold of you. They don't like us colonials much. Look, if you're so intent on running away, at least take a blanket. Here, take this one, I've got an extra. I still say you should go home. No one would dare bother you, not after this night, not if I and my fellow patriots have anything to say about it."

"Thanks, John, but there's enough fighting going on. I don't want to be the cause of more of it."

"All right, suit yourself," his brother replied.

Even though he had much to do and many responsibilities, John was worried about his younger brother. This was not a time to be out and about without the company of a stout band of men, preferably patriots. Even as a boy, he had wished he'd been able to do more to help his little brother, but he never seemed to be in the position to do him much good, always one step from destruction himself.

He was already ten when Nathan was born, and the death of his mother in the process affected him strongly. Not long after that he was traipsing the mountains and woods of New England and New York with his father, as they joined with other colonists to fight the French and Indians. He had been with his father when he died, although he did not witness the actual event. But he saw his bayoneted and arrow-riddled body shortly after. The British had been on their side then. Now they were the enemy. He hoped Nate was all right, but focused on the job at hand. Nate had made his bed. He was on his own.

16

"Just stay clear of the British," Nate's brother advised him as he started out on his way. "They're headed for Concord."

Nate had no intention of going to Concord. His path would lead him across country in a southeasterly direction to the south of the town. Although his destination seemed far away, he had no doubt it was well within walking distance.

Boston was a city he had only heard of, like those distant places across the ocean that you read about in books, but it was only twenty or so miles away, just a short day's hike.

There was a surprising amount of traffic on the road for the late hour, mostly militiamen rushing to their musters, but few paid him any heed. When he did get stopped he just told them he was with Isaac Davis' Acton Company, and they let him go. Most of the time, however, as he walked in the wee hours of the morning, he was alone.

He relished the anonymity and solitude of the night, and wondered why he hadn't done this before now. Running away was the best idea he'd had in a long time. He knew the general direction he wanted to go. He had seen his uncle and others head off on their way east, to Concord and Lexington, and on to Cambridge. Boston was only a short distance beyond that. Passing a small settlement southwest of Concord, he walked along a country lane and across a field. Then he cut through an orchard, eastward toward the Concord Turnpike.

Crossing a couple streams, he lost his bearing momentarily, but was soon on his way again, finding the direction by the light of the moon. He hiked through wooded trails, and over stone fences, he passed farmsteads and hamlets, until finally he hit the turnpike, a few miles southeast of Concord. There, sitting on their horses in the middle of the road were two British officers. They had detained a couple of men, who were arguing with them about being held up.

"I demand that you let us go," said one of the men, also on horseback. "We have an appointment in Concord. You have no right to detain us."

"I am sorry, sir," said one of the British officers, a major. "You will have to wait until we receive orders that civilians are to be allowed through again."

"You have no right!" bellowed the man, who happened to be Paul Revere on his way to warn his compatriots the British were coming. Luckily, the officers on patrol didn't know who he was and soon let him go.

Nathan was less interested in the argument than he was by the sight of the two British officers resplendent in their bright red uniforms and gleaming swords, atop their white chargers. A few other British soldiers stood nearby carrying rifles with long bayonets.

After gawking at the soldiers for some time from the safety of the woods, Nate cautiously made his way across the highway further down the road, and along the fringe of the trees that bordered the road at this spot.

After awhile the woods opened up into a series of wide fields and gentle hills that led him east and away from the highway, which cut to the south. The broad meadows interspersed with trees and streams were beautiful in the half-light. The landscape looked enchanted, bathed in the reflection of a luminescent moon. The haunting stillness of the night made him half-wonder if he had actually dropped off to sleep. Taking a swig of water from his gourd, he fished in his sack for something to eat. Finding a corn biscuit his aunt had made for him, he munched on it while he rested on a stone fence.

The sky was still black in the eastern sky, dawn yet hours away. He had been walking at a good clip for about three hours. He wondered where he was.

He figured he'd walk another hour or so, then find a place to rest until daylight. He felt he had put enough distance between himself and any posse his uncle might put together. They certainly wouldn't expect him to come all this way, in this direction – wherever it was. Still, he planned to lay low until he got his bearings and made it to Boston. Then he'd be free from his uncle once and for all. He dismissed all the talk of people in the city being terrorized by the soldiers. Instead, he took his uncle's view that people were just exaggerating and being hysterical. His uncle had been in Boston during another such false alarm and swore everyone was getting on as normal. In any case, Nate wanted to see for himself.

After walking a few more miles he came upon a long, narrow field behind a cluster of buildings. Finding a spot beneath a tree next to a chest-high stone wall, he curled up under his brother's blanket and instantly fell asleep. Content to see what the morning would bring, he felt as free as a bird.

Chapter 3

Lexington Green, April 19, 1775

Nate woke with a start, momentarily forgetting where he was. Men were yelling. He couldn't tell what they were saying but it had awakened him from a deep sleep. He rubbed his eyes and sat up slowly, looking around for the source of the sound, but he could see no one in the field before him in the dim morning gloom. The yells got louder. They were coming from the other side of the wall he was crouched behind. It sounded like they were saying, "Huzzah! Huzzah!" But what could it mean?

Slowly, he raised his head, inch by inch, until his eyes were just peeking over the top of the wall, which came up to his chest. The scene before him almost made him fall down again.

There, standing not more than 100 yards away, were sixty redcoats with their muskets raised, their bayonets gleaming in the early morning light. Nate had never seen so many British soldiers in one place in his life. They were standing in three long, compact lines, staggered so that each line could fire clear and over the shoulders of the preceding one. Nate gulped and ducked down as quickly as he could, but couldn't resist another look. No one seemed to notice him, everyone too intent on what was taking place in front of them. Another group of men was gathered at the other end of the green dressed in homespun country clothes, a rather rag-tag, motley crew. They had muskets, too.

Nathan's attention was directed to the officer leading the regulars in the vanguard. Riding on a large black charger, he had the grandest uniform Nate had ever seen, with ribbons and medals and gold braid enough for three men. He seemed especially agitated and was yelling at the top of his voice.

"Stand down, you damned rebels! Disperse back to your shanties and let us pass! No more will you spit on His Majesty's laws with impunity!"

He had on a wide cocked hat, with a red ribbon and medal attached to it. It gleamed like a jewel in the new day sun, attracting Nathan's attention like a lure attracts a fish. Whatever the man was saying, he was being particularly obnoxious. At least Nate thought so.

The officer's rant was drowned out by the huzzahs of his men. They were like mad dogs. Well, thought Nate, he could be just as crazy as the lot of them.

He primed his musket, and without thinking, brought it up and eased it into position, resting on the top of the stone wall. The noise and commotion of the men was increasing, growing to a fever pitch. Those on the other side began to yell and taunt the regulars in return. No one noticed Nate on the sidelines behind the wall.

He sighted his target and squeezed the trigger. Ping, the officer's gaudy hat went flying off, as Nate's mini-ball hit the red medaled-ribbon.

Perhaps it was the lack of sleep and the strain of the past few hours, maybe an impulse born of his lonely, bitter childhood. It could be that he just wanted to shut everyone up. Who's to say, but he couldn't have imagined what would happen next. If he had, he never would have pulled the trigger.

Nate ducked back behind the wall before anyone saw him and got ready to flee, but before he could move, sixty muskets discharged in unison. He had never heard such a deafening barrage in his life.

Despite the peril, his curiosity drew him to the top of the wall. Peering over it, he saw the sixty British regulars unleash another volley into the still forming group of militiamen seventy-five feet away. Nothing seemed to happen at first, but a third devastating blast cut down a dozen minutemen right before Nate's eyes. Thick grey smoke obliterated the British line as more volleys thundered out accompanied by dozens of white flashes.

Nate ducked behind the wall again as if they were all shooting at him, although as far as he could tell, no one had seen him. Scurrying away on his hands and knees, he crawled along the length of the wall to a field of tall grass, leaving everything but his musket and pouch behind. From there he sprinted to a wooded hill. Then he ran for all he was worth along a series of trails and pathways until he had gone several miles. He had no idea in what direction he was going, only that he had to get as far away as possible from that horrible scene.

No matter how far he ran, however, he couldn't get the terrible images of men being shot down out of his mind. The screams and yells of the wounded and dying still rang in his ears. It was like something out of a nightmare, though he had never dreamt anything as terrible as this. He had heard stories about the Indian massacres in the last war,

20

still in progress when he was born, but had never imagined seeing anything like the slaughter he had just witnessed.

Running in a southwesterly direction, he made his way back in the direction he came, finding his bearings again just short of Lincoln. He stopped to have a drink of water from a bubbling stream and take stock of the situation. He now had second thoughts about going to Cambridge. After what he just witnessed, he only wanted to go home, though nothing but trouble awaited him there. He didn't know where he belonged. Suddenly, the world seemed a very dangerous place.

He wandered about in a confused state for some time, until he noticed groups of men rushing by in great haste. They all seemed to be headed northwest toward Concord, every one of them carrying a musket. They had stern, determined expressions. He stopped one of them to ask where he was going.

"To Concord," answered the man without stopping. "The British have fired on our men in Lexington. Now they're marching on Concord. This means war. It's an wanton attack, is what it is. They shot our men with no provocation."

Nathan wondered if what he did could be called provocation. Did that mean he started a war?

"It was only a joke," he said, but there was no one there to hear him.

Colonel Francis Smith's British Light-Infantry on Road to Concord

Charley McBride had been marching since early morning, long before daybreak. He had been mustered and ready even before that. Although he had his musket and gear, they carried little in the way of baggage or artillery. So far it had been one big fiasco. Everyone had told them the colonials would never fire upon British regulars. Well, that had been a lie. Now several of them lay dead in the field behind him as the troops marched west to their objective.

They had boarded boats earlier, brought along the Common, where the 700 man force was bivouacked, and rowed silently across the Charles River to Cambridge, where they formed up into companies. Charley was marching in one of the leading columns.

It all seemed unreal to the young infantryman. He pondered his fate as he marched. Who would have guessed that he'd end up here at the end of the earth? He had seen the maps. Only a few hundred miles to the west there was nothing but unknown wilderness, as wild and untamed as Eden itself. England hadn't been at war in over a decade, with no other conflict in sight, and then this nonsense with the colonials. He didn't see what all the fuss was about and certainly didn't think it was worth marching out of his comfortable tent for. Now this!

It had happened so suddenly. A couple of the officers, incensed at their ill-treatment at the hands of the provincials, led two companies forward at the double-quick toward a group of militiamen at the other end of the Common in the center of the village. Charley's company hung back near a small parsonage and belfry, which had been ringing shortly before they arrived. They had strict orders not to shoot first, to only fire if fired upon, but their muskets were primed and everyone was on edge. There were dozens of colonials arriving by the minute, streaming across the fields and over fences and creeks. The ones standing at the other end of the common were a surly bunch, just asking for trouble. Then a shot knocked the major's hat off, probably a miss aimed at his head. He was lucky. Another inch lower and he would have been killed. They had returned fire with a vengeance.

Private McBride joined in with glee. Why not? They had been taunted and spit on, ridiculed and maligned since they got to this godforsaken place. There were still some good people, like the folks who had been coming to Boston for protection from the troublemakers. Too bad they were the minority. Now look what had happened.

There was so much noise and confusion no one really knew what was happening. Suddenly, without an order being uttered, they were firing and reloading and firing again, at anyone standing in the field in front of them. There seemed to be a lot of them, some who were firing back. All the pent up anger of the last few months, of being cooped up in a foreign city surrounded by a hostile countryside, had burst out. Who did these provincials think they were, defying the law of the land, firing on British soldiers? Let this be a lesson to them. Charley had fired again and again, until an angry and desperate officer slapped him on the head with the broadside of his sword.

"Cease firing! Cease firing!" he heard the officer yell. "Stop your shooting!"

For a moment, Charlie and his mates had been totally out of control. Order was soon restored, however, as British discipline won out over blind, brute rage. By that time, almost twenty colonials lay dead and wounded on the Green. Luckily, only two of his comrades had been hurt. Now they were on the move again toward Concord.

Chapter 4

John Daniels, Acton Militia, Punkatasset Hill, Concord, MA

While Nate wandered the trails between Lincoln and Concord, his brother John watched the British below him from a wooded ridge as they searched the Barrett farm for cannons and powder. He would have liked to attack them then and there, but his commander, Captain Isaac Davis, ordered them to keep marching to join up with the other militiamen on Punkatasset Hill. Things were happening fast.

They had gotten the alarm that the British were on the move around 3:00 AM, after most of the men had disbanded and gone home. They mustered a few hours later at the captain's home in Acton. Now they were on their way to Concord with little idea of what awaited them. Stragglers had been joining them since they left at 7:00 AM, so that they now had almost forty men.

Not only were they the best equipped and best trained company in the local militia, everyone one of them had a sharp, new, gleaming bayonet. John, for one, thought that they were more than a match for the thirty or so British regulars rummaging around for arms and powder on Colonel Barrett's farm.

It looked like Mrs. B was doing a good job of distracting and misdirecting them, but it was still an affront to his sensibilities to see British soldiers pushing his neighbors around. A small fire had been started near the barn, but John's company marched on.

As they passed Brown's Tavern, their fife and drums started playing a jaunty, martial air. The men picked up their step as they marched along to the music.

Rumor was rampant that the British had fired on a number of patriots in Lexington. Several had been killed, who were doing nothing but standing on the Green. Now the murderers were in Concord.

More than 500 militiamen from all over the area had converged on the town, some from as far away as Chelmsford and Groton. Soon John's company joined them on top of a small, flat-topped hill overlooking the Concord River with a view of the bridge. They could see about 100 British regulars formed up on its western end.

While John's commander conferred with the leaders on the hill, John looked out at the valley below. Concord appeared to be burning.

"Well, Colonel," one of the officers in the circle of men exclaimed loudly. "Are you going to let the British burn the village?"

"We don't know what's going on," replied Colonel Barrett of Concord, the officer in charge. "We better find out their disposition and numbers before we go barging in there."

"We know damned well their numbers," said the other militiaman, a lieutenant that John did not know. But he agreed with his sentiment. "We've been watching them march here for the last two hours, after they've killed dozens of our citizens. There are 700 British regulars in the village and another 100 standing right in front of us. I say we march before they burn the whole town down. I'll lead the charge."

"So will I," said another.

"No, we will do it!" many more cried out.

They all stood and watched as the colonel decided what to do. The smoke from Concord grew thicker. Flames rose from what looked like a bonfire through their field-glasses. Finally, looking around at his army, Barrett came to a decision.

"All right," he announced. "We will march to the defense of the town, but I want Captain Davis's company to lead the attack. We will need their bayonets in the vanguard when we storm the bridge."

John thrilled at the order even while he swallowed down the bitter taste of fear. The hair on his arms stood up as if to protect him from the cold. The next thing he knew they were marching down the hill toward the bridge.

They lost sight of the rickety structure as they rounded a bend in the road, and came upon it suddenly as they marched up a rise. Now there were only a few dozen yards between them and the river. The opposing force had retreated to the other side and was forming up. A few of their men jumped a stone fence and fanned out along the grassy bank.

John and his company were moving fast now, bayonets lowered, their captain in the lead with his brother, Ezekiel by his side. They ran in columns of two as they stormed toward the bridge, heads down.

"What do you think they're going to do?" asked John's friend, Abner, who was running beside him.

"I don't know," answered John. "But they have no right coming here and causing trouble. Hopefully they will see the error of their ways and go back to England."

Two more of Davis's Acton men were marching ahead of them.

"John," one of them said, looking back. "We will not be able to fire while running in line like this. When the time comes, we will kneel, while you shoot over our shoulders."

"Do you think they will fire on us?" asked Abner with a nervous look. No one answered him as they came to the bridge.

"Hold your fire, men," they heard their captain order over the din, as if reading their minds. "We have a right to march through. Let them see the bayonets, boys. That will clear the way."

They followed him as he leapt upon the bridge.

Suddenly, a tremendous barrage exploded in front of them, filling the east end of the structure with smoke. Everyone stopped, not sure what had happened. Several hats were blown off. From behind him, John heard Colonel Barrett yell in outrage.

"They have fired on us, damn them! They have fired!"

The two men marching in front of John dropped to their knees and aimed their rifles at the bridge. John and his friend, Abner, stood behind them with their guns raised. The British unleashed a second volley. The sound of a hundred muskets going off at once almost deafened them.

A mini-ball hit his friend, Abner, square in the face, smashing it in with a devastating wound and taking off the back of his head. John hardly noticed as the mayhem and noise rose all around him. His attention was riveted in front of him, where a musket ball had torn through Isaac Davis's chest, gushing out in a ten foot torrent of blood that drenched John and his comrades. In the shock and confusion he never even noticed poor Abner fall to the ground beside him, his face mangled so he would be unrecognizable. Men screamed, some in pain, some in anger.

"Fire! Fire!" the colonel yelled through the din, but no one had to tell them what to do.

John shot into the smoke-filled mass on the other side of the bridge at a barely visible officer on a horse. The man fell backward and disappeared. Then he charged forward through the smoke with his bayonet pointed forward, yelling a war cry he had never heard uttered before. To his ears it sounded like the howl of a madman or a savage beast.

There was one more volley from the other side of the bridge. Then all resistance evaporated as the militiamen swarmed across the intervening space. It was over in a few desperate moments, and what little he remembered, John drove from his mind, a horrid, slashing and stabbing frenzy at phantom forms only vaguely seen through the smoke and dust and spurting blood. Anyone left on the other side wearing a red uniform was shot, bayoneted, or bludgeoned, sometimes all three. One unfortunate man had his head cleaved in with a tomahawk. In the heat of battle men became animals. No quarter was given. When the smoke cleared, the militiamen were standing victorious on the river bank. They had done something no volunteer army had ever done before. They had defeated a force of British regulars and sent them flying from the field.

Several were for pursuing the retreating soldiers, but others of sounder judgment showed more prudence. The men milled around waiting for orders. A few, like John, followed the retreating force taking potshots at them as they fled. They soon came back to report to the Colonel.

"They've joined up with their main force," said one of the returning men. "There must be seven or eight hundred of them. It doesn't look like they'll be coming back."

"Good," said Colonel Barrett. "There's been enough killing for one day." He looked at the body of Isaac Davis, who was being carried back across the bridge.

"I say there's a good deal of killing left to do," said the combative lieutenant from the hilltop. "We outnumber them two to one. We can surround them and cut them off."

"There may be an opportunity for that, but for now we have to consolidate our victory and reorganize our forces. We have to wait for orders from the committee."

There were murmurings of consent from some. Others disagreed.

"Now is the time to attack, while we have them wheeling," said a major from Concord, one of the officers who had been leading the charge on the bridge next to Isaac Davis.

"No," Barrett said after some thought. "You may take your men up to that ridge of hills across the road. There is a stone wall there that will make good cover. Watch the road. Make sure they do not return."

With that he led the rest of the men, with their fallen and wounded comrades, back across the bridge to their starting point. It was a somber march, and many were having second thoughts after the terrible carnage they had just experienced.

John followed the major across the road where about 200 of them lined up behind a stone wall that ran along a ridge of hills overlooking the road. As he took his position he noted that the retreating redcoats had met up with reinforcements coming from the town. They stood in nice straight lines while they decided what to do.

John had his gun primed and aimed, pointing at one of the officers not more than 250 yards away.

"No you don't!" said the major, standing right behind him. "Don't go starting something you can't finish, young man. No one fires unless I tell them to," he added to everyone within hearing. "Let's wait and see what they are going to do."

So John waited with his musket resting on the wall in front of him. He felt terribly thirsty.

"Hey, boys," he said, to a group of lads who had followed the army after their victory. "Why don't you go down to the river and get us some water. The major will give you some canteens."

"And boys," he yelled, as they skipped off to make themselves useful. "Make sure to get the water upriver from the bridge."

Colonel Francis Smith's British Light-Infantry on the Road from the Old North Bridge

Charley McBride had never been so humiliated in his life, not to mention scared. He stood on the road from the village of Concord with a cluster of British regulars, light infantry like himself, and heavily armed, large-boned grenadiers. They waited for their commander, Colonel Smith, to make up his mind what to do. Their scouts informed them that there could not be more than 200 of the enemy on the ridge in front of them, the rest having retreated back over the bridge.

God, these provincials were a strange lot. He had never seen anything like that bayonet charge, not even from the German Hessian companies, who could raise your hackles with their simulated attacks, but this was different – this was real. These men didn't stop even when you fired into them at pointblank range, which is what Charley did. But the tide of bayonets was overwhelming and they had to give way. Soon he was running for his life, expecting a bullet or fourteen inches of steel in his back at any second.

Now they were standing on a tree-lined country road counting the survivors, who were about half of the three companies they had started with. Charley couldn't believe it had happened.

After the noise of battle, the quiet of the morning was startling, as if all sound had ceased in the world. No one said a word. Not even a bird chirp was heard in the clear late morning air. He rued the day he had arrived in this cursed country. Finally, after ten more minutes, Smith ordered them back toward the village. They were returning to Boston.

The scenes leading up to the action, and the battle itself, kept replaying in Charlie's mind. It was funny how things could change so fast, one minute full of confidence, the next, filled with doubt.

After the feeble defense put up by the local militia at Lexington, he had felt invincible, marching with such a formidable force against farmers and tinkers. That began to change when his company, who were milling around on the western side of the bridge, watched the men gathered on the surrounding hilltops start to swarm toward them. Things deteriorated fast.

First there was a rather unorganized retreat over the bridge to form up on the opposite bank. To their surprise the colonials did not stop, but kept coming at the double-step. When their commander tried desperately to form a defense, it was so complex and unpracticed, it resulted in a disaster. The enemy was on them before they had time to deploy. Many of the men fired high or not at all. Those like Charlie, who knew what they were about, made the enemy pay, but they were in the minority this day.

Since that time, Captain Parsons and his men had returned from Barrett's farm, where they were unsuccessful in finding any powder or cannons. The whole reason for them being there had proven fruitless, all of it for naught. Not only that. The blood-curdling tales Parson's men brought back were enough to make a grown man's blood freeze.

"It is the worst thing I have ever seen," said one of them, who had joined Charlie on the road. They were now marching through the mostly deserted streets of Concord. "They are nothing but a pack of blood-thirsty savages. There is no excuse for what they have done."

"What, what has happened?" asked a man from Charlie's company who was walking beside him.

"They have scalped prisoners and helpless wounded, leaving them on the ground with their brains seeping out, their skulls cleaved by tomahawks. It is nothing like I have ever heard tell of, except in stories about the war against the French and Indians, where such atrocities were commonplace. Nay, this is worse, for these are Englishmen. These people are nothing but dirty savages. This means war! What did we march all the way out here for?" he asked of the men around him. Charlie looked up, afraid an officer would overhear the heated talk, but there were none around. Half of them had been killed or wounded in the skirmish.

"Look around you," the angry non-com continued. "We should have conquered this village, or at least burned it to the ground. Instead we put out the fires for them and run home like a dog with its tail between its legs. Not a building has been so much as charred. They will pay for this, I swear, they will pay."

"That may be," said Charlie, looking about him, "only not today." Militiamen from miles around were gathering on the hills around them. "Today we will be lucky if we make it back to Boston alive."

They marched on in total silence, no fife and drums marking the time to their footfalls.

About a mile from the village, along a particularly pleasant stretch of county road with woods and pastures dotting the many hillsides and valleys, they came to a bridge over a small brook. As their flanking parties moved back to the road to cross the bridge, a shot rang out, then another. In rapid succession, the shots increased to a barrage and moved rapidly up the line toward Charlie and his company. He ducked just as bullets began to ping off the dirt and rocks around him, and ran to the side of the road where there was a chest-high stone wall. Two men dropped to the ground dead not ten feet away from where he crouched.

The mini-balls came from all directions, left, right, but mostly from the rear. It was impossible to see the enemy, who must have been all around them, hiding behind trees and bushes, rocks and walls, firing out of houses and barns. All Charlie could see was the puffs of smoke from their muskets as they shot at him. Not knowing what else to do, he started running along the wall toward the bridge, keeping as low as possible. His nightmare had only begun.

Chapter 5

Road from Concord, Massachusetts

Nate was getting hungry and figured it must be around noon. He had taken some food with him when he left his uncle's farm, but had left his pouch by the wall after firing the shot. The shot! Why had he done it? What could he have been thinking?

He wandered alone through the countryside as if he was on his way to school, but school had been suspended. Their teacher, the Rev. Smith, had joined the men in Acton mourning the death of their captain, who lay on his kitchen table with a hole through his chest. Nathan knew none of this, but he knew a battle had been fought and men had died - a battle he had started. He couldn't shake off that thought, which made his other troubles, even having a posse after him, seem trivial.

He walked in the general direction he had seen all the other men moving, militiamen rushing to join their companies at the news the British were moving on Concord. Unlike them, he moved at a slow, leisurely pace. He wondered vaguely what was going on. Had there been more fighting? Then he heard the shots.

It sounded like a hundred guns were firing at once. To his surprise, the sound was repeated, and then again, a constant barrage that lasted several minutes. Then all was quiet. He stopped and listened and then moved off in that general direction.

He had walked a mile or two, when he heard the lone pop of a musket, and then another. To his amazement, the musket fire increased as more and more guns were added, until the volleys grew to a crescendo and continued unabated. Nate wondered what could be happening.

Picking up his pace, he jogged in the direction of the sounds of battle. As he grew closer, he moved with more caution. Peeking out from the woods on a small hill along the highway, still a quarter of a mile away, he could see a long line of men in red coats rapidly marching eastward on the road. Shots continued to echo off the hills, as militiamen on horseback and hiding along the trail fired at the retreating columns almost at will. Nathan instinctively moved toward the fighting.

Part of him wanted to join in. Part of him was abhorred, mortified by the thought that he might have started the whole thing. Why did he have to go and do something so stupid? Maybe his uncle had been right after all, and he was just a no good troublemaker. He sure felt like one, and yet it might be fun to shoot a redcoat. Although he had nothing against the British, he didn't like the way they were acting, especially when they shot everybody standing in front of them. They *wanted* to shoot Americans, he realized. They just used his harmless prank as an excuse. With that thought, he hefted his musket and headed toward the thickest of the shooting, where the British were bunched up as they filed through a narrow spot.

Coming over a ridge that gave on to a field of apple trees surrounded by a stone wall, he noticed that much of the shooting came from a farmhouse a short distance from the road where the regulars had to pass. He made his way in that direction, keeping low, using the walls and trees for cover, until he came to a wide field of high grass that sloped down from the orchard to the rear of the house. He crawled to the edge and peered out unseen.

He could hear the shouts of the men firing from the house. They yelled with glee when they saw one of their bullets hit its mark. There must have been four or five of them from the sound of it. Then Nate heard another sound, this one barely audible over the wind and other noises, but ominous just the same, like the swish, swish, swish of a broad sickle.

Suddenly, a line of redcoats rushed out of the trees that hid the road from view, and ran toward the house, their bayonets gleaming in the early afternoon sun. Nathan gulped in horror. He wanted to cry out a warning, but fortunately for him, he could utter nothing but a tiny squeak.

He watched in dismay as a dozen infantrymen rushed into the house shooting, clubbing, and stabbing. Then he heard the screams of the fellows who only moments ago had been yelling in triumph.

Nate turned to flee, but just then someone burst out of a window and ran screaming across the yard near where he hid in the deep grass. A British infantryman was right behind him brandishing his bayonet. The militiaman sprinted toward a well at the end of the yard, just a few feet away from Nate. Putting the well between him and his pursuer, he dodged and darted this way and that as the redcoat began stabbing at him. Nathan watched in horror when the man made a dash for it and the soldier jabbed him in the side. The long, steel bayonet went in all the way to the hilt. Nate buried his head in the ground when the soldier again stuck the man, who howled in pain, and began stabbing him over and over.

He hid there with his head buried, while the fighting raged around him. The sounds of battle were almost as bad as the sight. He prayed no one, not militiaman or redcoat, would spot him.

Slowly, the sounds of war moved away until all was quiet. He looked up to see two more bodies lying beside the unfortunate man he had just seen murdered.

"John!" he exclaimed, realizing that his brother might be among the dead or wounded. Becoming concerned for his brother, he followed the sounds of battle as it drew east, hiking down the road toward Lexington. He was stunned by the violence, shocked by the bloodshed. People were acting like beasts. All semblances of human decency and civility had disappeared. Was this all his doing?

He had to find his brother.

The fighting followed the columns of British regulars as they marched at the double-step toward Lexington. Nathan followed warily. He hadn't gone far when he heard a shout from behind him.

"Hey, you, where are you going? Who might ye be?"

Nathan turned in alarm, but relaxed when he saw it was a militiaman.

"No one, sir," he said. "I ain't going nowhere. I'm looking for my brother."

"And who might that be, lad?" asked the man, who appeared to be in charge of a group of fighters. He had a red ribbon tied around his arm.

"John Daniels," answered Nathan. "He's with Captain Isaac Davis's company from Acton."

"Ah, poor Isaac, such a brave man. It is a shame he has gone to meet his Maker, he and many other good men."

"John? Not John!" exclaimed Nathan in alarm. His brother was all the family he had left in the world after what had happened.

"No, do not worry. John is still with us and a very good man he is indeed, for he was right behind the intrepid Captain Davis and helped win the bridge. Their names will go down in history this day. So you are John Daniels' brother. I did not know he had another sibling his age."

"I am only fifteen," said Nathan, embarrassedly.

"Fifteen, why you look to be a young man of nineteen or twenty. You are a big lad, are you not?"

"I guess," stammered Nathan. "Is my brother nearby? Can you direct me to him?"

"We can do better than that, my boy. We can take you to him. My name is John Ford, of the Chelmsford militia, but you can call me 'Sergeant, sir'. Is that understood?"

"Yes, sir, Sergeant, sir," replied Nathan snapping to attention and looking straight ahead.

"Good, now that we've got that settled," said the sergeant, smiling slightly, "you can follow me."

"Yes, sir," answered Nate, saluting.

"Relax, boy," said Ford. "You're not in the militia yet. You will have to wait a few years. We will have to see what Sergeant Daniels wants to do with you."

As he led Nathan along the road to Lexington the sound of gunfire increased in the near distance.

"The British must have met Mister Parker and his company," observed the sergeant. "They are taking their revenge for what happened to them in Lexington this morning."

Nate cringed at the mention of the place, the scene of his unfortunate prank. He felt exposed, as if everyone could tell he had caused it all.

"You are a long way from home," said the sergeant as they walked. A few other men walked behind them with their rifles raised and alert. "You came all this way just to find your brother or did you come to fight? You have a rifle. Are you prepared to use it?"

"I don't know," replied Nathan, looking around him at the ground. There were bodies everywhere along the road, mostly redcoats, but patriots as well, dozens of them. He had never seen a dead person before, except when his grandmother had died. Now there were dead men lying all over the ground like they had been dropped from the sky. That was bad enough, but the condition of the bodies was even more disturbing.

Many had been mutilated, their faces bashed in by the butts of rifles. Some had dozens of stab wounds, as if a whole company had bayoneted them. There were some with parts of their bodies missing - ears, noses, fingers, hands - as if people had been collecting trophies.

He had never seen or heard of anything so atrocious in his young life, not even tales of the last war with the French and the Indians.

The sounds to the east and Lexington had increased to a storm of musket fire. Nate could only imagine what was happening there. They followed the trail as it bent to the left away from the road and up the side of a small rise, to a hill overlooking the town of Lexington. As they approached the top, he saw about 200 militiamen milling about. The sound of gunfire came from the Common below, where Parker's company was wreaking havoc on the retreating columns of British regulars, though little could be seen through the smoke of battle.

"Your brother is over there, by the edge of the clearing," announced the sergeant, who was intent on what was happening below. "Good luck, lad."

Nathan followed the man's gaze and spotted John among a number of other militiamen, near the edge of the woods where the trees fought to overtake the bare, rock-covered hilltop. There was a British officer on his knees in the middle of the group.

"You have told us nothing that we don't already know," he heard his brother say sharply as he leaned toward his prisoner. Then, without warning, Nate's brother kicked the kneeling captive in the chest, sending him sprawling backward. The men around him laughed.

Nate's mouth opened in shock. His brother had no call to do that. Nate looked at him questioningly and called out his name.

"John, John, it's me, Nathan," but his brother could not hear him through the shouts of the other men, who were yelling at the prone officer as they jabbed him with their bayonets.

Nate tried to make his way through the crowd that surrounded the scene. As he did, he heard the screams of the terrified redcoat. Finally, Nate made it to the front of the throng. One of the men - was it his brother – was stabbing his bayonet into the helpless prisoner, making him double over like a skewed worm. Soon others were doing the same, so that each one got a turn. It was revolting, but Nathan, in a state of shock, could not turn away even though he wanted to, due to the press of the crowd. At some point he passed out, for the next thing he knew he was looking up at Sergeant Ford.

"Are you all right, lad?" he asked, looking at Nate with concern. "Here, take a swig of this. You probably haven't had anything to drink all day."

"No," Nate moaned. "Yes, I mean, no, I haven't drunk nothing since this morning."

"You just take it easy. You have had quite a shock. The brutalities of war are not a pretty thing to see."

"Why, why did they do that?" Nate asked in confusion. "The redcoat wasn't doing nothing."

"War does strange things to men. There's no accounting for what a person will do in the heat of battle. It was the same in the last one. Our men are maddened by bloodlust and rage. They wish to inflict pain and death on the British for what they did this morning. Do you know that they fired on our men, men from this very town, men who were doing nothing more than their God given right to stand and breathe the air? They marched out here like tyrants to seize what is rightfully ours. They killed dozens of our people, our friends and neighbors, without any provocation."

There was that word again.

"What does provocation mean?" asked Nathan, wishing he had listened more to his teacher in school.

"Without provocation is when you do something to somebody for no reason, when they haven't done anything to you, like you said of that British officer. Those are the wages of war. They fired the first shot! They killed our people for no reason!"

The sergeant almost shouted these words he had become so incensed. Then he calmed himself.

"I alone must have killed half a dozen men today, and I take no pleasure in it. It is a terrible thing to kill a man, no matter what he has done. What you saw today resulted from poor training and lack of discipline. That will change now that we are in this for earnest, but in the meantime, when the blood of young men is hot with the passions of a life and death struggle, there will be no controlling it."

Nathan soon recovered and sat up, intent on talking to his brother. He wasn't so sure he wanted any part of the militia. Before he left the sergeant, he thanked him for his help. Then he asked him a strange question.

"What if they didn't fire the first shot?"

"What?" asked the sergeant, not quite understanding.

"What if it wasn't the British who fired first? What if someone else did?"

"What are you saying? Where did you hear that? That is preposterous. I have talked to Captain Parker personally, and to Mister Hancock. They were both there and swear that none of our men fired first. Half of them weren't even armed. Why do you ask such a silly question? It was the British. They started this."

He looked at the boy harshly, but Nate had already turned to seek his brother. Ford felt bad for him and hoped John would watch out for him, but had too many other things to worry about. So he went about his business, organizing his company and finding someone, anyone, in authority.

Chapter 6

Nate found his brother standing alone not far from the remains of his prisoner. He did his best to avoid looking at the mutilated corpse, but it was difficult to ignore. It seemed to fill his peripheral vision like a sliver in his eye.

"John," he said, in a shaking voice. "It's me, Nathan."

"What are you doing here?" his brother replied, looking at him sternly. "I thought I told you to go home. You don't belong here. Get out of here!"

"But John," he stammered. "I need to talk to you. I'm in a heap of trouble."

"I don't have time to worry about your problems. I told you everything will be all right. Don't worry about Uncle Jacob. He's being taken care of, now go home. Go on, get out of here!"

He said it with such force and with such hate in his eyes that Nathan staggered away as if slapped. He was dazed. Tears blinded his eyes.

Suddenly, a strong pair of arms grabbed him, just before he would have stumbled down a rock-strewn embankment.

"Hold it there," said Sergeant Ford. "Watch where you're going. You'll fall over that ledge. Here, you forgot this."

He stepped back and handed Nate his musket.

"You don't want to forget this, do you?" he said. "That's a nice piece, finer then some of the men have. Where did you get it?"

"It was my dad's. He fought in the war."

"Is that his name there?" asked the sergeant, pointing to a small metal tag on the stock."

"Yes, sir," said Nate, holding it up for inspection.

"So, you are Captain Nathaniel Daniels' boy."

"You knew my father?" asked Nate.

"No, not personally, but I fought in the war and know of him. He was a brave man and good leader, a war hero from what I hear. He would have been given a medal if not for British arrogance and personal jealousies."

"You seem to know a lot about him," observed Nathan, wishing he might have more time to talk to the older man.

"You should be proud of him. He would not condone what you saw here today, but don't judge your brother too harshly. He is new to all this and under a lot of pressure. He will sort it out. He's just not up to dealing with people right now. I think he's right, though. The best thing for you to do is go home and take care of your family."

"I don't have any family," said Nathan defiantly.

"You have a family name," replied the sergeant. "You have to live up to that. It's not safe to be out here. Your brother and I have a lot to deal with and can't be saddled with watching you. But I know how you can help us, if you want."

"Yes, sir, anything. What can I do?"

"Well, you can go home, gather up all the food and beverage you can muster, and bring it back to us here. It can't be much past two. You could go and be back by supper time. We'd all be much obliged. It would be doing us a great service and help your country."

"Yes, sir, Sergeant, sir," Nate said sprinting off. Finally, he had a purpose.

Cutting across country, he avoided the highway and its mutilated corpses, heading west toward Concord and his home beyond. He wanted to tell someone his terrible secret. If they knew it wasn't the other side's fault, that neither party had fired first, maybe everyone wouldn't be so mad at each other. But he was afraid of what they would do to him. He was already in enough trouble. After what he had seen, he didn't want either side to be mad at him. He just wanted to disappear. He held his mission in his mind like a shield to protect him from his own guilt and worry.

He had been walking at a good clip and had already reached the half-way point of his ten mile hike, but had not seen a soul. The farms were abandoned, the houses boarded up. Everyone had either fled or joined the militia, who now numbered over a thousand men, in their relentless attack on the British soldiers.

A half hour later, Nate reached his aunt and uncle's farm, and looked around cautiously. The place seemed deserted. His uncle's horse was not in the pen and the barn was empty. He peered in a window but saw no one. Going to the back door, he knocked quietly. The only sound was the clucking of the chickens, out of the coop and looking for their dinner. It was late in the afternoon. He would have to hurry if he was going to get back in time for supper.

"Aunt Margaret, are you here?" he called out, as he quietly opened the rear door to the house.

"Who is it?" he heard a frightened voice say from the hallway.

"It's me, Nathan. Where is everyone? Are you all right?"

"Oh, Nathaniel, it has been just terrible," she said, coming into the kitchen where he stood. "Your uncle had to flee for his life to Boston. They came for him this morning with ropes and pitchforks. I thought they were going to tar and feather him, or worse. He was able to get away on his horse. I am to follow as soon as I can, but there are so many things to do. I cannot go and leave everything. Oh, Nathaniel, what am I to do?"

"Don't worry, Aunt Margaret. I will help you. Are you all right for now? I have to do something. Then I will come back and take you and your things to Boston."

"Oh, don't leave me, Nathaniel. I am so afraid here alone. Everyone has gone mad. It's all so crazy."

"You don't know half of it, Aunt Margaret, but you are safe here. No one will bother you if you tell them you are with John and me. Now I have something to do."

"Why, why do you have to go? Why can't you stay here with me?"

"I've done something terrible, Aunt Margaret. I have to make up for it somehow."

"Oh, don't worry about Mister Weekes and his boy. They have gone to Boston, too."

"No, it's not that. I started it. I started the war," he blurted out finally able to hold it in no longer. He had to tell someone, confide in someone. His aunt was the only person he knew who would be safe with the knowledge.

"Oh, don't be silly, Nathan. How could you have started anything?"

"No, Aunt Margaret, it's true, I was there."

She was going to object again, sure her nephew must be exaggerating, but the look of anguish on his face made her hold her tongue.

"Last night when I ran away," he continued. "I walked all night. I was going to Boston, but only made it part way, near Lexington, and fell asleep behind a stone wall. When I woke up there were 100 British soldiers there on the Green. Some of our men were standing not far away at the other end of the field. They were all yelling at each other. I thought it was kind of funny. There was an officer on a black horse with a big hat that was really yelling loud and saying bad things, riding back and forth like he owned the place. I thought I'd knock a little stuffing out of the cocky bastard."

"Nathan!" his aunt said in shock. "Please don't talk like that. God knows we have done our best with you, but we can't be to blame for you not getting any proper upbringing. The Lord only knows your grandmother couldn't tame you."

"I'm sorry, but I'm a man now, and I will talk the way I want."

"Your uncle is a man, and he don't talk like that."

"Oh, yes he does. You should have heard him cuss me out last night. And I've got news for you. It was me who fired that first shot. I shot that hat right off that big-mouth British officer's head, like he was a contest at the fair."

"Nathaniel, what you are saying?" whispered his aunt, even more shocked at his latest revelation than his cussing. "Don't say things like that. People might hear you."

"Maybe they should. It might make things right again. People are mad because they think the other side fired first. If they knew the truth…"

"They'd be mad at you," his aunt finished for him. "There's no telling what people might do. You'd better not tell anyone, not even your brother. We'll take the secret with us to the grave."

That seemed a bit extreme to Nathan, but he agreed. It was probably better that no one knew.

A short time later, after promising to return to help his aunt, he was headed back to Concord laden with enough supplies for twenty men. He moved slowly, but deliberately, carrying the supplies on his back and in his strong arms like an oxen under an impossible load, his musket slung on his shoulder.

"What are you doing, Daniels?" a voice called out. He turned to see the closest thing he had to a friend, a school chum named Francis, who was a year older, and like him, had a distinct dislike of school, as well as a habit of getting into trouble.

"Hi, Francis. I'm bringing food to our men. They're fighting the British in Lexington. There's a real battle going on."

"I know, we've been trying to find them all day. That's why we're here in Concord. You should see all the dead soldiers. Three men from Acton were killed too. One of them was Mister Davis."

"I know. I heard. I was just with my brother, John. It was pretty bad." He didn't tell them what he had seen.

"You look like a pack-mule under all that stuff," laughed another boy, Ben, also from Acton. "Why don't you join us? We are bringing food to our fathers, who are fighting, too. You know where they are?"

"Sure, I'm going there now. Follow me."

Loading his burden onto a horse the other boys were leading, they started off down the road east to Lexington.

They soon saw the first of the mangled, dead bodies along the road from Concord. Some of the boys shook with fear at the sight. Some grew pale and looked about to get sick. A few went home. Nate had a mission to perform, so kept going and tried to block out the terrible vision, carrying his secret guilt with him like a chain around his neck.

"What's that?" said one of the boys, on hearing a loud boom. They were already scared and on edge. The loud sound made them jump.

"A cannon," answered Nate.

"I wonder whose?" asked his friend. "Do we have any cannons?"

Nate thought for a moment. He had seen a lot of soldiers on both sides, but had not seen any cannons. Since he didn't know, he thought it best to keep up a brave face so the rest of them wouldn't get scared and leave.

"It's probably one of ours," he said confidently. "I saw a lot of British on the road. None of them had cannons and they didn't get ours. So don't worry."

That seemed to reassure them. They continued on with some reluctance, but he could tell they were all frightened.

He thought it was funny that some got scared, and wondered why he didn't, at least not now. He had seen things he never thought he would see in a dozen lifetimes. He had seen what could happen to a person in battle, and yet he wasn't afraid. Maybe it was because he didn't have anyone to care about him.

A short time later, one of the boys, Ben, cried out in alarm on spotting a body by the side of the road. Nate was surprised, for they had passed several such sights, some much worse. What was it about this one that alarmed his friend so?

"Pa! Pa!" Ben cried. "That's my father!"

Jumping off the horse and running over to the body, which was crumpled by the side of the road, he turned it over carefully.

"Pa! What did they do to you?" Looking at Nate and the other boys, he cried, "They killed my pa!"

42

The boy turned back to his father's battered body, sobbing loudly. Nate held his shoulders and drew him away.

"Don't fret," he said. "We'll take care of him. Best you move on. There's nothing you can do here."

The boy tried to go back to his father, but Nate held him firmly.

"Take him on," he ordered Francis and the other boys. "I'll take care of his pa."

They moved on with the sobbing boy, while Nate went back to take care of the body, covering him with a blanket they had. Then he followed the group as they made their way east to Lexington. Nate hoped that none of the other boys' fathers, who had left early that morning when the alarm was sounded, had died today.

They soon came to the encampment where Sergeant Ford greeted them with surprise.

"You returned, my young friend. I wasn't sure you had it in you. We might have to enlist you after all. Yep, we just might have to sign you up. Can you shoot?"

Nathan was going to tell him about his shot that morning, but suddenly remembered what his aunt had told him and said nothing.

"Why so morose?" asked Ford, noting the youth's silence.

"We found one of the boys father on the road back there," Nate answered. "He was dead. He was shot up something terrible. He's by the side of the road under a big tree about a half mile back. I put a red blanket over him."

"That is too bad. I will have some of the men take him home so he can have a decent burial. I'm afraid many more good men will be buried today."

The other boys went to their fathers, who were all together with the rest of the Acton men, while the sergeant distributed the food and water. Nate found the boy whose father had been killed, sitting alone, and brought him something to eat.

"I ain't hungry," said Ben. "What am I going to tell my ma?"

"That your father died like a hero just like mine. We're sort of brothers now."

"What am I going to do?"

"The sergeant said they are going to bury your father with full military honors. You should be proud. Now you have to carry on. That's what he would have wanted."

Nate wasn't bothered when the boy began crying on his shoulder. He figured Ben needed a good bawl. He knew he did. Sergeant Ford came by a short time later with a detachment of men taking the boy's father back home. His friend went with them.

Nate needed to talk to his brother, John, and wandered the camp looking for him. The men mustered out and marched down the hill with fifes playing, off to continue the battle and let others rest. It was a sustained onslaught that had continued from the town of Concord all the way past Lexington, where they now were, a force of over 2000 men, and they were still coming. Nate's brother did not appear to be among them.

"What are you going to do now?" Sergeant Ford asked, before following his men east.

"I am not sure, Sergeant, sir," answered Nate.

"I was afraid our men would be dejected, scared, but they are happy and in high spirits," observed Ford, "eager to continue the glorious battle. We have the British on the run. The fun has only begun."

"I would like to find my brother," said Nate. "He was here earlier. Maybe he will be among those returning from battle. I should wait for him."

"I think he may have left and gone home, Nathan. Perhaps you should do the same. You look tired. You can come back in the morning with more supplies, if you have a mind."

"Maybe," Nate replied. "I still have something I must do."

Colonel Francis Smith's British Light-Infantry on Road from Lexington

It had been the worst few hours in Charley McBride's young life. From the bridge where he had first been fired on, to the deadly ambush at the last hill, he had been under almost constant musket fire. Out of ammo, out of food, and short on water, what had been an orderly if hasty retreat had become a full-fledged rout, as men threw down their arms and accouterments and ran for their lives. Charley, who barely had the strength to stand, stumbled after them, fearing for his life.

Suddenly, an officer on horseback reared up before him.

"Hold the line," he yelled. "March in order."

Charley ignored the order and darted around him as the officer repeated his exhortations to others in the ragged line. No one obeyed.

Then a miracle occurred.

At first Charlie thought his eyes were deceiving him, that he was seeing a mirage. A long line of British regulars stretched across the highway in front of him, and they had artillery. Thirteen hundred men from Percy's brigade had come out from Boston to reinforce Smith's beleaguered troops and guard their retreat. As he watched, they discharged a cannon that blew the corner of the meeting house apart, scattering the Yankee rebels hiding inside.

"We might make it out of this alive yet," Charlie muttered to the man running beside him, as more of the British artillery began to discharge their guns, blowing up more houses around the Green. Hobbling for all he was worth through the thin red line, he made for the rear.

"Form up men, form up," an officer was saying. "Keep the line moving."

This time Charlie and his comrades obeyed and began to march in order east toward the town of Menotomy.

Exhausted, drained, and drenched with sweat, Charlie hurried on as best he could, happy to be moving to the rear, toward Boston. Just when he thought he was safe behind Percy's reinforcements, however, he was peppered with shot from the front, as bad if not worse than what he had just escaped.

"Bloody hell!" yelled Charley, ducking behind yet another stone wall under a hail of bullets. "It's worse up here than it was back where we were." A musket balls whistled by his ear, as someone fired at him from another angle.

They were pinned down where they squatted.

"Where's all the shooting coming from?" Charley asked.

"It seems to be coming from all directions," his mate yelled back, "They're coming out of the woodwork. The whole colony is in an uproar. There must be thousands of them, and they all have muskets."

Crouching behind the wall, Charley tried to think things out while he caught his breath. He was so exhausted, hungry, and scared he could barely move. The impulse to curl in a ball and go to sleep was almost overpowering. Only the fear of being left behind and butchered made him get up and run along the cover of the wall.

Then to his relief, two of Percy's guns unleashed a barrage at the houses beside the road where militiamen were firing from, and cleared a swath through a swarm of rebels on horseback circling around them. Still the incessant musket fire went on.

Soon Charley and the rest of Smith's men were moving forward again, heading for home as best they could. Charley had dropped his musket miles back. He had no cartridges anyway, not one mini-ball to his name. He would have thrown rocks if he had the strength, but he was ready to give up and find a ditch to lie in.

"Boston didn't seem that far away this morning coming out," Charlie lamented. "Now it feels like a thousand miles away."

He was beginning to wonder if he would make it home alive.

Just then a cannon rumbled by pulled by a haggard mule. Without thinking, Charlie joined another man and hitched a ride. No one seemed to pay them any mind, each encompassed in his own misery, as they fled back to Boston.

Chapter 7

Nate was on his way back to Acton to help his aunt pack and move to Boston. It was getting late, but there was still some daylight left. Although it had been only fourteen hours since the fateful shot, it seemed like an eternity, so much had happened.

He thought he might go with his aunt into Boston, but now he was not so sure, not with his uncle there. He was walking past Concord, through the large pastures and common fields between that town and the village of Acton, when he spotted a lone figure on the road ahead of him. Nate stopped and called out.

"John! Hey, John! Hold up, it's Nate!"

The person did not appear to hear him and kept on up the hill. Nate took off across the meadow to cut him off.

"John! John!" he continued to yell as he sprinted after the figure.

The man stopped walking and turned to face him as Nate ran up.

"John, I wanted to talk to you."

His brother didn't answer, but stood looking at him with a stern expression. Finally, he spoke.

"You should not have seen that. You should not have seen what we did."

"It doesn't matter, John. I understand. I need to talk to you."

"I don't think Uncle Jacob or Mister Weekes will be bothering you now if that's what you're worried about. They have gone to Boston."

"I know. I saw Aunt Margaret. I was going back to help her pack and take her there."

"You're not going with them are you? You will not like Boston these days, I'll wager."

"Why aren't you fighting with the others?" Nate asked, noticing his brother didn't have his gun. "Where's your piece?"

"I've done enough killing today to last me a lifetime," answered his brother. "I never want to shoot another man as long as I live."

"What about the war? I thought you wanted to get rid of the redcoats. They don't belong here is what you said. I thought you hated them."

"Freedom and liberty are one thing, but what I saw and did today is another matter. I never imagined myself or my friends capable of doing such things. I saw a man scalped and was glad."

His eyes seemed to glaze over with a faraway look. He started laughing in a strange way that made Nate nervous.

"John, I have to tell you something. It's very important."

"What can be so important after today, when so many died? I killed so many people, oh my God."

"John, listen to me!" He grabbed his older brother by the shoulders and shook him. His brother seemed to look at him for the first time."

"Yes, Nate, I'm sorry, what is it? What do you want to say?"

"It's just that last night, while I was running away, I stopped to rest for a short time beneath a tree behind a stone wall. When I woke up this morning there was a commotion. It was on the Green in Lexington. There were a bunch of redcoats all yelling and an officer on a horse. Our men were standing a short ways away, just milling around, you know. But it was funny 'cause it was kind of early in the morning for a meeting."

"You were at Lexington this morning?" his brother said, focusing more intently on what he was saying. "You saw what happened?"

"Yes, I saw everything."

"How did it start?"

Nathan didn't answer, but hung his head then looked away.

"Well, tell me, what happened?" his brother demanded.

"There was this major or something, on a big black horse, a real blow-hard, all huffed-up and prancing about yelling. He had on a big fancy hat with a ribbon on it, the kind we would have knocked off someone's head just for laughs, a real dandy. I had my musket, so I shot it."

"Shot what? What did you shoot?" his brother asked, as the import of Nathan's words hit him.

"His hat. I shot his hat off."

John stared at his brother as if he had turned into a wolf.

"You shot the British officer's hat off?"

"Yes," said Nate sheepishly. "He was such a big blow-hard. I thought I'd shut him up."

"Then what happened?"

Nate gulped and shook his head, finding the reliving of it in the telling almost as bad as the real thing.

"Oh, John, it was terrible. Those redcoats let loose such a volley as I've never seen or heard tell about. They kept firing, dozens of times, just mowing down our people."

John stood there in shock, shaking his head as if he didn't believe it. But why would his brother lie about a thing like that?

"You're not making this up, are you? Because if you are…"

"No, John, it is the God's honest truth. That's why I wanted to talk to you so bad. What should I do?"

"Don't tell anyone. Don't tell a living soul. Oh, my God. Do you know what you've done?"

"Yes, you don't have to get all riled up about it. I've already told Aunt Margaret. Do you think she will tell Uncle Jacob?"

"If she does, you must deny it. Say you were just joking, trying to scare her for being mean to you."

"Aunt Margaret has not been mean to me," insisted Nate.

"It doesn't matter!" yelled his brother. "Just deny it and don't tell anyone else. They would hang you if they knew."

"Who, who would hang me?"

"Everyone!"

Talking to his brother had not made Nate feel better as he thought it would, just the opposite. John's reaction to the news made him feel even worse, as if all his fears about it had come true.

"What am I going to do?" he cried in anguish.

"Nathan, I can't deal with this right now. All that has happened today is your fault, you stupid little…"

He broke off his tirade seeing the effect his words were having on his little brother, but he could hardly contain himself. He wanted to ring Nathan's neck, but felt sorry for him at the same time. Perhaps if his own soul was not so heavily burdened with guilt he would have been more understanding, but the revelation was just more than he could accept.

"I cannot look at you right now. Get out of my sight!"

With that he turned and walked away.

Nate watched him go, feeling worse than he had all day. The full magnitude of what he had done finally hit him. Even worse, his actions had caused his brother, his only link with his family, to turn his back on him. Overwhelmed with guilt and anger, he swung his musket, butt first, against a tree, shattering it into several pieces.

The sudden impulse had overtaken him in a moment. He stood in shock, realizing he had just destroyed the only thing he had of his father's. He screamed in anguish.

Crying like a baby, he picked up the broken pieces of his gun and walked slowly toward the village, carrying it in his arms like a dead child. Maybe Mister Thomas, the gunsmith, could fix it. If only someone could fix his shattered heart.

Not far from where Nate and John stood by the side of the road, two boys hid in a thick cluster of trees. One of them was Jedediah Weekes, the boy Nathan had hit the day before. He indeed had a wire securing his jaw so it would heal where Nate had broken it. That didn't prevent him from waiting at this precise spot on the road from Concord in the hope of ambushing his nemesis, Nate Daniels. He knew Nate was with the other Acton boys and would be returning along this very road, hopefully alone. He had been waiting several hours and was about to leave when he heard Nate yelling his brother's name.

Seeing them together had discouraged him at first. John Daniels was a grown man, a fighting militiaman, though he appeared to be unarmed. Nate *was* armed, however, and that could prove an obstacle as well. But when he saw John leave, and watched Nathan smash his gun against a tree, he realized his chance had come. He had his enemy just where he wanted him.

"Let's go," he grunted to his companion, as he began to rise from their hiding place. He had his father's handgun.

"No, Jed, wait," said the other boy, a tall, thin youth with hawkish features. He was also considerably more intelligent than his large red-headed friend. "Did you hear what he just said?"

"No, what?"

"If you go shoot him now, you will be the criminal. The shot will be heard. You'd be hunted down. What if you miss? His brother is not far off. But we can use what we just heard. Your friend Nathan will be the hunted man. By the time we are through, he will be the criminal, with the redcoats and the rebels both after him. Then we can do anything we like to him."

Jedediah was going to object. After all, putting a bullet in Nate would give him great satisfaction, especially considering the pain and discomfort his every waking moment had been since Nate hit him. But as his friend, Simon, explained it, this might be much better, so he went along. The more he heard of his friend's plan, the more he liked it.

Colonel Francis Smith's Brigade with General Percy on Road from Concord

For the last three hours Private Charles McBride, of the British 3rd light-infantry, had been battling through the village of Menotomy, fighting for every inch of road back to Boston. From house to house, and yard to yard, it was a fierce, brutal struggle with him-or-me, no quarter given, every man for himself. Somewhere along the trail of carnage he had picked up a musket with a bayonet, and a cartridge bag full of powder from one of the dead. He had also been able to slake his thirst at a local well, but that had been only after the most intense life and death fighting.

Sick of being ambushed from every house they passed along the road, having pot-shots taken at them only to have the culprits flee on horseback when he drew near, Charley and a few of the men had had enough. They decided to form a deadly flanking action.

Coming upon the rear of a house where the rebels were making a stand, they hit them like a flash-flood from behind, smashing into the militiamen as they waited behind windows and doors. Finally, they were getting their revenge for the slaughter they had endured at the hands of the damned Yankees.

In the initial rush, Charley shot a man hiding behind a stack of shingles. Not stopping to reload, he ran to the wounded man and bayoneted him again and again.

With grim determination, the twenty-year-old British light-infantryman reloaded his musket and looked for his next target, a rebel fighter exiting the house. He shot him down without moving. Then he shot another from the doorway, who was fleeing through a field next to the house. He looked down at the man lying across the doorstep. He was dressed in what looked like his wedding suit and reaching up at him for mercy. Without hesitating, Charley stabbed him until he stopped moving.

After that he had thrown down his gun and was now running as fast as he could toward Boston. He did not run for long.

Stopping exhausted by the side of the road, he lost whatever he had left in his stomach. It was then he realized that for the first time in almost ten hours no one was shooting at him. A quiet had descended on the world, where only the shuffling of the army's leather boots could be heard marching along the dirt-covered road.

Charlie noticed that the column was taking the left-hand fork toward Charlestown instead of the expected route to Cambridge and the bridge across the Charles. He wondered what this could mean and became concerned.

"Where are we going?" he asked the first officer on horseback he encountered. "Why are we not going over the bridge at Cambridge as we did coming out? That is certainly the shorter distance."

"Because the rebels have blocked the bridge and are waiting to ambush us," replied the major. "General Percy knows what he's doing, Private. The road to Charlestown is by a narrow neck of land we can easily defend. And the guns in the harbor will cover us. It is our best means of escape."

"But we'll be trapped out there. We won't be able to get out."

"You forget we have our fleet. They will be able to ferry us off with no problem. We will be safe there."

Private Charlie McBride didn't argue but followed along, shuffling like a drunken man. Dusk had fallen. They halted at a hill commanding the western end of the peninsula. The village of Charlestown lay below them. It still seemed like a long way from home.

He looked out over the water to the north, and west at the opposite shore, across the Mystic River and over the Charles to Cambridge beyond. As far as he could see, the dark shores were covered with countless small fires, as the surrounding militiamen bivouacked for the night.

"There must be thousands of them," he observed out loud.

"10,000 if there's a dozen," said a non-com from Smith's Grenadiers. "I'm afraid we did not accomplish anything today except stir-up a hornet's nest."

Charlie McBride thought that pretty much summed it up, and wondered if he would ever get off this bloody continent.

Chapter 8

Nate made his way back to his aunt's house south of the village of Acton, depressed and numbed from his harrowing day. When he got there it was already dark. The wagon was half packed.

"You should have waited," he scolded when he saw all the heavy things his aunt had carried to the cart.

"There's no time to waste. Boston will be locked up tight as a jailhouse after what happened today. Where have you been? I hope you have not taken part in the fighting."

"No, Aunt Margaret, I was just bringing food to the men. They hadn't eaten all day. John was with them."

"Oh, Lord, don't tell me that. This is all so terrible. What am I going to do?"

"Don't worry, Aunt Margaret. I will take you to Boston and Uncle Jacob. Everything will be all right."

He wished he felt as sure as he sounded, but he was filled with heavy doubt and anxiety. Yet he soldiered on, concentrating on the task at hand - helping his aunt. That's all he let himself think about as he loaded the wagon with her belongings. Many things had to be left behind.

"We only have one horse to pull everything, Aunt Margaret. We don't want to overload it. You have to ride too, you know. It is a long way to Boston."

"I can't leave without my bed, Nathaniel. I have had it since I was a young girl."

"It is too big. You can't take that and the chairs. There will be beds where you are going, and chairs for that matter. They will have to be left behind."

"No," she cried. "They were left to me by my mother."

The scene, which was playing out throughout the colony, was long and heartrending, but in the end cold hard reality won out over cherished sentiments and memories. They finally left the farm with most of her beloved possessions still inside or sitting on the front lawn, making the place look even more forlorn and deserted.

It was getting late. Nate was dog-tired. So much had happened. Yet he went on. He had one more thing to do.

"Your things will still be here when you return," Nate assured her, as he latched the door and jumped on the wagon. Soon they were headed along the road east to the turnpike and Boston beyond.

It wasn't long before they were stopped by armed men barring the highway.

"Where ye be going?" one of them asked.

"To Boston," answered Nate truthfully. "I am taking my aunt there to be with my uncle."

"Only collaborators are in Boston," another remarked. "What are you going there for?"

"I don't know nothing about that. My brother is John Daniels. He's with Isaac Davis's company from Acton. He was at the bridge in Concord today. We are not collaborators, but my uncle is stuck in Boston and my aunt wants to be with him. Now please let us pass. After I take care of my aunt, I'm going to join my brother."

"He's all right," said one of the men. "I know John Daniels. He was with us today along the road. Your brother is a good man."

"I know, but I am obliged to help my aged aunt, so please let us go."

Nathan's story was good, made up on the spur of the moment, and they were soon on their way again, Nathan leading their old nag by the bridle.

As they gained the turnpike near Lincoln, they headed southeast toward Watertown, missing most of the ruin and horror further north along the road through Lexington and Menotomy. From Watertown he planned to head for Roxbury south of Boston, following the instructions his uncle had left his aunt.

To his surprise they were joined on the road by a mass of men.

"Where is everyone going?" he asked of a knot of them who had overtaken him.

"Have you not heard? The British have shot our men at Lexington today. This is war! We are going to guard the Neck. They will not sally forth to kill our men unimpeded again."

"My aunt and I need to get to Boston."

"I do not think they will let you pass tonight, boy, either side. This is not a time to be out with your old aunt. Go back home."

Mounting the wagon, Nate grabbed the reins and moved them forward ahead of the walking men.

Riding through the village of Roxbury, Nate was struck by the number of campfires. They dotted the entire countryside as he descended the hills toward the narrow neck of land separating Boston from the mainland. Other than this thin strip of sand, mud, and rock, if you wanted to get into or out of Boston, you had to go by boat.

He could see a large fortification of some kind, half-way across the isthmus. Torches and lamps lit the darkness. The fires of the patriot forces blocked the approach to the Neck, where Nate and his aunt were stopped again.

"You will not get past the fort," the sentry informed them. "That is unless you are collaborators, in which case you'd better leave the colony."

"My uncle is stuck in the city. He doesn't want to be there, but he must stay with his goods if he and my aunt are not to be ruined. She is old and wants to be with him."

"Who is your uncle? What is his name and what is his business?"

"I do not know why I should say. I am only trying to help my poor aunt. I know nothing about all this. He is a merchant, that is all. Mister Jacob Daniels. My brother is John Daniels with Isaac Davis' Acton Company. He was on the bridge this morning in Concord, and has been fighting against the British all day."

"Then I suggest you join him and do the same, and let your Tory aunt and uncle fend for themselves. No one is getting in or out of Boston unless the Council says so, so shove off."

"That is not fair. They are not Tories, just poor old people trying to protect their goods."

"How do I know they are not collaborating with the British? You will have to wait until the matter can be reviewed by the council. Now go back home."

Nate turned the wagon around, but he had no intention of going home.

As he trudged back up the road, he looked about him curiously. There were groups of men everywhere. Over 4000 had spontaneous left their homes and families from miles around to come to the aid of their fellow colonists, and they were still coming.

Some wore simple homespun country clothes and slouch hats. Some were dressed in their Sunday best. They occupied every part of every field. They stood in peoples' lawns. They camped on every common. They bivouacked along all the roads. Some stared back at him. Nate noticed one man who seemed especially intrigued with his aunt's fancy clock. He had a wagon of his own filled with large barrels.

The clock was a family heirloom, bought in better times in England when his aunt's father was there on business. It was the only thing of all her prized possessions that she could absolutely not part with. If the clock stayed, she had insisted, then so did she. So he had brought it along, even though, because of its size and delicacy, it made the trip that much more difficult. To hear her say it, the piece was priceless. Apparently someone else thought so, too.

"Where you going with all them things?" the man asked when Nate stopped the wagon next to his.

"Sorry, sir, but what business is it of yours where I be going?" he replied intrigued but naturally suspicious.

"None, young sir. I don't mean to pry, but these are dangerous times. Perhaps you could use some assistance. Are you from around these parts? Or are you coming from the city like a lot of folks, leaving the sinking ship while they have the chance?"

"Neither. We are from Acton. I am bringing my aunt to Boston to be with my uncle, who is stuck there due to his business."

"That may be, but if he and your aunt know what's good for them, they will be leaving like most of these good people here."

He pointed to the main road leading through the village. Being so caught up in his own private struggles, Nate had hardly noticed the steady stream of wagons, buggies, and carriages exiting the city of Boston, one long line of people fleeing the soon to be sealed off seaport.

"It is not my choice to make. All I know is that I promised to help my poor aunt, who has had to leave her home and wants only to be with her husband. If all these people can leave, why can't we go in?"

"You will have to ask the Brits that question. From what I understand, the militia has been ordered to not allow anyone in without written permission."

"How does one get such permission?" asked Nathan, trying to stay up with the fast moving events.

"You'd have to talk to someone in the Committee, or one of the generals."

Suddenly, what Nate thought was going to be a simple task had become an impossible ordeal.

"What do you have in them barrels?" he asked, a vague idea forming in his frazzled brain.

"Oh, nothing, but they will soon be filled with the finest Jamaican rum this side of the Americas."

While they talked, the man continued to eye the contents of Nate's wagon, his gaze resting repeatedly on the elegant, grand pendulum clock.

"That is a nice clock you have there," he said finally, pointing to the back of the wagon. "I have not seen the likes of it since I was last in London. It won't last long sitting in the back of that wagon. If it doesn't get wrecked it will get stolen by desperate men."

"I doubt that," said Nate, a bit offended at the man's presumption.

"Would you consider selling it?" asked the man.

"It is a priceless family heirloom," answered Nate. "It's not for sale."

"I was only thinking what a nice price a fine clock like that would fetch. I will give you a hundred pounds for it."

Nate was momentarily taken aback by the large sum the man was offering for his aunt's clock. With cash like that, getting into Boston might become much easier. Suddenly, his aunt, who had been silent up to this point, overwhelmed by the scene around her and fretting over her fate, spoke up.

"The clock is not for sale," she informed him. "Not now, nor ever."

"Please excuse me," Nate said to the man, and pulled the wagon up a short distance.

"Aunt Margaret, do you want to get into Boston and be with Uncle Jacob or not?"

"Of course, but what has that to do with selling my prized possessions."

"It is the only way we can get in. A hundred pounds is a lot of money, enough to bribe the guards with if we need to, and I have an idea, but I will have to sell the clock if we are to make it work. It is this or turn around and go all way back home, and as this man said, the clock is not likely to survive the journey. We were lucky to get this far with it, but it is the key to getting into Boston. Trust me."

His aunt was beside herself with the dilemma facing her and wrung her hands in anguish, praying out loud to the Lord to deliver her. In the end, she relented and placed her life in her fifteen year old nephew's hands. Nate not only sold the clock to the man, but everything in the wagon except a few trunks of clothes and personal belongings. Besides the 500 pounds he got in return, he obtained three of the man's large but empty barrels, and two smaller ones full of rum as a bonus.

They ate an impromptu dinner of cabbage and potato soup, purchased at a stand, one of many setup to feed the mass of hungry militiamen who were arriving at Roxbury by the minute from all parts of the colony.

A short time later, after observing a change of the guards at the militia post on the Neck, Nate jumped on the wagon and started forward. Now that he was actually executing it, he wasn't so sure his plan would work. It had sounded good when he explained it to his aunt, who was less than enthused with what he had in mind, but she had gone along in the end. Now he was beginning to have doubts. He had to admire her for her gumption. He just hoped the trip wouldn't be too hard on her. It was too late to turn back now.

He pulled the wagon to a stop as the guards stepped out in front of him.

"What be your business?" the man in charge asked.

"I am bringing spirits to the patriots in Boston."

"Oh, you are, are you? By who's orders? Let us see your papers."

"I don't have no papers, sir, only the best rum this side of the islands." He hoped he sounded like the man he had bought it from. "It is for Mister Sam Adams himself."

"Mister Adams? Is he not with Mister Hancock out in Concord?"

"That was earlier. They are in Boston now, but it's a secret. I am to take this to him and his companions."

"I don't know," said the sentry, uncertain what to do. Each man was on his own in the come-as-you-are army. No one really seemed to be in charge. It would be easy to make a mistake that could cost him his honor. "You need papers."

"Didn't you hear me? This is secret. No one is to know, but perhaps this will help you see us through."

Nate got off the wagon, went to the smaller of the barrels, and ladled a pewter cup full of dark golden liquid.

"Taste this and tell me you are not going to let me deliver it to Mister Adams."

"Ah, that is good drink," said the man, slurping down half the mug in one gulp. "Top of the line, I would say."

"It would be a shame to deprive Mister Adams of his cups. I doubt he would take it kindly."

"Well, perhaps it can't hurt, can it boys?" replied the militiaman.

"No," said his mates, who were crowding around waiting for the cup.

"Perhaps one more," said the man, squeezing in front of the others.

"Better yet," said Nate, anxious to get moving. "I will leave this small barrel with you and your good mates, compliments of the good Mister Adams."

They all cheered him as he moved through the guard post and across the Neck.

The site of the fortress as it loomed up out of the darkness midway across the causeway caused Nate to shudder. The giant fortification of stone and rock, with its forbidding barricades lit by torches and lanterns, looked like a crouching dragon. It rose up mountain-like, several stories above his head.

The massive wooden gate was opened, but guarded by a phalanx of men in red. It looked like they were expecting an attack any minute. While the road going in was practically deserted except for Nathan and his wagon, that leading out was lined with carts and wagons, and people on foot and in carriages, all rushing to get out. Nate gulped and went on with his ingenious but dangerous plan. He was worried about his aunt, lying in the barrel.

He had made it as comfortable as possible, stuffing it with soft pillows and blankets, and had lain it sideways, wedging it in tightly so it would not move. But it had been a half hour since she had slid inside it and he was worried how she was doing. Even more importantly, he hoped she'd be quiet.

"Where are you going?" asked a sentry in a red jacket, a sergeant by the stripes on his arm. "How did you get through those rebels? They have let no one in. They are getting ready to attack, I'll wager."

"I do not know about that, but there sure are a lot of them. I have something here for the general."

"Who? What general? What do you have? Who are you?"

"My uncle is a well-known merchant in town. He has sent me down to the south shore to fetch these barrels from his ship. It is a gift for the general."

"What general? General Gage?"

"Yes, General Gage and his men. I have three barrels of the best rum this side of Jamaica."

"Nothing gets through, but that we check it," the guard announced, barring the way.

"You can do better than that, Sergeant," replied Nate. "You can taste it."

With that, he jumped off the wagon, led the man to the rear, opened a small barrel, and scooped some of its contents into the pewter cup. Before long he was passing it around to a group of men, all of them wearing red coats.

"We must give you an escort," offered the sergeant.

"Ah, no, sir, that will not be necessary," answered Nate, thinking fast. "This is supposed to be a surprise. It will be spoiled if your men come with us. Let me go on to my uncle's place in town so that it may be delivered properly as I was told."

Although everyone was on edge because of the anticipated invasion, Nate's story seemed plausible enough to the men on duty, especially after they got to keep the small barrel of spirits for themselves. So they let him pass. Now all Nate had to do was find his uncle.

Colonel Francis Smith's Brigade, Boston Commons

Charlie McBride had finally made it back to Boston, rowed across the harbor in a ship's boat a little after midnight. He staggered to his quarters, a simple tent pitched among a thousand others on the city's commons, where sheep and cows used to graze before the British came. He was cold and tired and hungry beyond imagining, but more than anything he was angry - at his commanders for the waste of it; at the provincials for their hysterical and ruthless response. What kind of people were they? They were certainly not good, sane Englishmen. As he waited for his pot of tea to boil, he was besieged with questions from those who had remained behind.

"What happened?" asked one of his mess mates, who as yet had heard nothing about the battle. "Did all go well?"

Charley just looked at him with a blank expression. He was numb with shock, stunned with the memory of what he'd just gone through. He couldn't believe his mate's question. How could he not know?

"You do not know? You have had no word?"

"No, Charles, we have not heard a thing. No one has told us anything. You are the first to return."

"Then you have sorrowful news to learn."

More men stopped by to listen as they passed. Others came up, attracted by the activity. Before long, Charley had a crowd of twenty regulars around him all eager for news of the day.

60

"They fired on us in the morning as we approached a town green. We returned fire, killing a dozen, and cleared the field. Then we moved on to the town of Concord, where they have their arsenal hidden. They fired on us again there, and attacked us as we stood next to a bridge, all without provocation. They are mad, these people. They have lived in the wilderness too long and have become like savages. They scalped our men, helpless wounded prisoners."

This revelation caused a chorus of groans and exclamations.

"But that was nothing to what happened afterward, as we tried to return to Boston. I must have marched sixty miles today, half of that under the most extreme duress. We were literally running for our lives under a continuous, galling fire. We did the county folk no harm. We burned none of their homes, but they came out of the houses and woods to harass and kill us as if we had murdered their children. There were thousands of them swarming around us like buzzing bees, shooting. They waited behind every turn in ambush. They crowded the mountain tops like crows, and swooped down on us like wolves. No retribution can be too great for what they did to us this day."

He shuddered as he reached for a hot cup of tea and some hard biscuits. Someone had started a make a soup from a collection of fresh carrots and greens.

"The word is they are going to attack tonight," one of the men standing by observed. "We have to sleep with our arms. There are thousands of them surrounding the city."

"Yes, I'm afraid we are being cut off," answered Charley, taking another sip of tea. "Thank God for our Navy. Otherwise, we would be completely surrounded."

"Yes, as long as we control the waters, we will be all right," the man, a grenadier, agreed.

"If we have control of the water, why don't we blast them?" asked another, standing with his musket by his side. "What is Admiral Graves waiting for? Our ships should be bombarding that peninsula across the harbor to the north. We should be clearing those damned rebels out. Why sit here like ducks waiting for them to attack? I say let's go at them."

"That is fine for you to say," replied Charlie, tired to his bones and still famished after two bowls of watery soup. "You have not endured what we have. Half of us are more dead than alive. This army is in no shape to attack, not after what we've been through. Let the provincials come. I'd like to see their bodies piled up along our walls and streets, for that is what would happen to them if they try to come in here, despite my fatigue and pain. But I will not venture out again until I am once more whole, and that will take a good night's sleep and a hearty breakfast. There are many like me who feel the same, including our brave General Percy, who saved the day. Without him and his men, I know not what would have become of us. There were many times when I would not have given a farthing for my chances."

No one said much after that, as some were mustered out to double the picket lines. Others, like Charlie, tried to sleep amidst the stir of the army as it prepared for battle and the anticipation of attack.

Chapter 9

King Street Inn, Boston

Jacob Daniels was beside himself with worry. It was bad enough he'd had to flee his home only steps ahead of a mob, but he had not heard a word from his wife, who he had to leave behind. Now, because a few rabble-rousers had been shot, the whole country was in uproar and talking of war.

How could British regulars, elite grenadiers, be bested by mere militiamen and farmers, and then chased all the way back to Boston? He still didn't believe it, although the state of military activity indicated something momentous had happened or was about to. Still no word from his wife, he did not know what to think. When he did hear something, it was enough to make his blood boil.

His associate, Mister Joshua Weekes, had also been forced to leave home and property, like many loyalists, and flee to Boston. He had recently stopped by to give him some news. It was not good. Not only had his wife not yet started for the city, but his truant nephew had done something so terrible, so reprehensible, he still did not trust the truth of the matter.

The Weekes boy, still unable to talk because his mouth was wired shut, had overheard a conversation between Nathaniel Daniels and his brother, John. A second boy, who was with Jedediah at the time, was able to corroborate his story and fill in the details. If what they said was true, his nephew had done something that made his other sins pale in comparison. Even more troubling to Jacob, his reputation in the community might be tainted by his nephew's treasonous activities. If only he could get his hands on the boy. He would make him mend his rebellious ways.

Less than a mile away, Nate led his horse and wagon up the steep, narrow, cobblestone streets of Boston as he tried to orient himself and find his uncle's dwelling. He had the address written on the directions his uncle had given his aunt, but the paper was so smudged and wrinkled, and the streets so dark, he could barely read the writing. It looked like three numbers – one, seven, something - and 'King Street'. He had no idea where that was.

There were redcoats all around him, regular British infantry and grenadiers, marching and running in all directions, but no one gave them much heed, familiar as they were with seeing refugees in wagons. He stopped at a quiet spot and went to see to his aunt.

"Are you all right, Aunt Margaret," he asked, as he gently pried open the lid and peeked inside the barrel.

"Yes, Nathaniel, but please get me out of here. I'm like to suffocate with the smell of rum."

"Did Uncle Jacob tell you how to find him?" he asked, once his aunt was out.

"He mentioned something about a Prancing Pony, across from the Prancing Pony, on King Street, I think he said it was."

Leaving the empty barrels in an ally, they continued on their way.

"Aunt Margaret, I cannot continue another step," Nate said after a short while. "I am so tired. We must find a place for the night. We can look for Uncle Jacob in the morning."

"That is fine with me. I too am exhausted. So much has happened today, it seems like a week has passed."

They found an inn at the top of the hill and got a room for the night, with a bed and clean sheets for his aunt. Nate had all he could do to stable the horse, before he fell asleep in the back of the wagon on a little pile of hay.

The next morning he was up with first light, asking directions to King Street and the Prancing Pony. It was not far, and during the short ride there, Nate tried to think of what he was going to say to his uncle. He wasn't looking forward to the meeting. First, he'd have to explain the empty wagon. What had happened to all their possession? The 500 pounds would help and replace the furniture, but still it would not go over well. Then there was his running away. He hoped the fact that he had helped his aunt and brought her safely all this way to Boston would count for something. He could say selling the furniture was the only way he could have gotten into Boston, which as far as he could see was the truth. He didn't have a boat and the city was under high alert. He would find out what was going to happen soon enough. The sign on the Prancing Pony came into sight.

Hitching the horse to a post and pulling up his breeches, Nate led his aunt into the rooming house across the street and asked for his uncle.

Jacob came downstairs a short time after being informed his wife and nephew had arrived. He wore his old uniform from the French and Indian wars, and his most severe expression. He also had his sword hanging in its scabbard on his side.

Nate swallowed hard when the old man peered at him.

"I have brought Aunt Margaret to Boston," he said hurriedly, before his uncle could speak. "She asked me to. We had to sell all the furniture to get into town."

"How are you, Margaret?" said Jacob, coming down the stairs and going to her, completely ignoring his nephew.

"Fine, now that I'm here. Nathaniel was very good to bring me. Oh, what a harrowing experience. There are soldiers and militiamen everywhere. All they talk of is war. Oh, Jacob, it was horrid. I'm so thankful to Nathaniel."

"You are safe now. Those rabble-rousing bullies can't harm us here."

Looking up at Nate when he said this, he continued, "What have you got to say for yourself?"

"Nothing, all that's over now."

"Oh, is it? The Weekes boy and his father are in Boston you know. I just talked to Mister Weekes today. He is still pressing charges. You showing up here is quite convenient."

"I'm not staying," announced Nate, getting nervous and looking toward the door. "I just brought Aunt Margaret back. Then I'm going."

"What you did to young Weekes is only the beginning of your troubles, I'm afraid."

"I didn't do anything to him. He hit me first. Anyway, it happened in Acton. We are not in Acton now."

"We are in His Majesty's jurisdiction, which despite what people like your brother say, is every inch of this great province. You will learn to obey the King's laws. You have done a very grievous thing, young man, most grievous indeed.

"What are you talking about? Jedediah started it. You said he would be all right. What do you mean, grievous?"

"Where were you yesterday morning?"

Nathan stood silent for a moment, frozen at the mention of that morning. He remembered all to well. Why would his uncle bring that up?

"Nowhere. I was coming here to Boston to get away from all of you. Now here you all are."

"That's right, we are all here, and so is the British army. You can't run away."

"You can't keep me here," objected Nate, edging toward the door.

"Where were you yesterday morning?" his uncle demanded.

Instead of answering, Nate bolted for the door and out into the street. His Uncle ran after him, his sword raised.

"Stop him. Stop that boy," he yelled.

Two army officers, in bright red uniforms, grabbed Nate before he had run ten feet.

"What have we here?" said one of them, peering at him

"What are you doing?" cried Nate struggling in the men's arms. "Let me go. Let me go."

"Nathan Daniels," his uncle intoned, coming up and holding a piece of paper in his hand. "You are arrested in the name of the Crown for treason most high, for firing on his Majesty's troops without provocation."

Nathan stopped struggling. He could hardly believe his ears. How had they found out?

"Take him away," Jacob ordered, as the men led him down the hill by the arms.

"They hang men for treason," one of his guards, a large-boned grenadier, whispered in his ear.

Nate remembered what his brother had told him.

"It's not true," he pleaded. "What he said. It's not true. It's a lie made up by Jedediah Weekes for me hitting him. You got to believe me. I didn't do it "

The two men had heard it all before from their own miscreant men and only laughed at the boy's pathetic pleas.

As they neared the bottom of the hill, Nate could see four more soldiers waiting for them at the corner. He stiffened and tried to halt, but the two guards dragged him along.

The street they were on ran down another steep incline toward the docks. Just before they reached the bottom of the first hill, something whizzed by out of the corner of Nate's eye. It all happened so fast he hardly had time to blink. His two guards went sprawling to the ground, their guns flung high in the air. Whatever it was that hit them continued past the startled men at the intersection and zoomed down the next incline. In the meantime, a pair of hands grabbed Nate and pulled him into an alley, where he was placed on a small, flat cart and sped down another hill. It all happened so fast he wasn't sure what was occurring.

"Hold on," the boy steering the cart yelled as they whooshed down a steep side street. "It's going to be a bumpy ride."

Nate held on for dear life as they careened down the slope at a tremendous speed, rattling over the cobblestone street. Just when it looked like they were going to crash headlong into a high brick wall, the driver yelled out.

"Left! Lean to the left!"

Nate did as the boy ordered, and leaned far to the side, closing his eyes as they barely missed the side of a building. On they went down a dark, narrow alley, scraping barrels and cans of trash in their headlong rush. At one point they ran through a long, low tunnel, only four feet high. Nate instinctively ducked his head. They came out in a flat, open area near the docks.

"We will be all right here," said the boy sitting in front of him as they slowed down in a wide dirt track. There were teams of horses pulling heavy wagons everywhere, filled with items of every description. The dockyards and harbor were within plain view. Seagulls cried as they circled in the air.

"Who are you? Where did you come from?" asked Nate in stunned excitement. "I have never seen anything like that before in my life. What do you call this thing?"

"I'm Jeremy and this is a sled with wheels," he replied pointing to the cart they had just gotten off. "In the winter time we put blades on them and slide down the streets on the ice."

"Wow," said Nate looking at the cart and his new friend. "That was something. You knocked those soldiers over like bowling pins."

"What did they arrest you for and who was that old man?"

"That was my uncle. I had some trouble back home in Acton that followed me here. That's what I get for trying to help my aunt."

"He sounded like a King's man."

"That he is."

"Then you must be a rebel," said the boy, stopping and looking at him.

"No, no, nothing like that," Nate said hurriedly, worried he had been found out again. "The boy I had the trouble with was the son of an important man in our town. I guess you could say he is what they call a loyalist, that's all. I ain't rebelling."

The boy looked at him hard.

"That's too bad, because we are. We hate the redcoats."

"Then why are you staying here in Boston?"

"Because our parents are here, but that doesn't mean they're collaborators."

His new friend, Jeremy, led him across the docks to a line of wooden sheds. Sneaking in the back of an especially dilapidated building, he led Nate up a couple of flights of rickety stairs to a large empty storeroom. A few boys, sitting on barrels at a table in the corner, stirred and looked up.

"Hi, gang," said Jeremy. "This here is Nate. He's from Acton."

"Where's Acton?" asked one of the boys.

"Out west, about twenty miles, just past Concord," answered Nate.

"Concord!" several exclaimed. "You're from there."

"Yes, I saw it all. It was horrible. I'm afraid this is war. The minutemen might attack Boston at any time."

"Wow," the boys said in chorus.

"What did they arrest you for?" one of the bigger boys asked.

"For treason I heard them say," Jeremy answered for him.

That elicited even more oohs and ahhs.

Jeremy had brown hair cut in a bowl but was fairly well dressed, with clean pants and a white shirt, and appeared to be about fourteen, slight of build. The other boys ranged from age eight or nine, to Nate's age, fifteen. There were eight of them in all, but he got the impression there were more.

"Where are the ones who saved me today?" Nate asked.

"That was Sammy and Pete," said Jeremy. "They'll be back soon. They drove the attack sled, while I did the pickup. We do it all the time, especially in the winter when the roads are iced and covered with snow."

"Well, that was the neatest thing I ever saw. You knocked those redcoats down like they was bottles. Boy was that funny."

They all had a good laugh.

"Do you fellows live around here?" Nate asked.

"Yes, we go to the Queen Street School," answered Jeremy. "But it's closed because of the redcoats. We formed a gang when they came. We're helping the rebels."

"Gee, what do you do?"

"Oh, we do errands and watch the soldiers, and sometimes get supplies for our parents, who are not allowed to leave the city."

"Why not?"

"Cause they are hostages," Jeremy replied. "To make sure the rebels don't try anything. Say, how old are you, anyway?"

"Fifteen."

"Fifteen!" exclaimed Jeremy. "Why that's no more than Peter's age. You look almost like a grown man."

"I guess I'm big for my age."

"I'll say. Hey, we could use a fellow like you."

King Street Inn, Boston

Jacob Daniels sat brooding in his lodgings on King Street. He was quite upset. He was happy and relieved to have his wife back with him, but angry in the extreme that she had been forced to sell all their possessions, some of which were irreplaceable, and was stuffed in a rum barrel. The story that it was the only way to get into Boston was patently absurd. All they had to do was send a message to the address he had given them announcing their arrival, and all would have been taken care of. Instead, that fool nephew of his had bartered away all his possessions for less than half their worth and made his poor wife lie in a rum-soaked barrel for two hours. He could have thrashed the boy with his own hands, he was so mad.

That was bad enough, but the assault on the two soldiers and Nate's subsequent escape had been the last straw. Nathan could not be allowed to get away like that, not after what he had done.

He had gone to Province House immediately to talk to General Gage, where he walked the entryway for hours with dozen of other petitioners waiting for someone to talk to. Only to finally be faced with a bored, arrogant official.

"I tell you major, this is of the utmost importance," he had insisted. "The general needs to be informed immediately. I must see him."

"I'm sorry, sir," said the aide. "But General Gage has had a strenuous day and has much to do. Perhaps his adjutant could be of service."

"No, this is for the general and him alone. It impacts directly on the activities of yesterday morning and could change the whole nature of the war. You must let me see him."

"No, sir, I'm afraid that is not possible."

"You blasted fool! Let me see the general!" Jacob had yelled in frustration.

"What seems to be the problem here?" General Gage entered the room from the next office. "How am I to concentrate with all this shouting?"

"Sorry, sir," Jacob had said, when the major was slow to respond. "But I have information about yesterday morning that is of the utmost importance."

"Well, then," said Gage, looking sideways at his subordinate with a smile. "Why don't you come in and have a seat."

That had been a day ago.

Jacob smiled but his eyes remained hard as he gazed out at the street below. The general might have pooh-poohed his accusations, but he knew better. Nathan was a menace. If the army wouldn't help him, he'd help himself. Money talks and would make others look up and take notice. The boy had to be caught and brought to justice.

Chapter 10

John Daniels was having a tough time of it. He wandered the countryside, unable to eat or sleep. When he tried the former, he would get sick and gag, unable to get the images of blood and slaughter out of his mind. If he attempted the latter, his dreams were filled with the most hideous visions of murder and mutilation. The worst part was that he was the one doing all the killing and butchering. He did not know if he could live with the monster he had become.

It had all started out so noble and honorable, free men defending their homes from foreign invaders, but it had turned into something totally different, something dark and sinister beyond his imagining, where humans became animals and animals devoured men. The things he saw and did that day could never be erased from his memory, except through death. The thought had come to him more than once. It was a good thing he no longer had his musket.

There was no one he could talk to. No way to explain the things he'd done. How had all this happened? The answer left him grabbing his head and bellowing in rage.

"Nathan! Nathan! How could you? How could you do this? You stupid little fool! Damn you."

His curse made him pull up short.

"No, I take it back," he said to the empty sky. "It is not the poor boy's fault, not the way he was brought up. Jesus, Mary, and Joseph, help us. Help me!"

He was on a backwoods trail, seldom used, with the sun filtering through the old-wood pines like light through a stain glass window. He fell to his knees and folded his hands in supplication.

"Help me, oh Lord, for I have sinned. Oh, God, I am so sorry."

With that he was overcome with grief. His sobs echoed in the forest.

Queen Street, Boston

Nate was running with the gang, learning the lay of the Boston streets - which ones were conducive to sled raids; where to hide when being pursued; the cutbacks and byways that made city blocks nothing more than a hop, skip, and jump away.

Jeremy seemed to be the informal leader of the group even though he was not the oldest. It was he who had started the gang, and his natural intelligence and instinct for covert activities made him a natural.

Theirs was apparently not the only group of boys loose in the city. One of their worst rivals was another gang from Boston Latin School with decidedly loyalist leanings. They seemed to instill a special terror in the boys from the Queen Street School, who dreaded them more than the British and avoided their territory as if it were the devil's ground.

It was Saturday morning. Nate was sitting in their makeshift clubhouse on a barrel, telling the boys what he had seen at Lexington and along the road to Boston three days before. He did not disclose his part in the affair, but all ears were trained on what he had to say. At each point in his narrative, there were exclamations of disbelief and shock. Suddenly, a boy came running up the stairs and into the room yelling.

"They've got Peter! They've got Peter!"

Peter was one of the boys who had rescued Nate from the soldiers. Nate was on his feet in a second.

"Who's got him?" he asked. "Where?"

"The boys from the Latin School. They grabbed us as we were crossing the square to our lookout to watch the British on the Commons. I got away, but poor Pete had two or three of them on him. They was beating him terrible."

"Take me to them," ordered Nate.

"Wait, Nate, there are too many of them," counseled Jeremy. "They are too big."

"I don't care," said Nate. "Take me to them."

They followed Samuel, a skinny thirteen-year-old, to where Peter had been taken, deep in Latin School territory. Jeremy tried to talk Nate out of going the whole way. They walked in a group, looking around furtively, but Nate moved with a purpose, concerned about what might be happening to his friend. He had no fear of his opponents, only for Peter.

"Nate, you don't know what you're up against," said Jeremy. "These boys are mean. They'd just as soon crack your skull open with a crowbar as look at you."

"I don't care. I've got to help Peter after what he did for me."

"You will be no help to Peter with your brains splattered on the ground."

"We will see whose brains get splattered."

"Here," said Samuel quietly, peering around the corner from the alley they had been walking in.

There in the middle of a sundrenched square near the docks, stood a half-dozen boys. In the middle of them was their friend, Peter, standing beneath a street lamp, over which a rope was dangling.

"They're going to hang him," uttered Jeremy. "We have got to get help."

Without a word, Nate strode out into the square and walked rapidly toward the knot of Latin School boys. His gang, all except Jeremy, stayed hidden, watching from the shadows of the alley.

No one noticed him as Nate reached the throng and pushed his way to the center, where they were about to put a rope around Peter.

"This is what we do to traitors," a big boy with rough features was saying.

"Leave him be," yelled Nate, pushing the boy with the rope away and pulling Peter toward him. Tucking him under his large protective shoulder, Nate started walking away.

"Hold it!" yelled the boy with the rope, grabbing Nate in a bear hug.

Before he had a chance to get a firm grip, Nate spun on his heels with a thunderous round-house punch, hitting the other boy straight on the top of the head. He fell to the ground so fast it looked like he'd been hammered into it. In an instant, the other Latin School boys were on Nate, all of them seeming big for their ages, thus the fear they instilled.

Nate never stopped moving, left, right, left, right, his large legs braced. He swung his big fists in hard round-house punches, one after the other, with such speed and power he was knocking people out as soon as they came near him. The blood was literally flying around him. Unmovable, but constantly moving, his fists flew like jack-hammers pounding stone.

Before a few minutes had elapsed, the half-dozen Boston Latin School boys lay about him on the ground, many not moving, while the others, bruised and beaten, got up and limped away.

Nate stood frozen to the spot, his arms hanging stiff at his sides, his mouth open, breathing hard. The other boys stood behind him, stunned in amazement. Nate was surprised himself. Other than the

73

time he hit Jedediah, he had never even been in a fight, but the fear and adrenaline had taken over and his big body just followed along. He didn't know if he felt good or bad. He was elated and upset all at the same time, mad at the boys he had just beat up for making him do such a thing.

"Gosh!" Samuel exclaimed. "I've never seen anything like that before in my life, even with grown-ups fighting. I could hardly see your hands they was moving so fast."

"You hit them so hard I could see the teeth flying out of their mouths," said Peter.

"Come on," said Jeremy, looking around nervously "Let's get out of here before they come back with soldiers."

They grabbed Nate, who was standing there looking at the boys lying around him, and led him away. He seemed a little wobbly and shaken, as if he was the one that had been punched, but no one had laid a hand on him.

"That was something," observed Jeremy quietly to his new friend, looking at him as if he was a wild, only partly-tamed animal, who could turn at any moment.

"I don't know what came over me," replied Nate. "I guess I got kind of scared."

"Remind me never to scare you," said Jeremy.

A few days later, emboldened by their success against the Latin School gang, Nate and the boys investigated a warehouse on their turf. It sat next to the Wharf and did not appear to be guarded. Breaking in through a rear window, they inspected the place, hoping for something they could use or sell. It was just getting dark, but there was enough light filtering in through the many dusty windows to see.

"Look at this!" Sam yelled.

"What is it?" said Peter.

"Gunpowder!" answered Jeremy. "There must be a dozen barrels of it!"

"What are you going to do?" asked Nate.

"We can smuggle it out of the city the same way you got in," suggested Jeremy. "My pa says the militia needs gunpowder."

Though Nate had earned everyone's respect, and was now the acknowledged champion of the group, the one they wanted by their side in a rumble, Jeremy was still the gang's leader. He still called the shots, but with Nate by his side, they were a force to be reckoned with.

"I don't know," said Nate pondering Jeremy's idea. "That might have worked once, barely, but I don't know if it would work again."

"We have to do something," insisted Jeremy, not yet ready to give up his plan. "Pa says the patriots won't attack because they don't have enough powder. A few hundred pounds of it might make a difference and help the cause. It is just sitting here for the taking. They don't even have it guarded. We could do it tonight. There is no moon."

"Can we get a boat?" asked Nate.

"My dad has one tied at the docks," volunteered Timothy, one of the boys. "It's big enough to carry all those barrels and a crew of four."

"Can you borrow it?" asked Jeremy.

"I don't know. My pa will want to know what we want it for. There are men with the boat who will only obey him."

"Hmm," murmured Jeremy. "I have an idea."

"I know where there's a wagon," Nate informed them, starting to like the notion the more he thought of it. He had a need to leave the city. He might as well kill two birds with one stone.

Later that night, Nate made a surreptitious visit to the stable near the Prancing Pony, where he retrieved his uncle's horse and wagon. Taking it back to the warehouse at the end of Hancock Warf, he and four of the boys loaded the twelve half-barrels of gunpowder - 600 pounds of it - into the cart. The two sentries, who showed up shortly before Nate returned with the wagon, were lured away by Peter and a couple of the other boys, who after providing suitable provocation led the guards on a wild-goose chase through the back streets and alleys along the harbor.

Now they were transporting the powder across the North End to Barton's Point, where the boat was waiting. It was the closest location from Boston to Cambridge across the Charles River, and Jeremy reasoned it was the best place from which to make their getaway. Timothy, the boy whose father owned the boat, had bluffed the men at the boatyard, saying that he had permission to take the craft on an errand for his father. He had forged his parent's signature on a letter to that intent. It helped that he was able to bribe the dock men, who were already friendly to the cause, with some spirits they had also pilfered from the warehouse. He was now waiting at the Point with thirteen year old Benjamin Russell, for Nate and the rest of the gang to arrive.

Packing the half-barrels of gunpowder in large crates of rags and old clothing that they had obtained from the school earlier, Nate and his fellow conspirators pretended to be on their way to the almshouse in the west part of town, next to the Charles.

The street from Hancock Warf to the turn-off to Barton's Point led straight across the north end of town. So far they had seen no soldiers. They were almost to the Point road when their luck ran out.

"Who goes there at this late hour?" asked the corporal in charge of the sentry point.

Jeremy and Nate were sitting in the front of the wagon, while Samuel rode on top of one of the crates. A few small barrels of rum sat among the crates.

"We are taking rags and clothes to the almshouse," answered Jeremy. "We have collected this on behalf of the poor people of Boston, and hope to keep ourselves from the poor house in the process."

Jeremy seemed happy to see the soldiers and talked pleasantly to them, even offering them a drink from one of the barrels. It had just the effect he had hoped it would and diverted their attention.

"Who is this rum for?" asked the corporal, sampling the contents of the barrel. "Surely the almshouse has no need for it."

"No, sir," answered Jeremy. "It is for the manager of the house and his men. He is making the whole thing possible."

"Hmm, I see," said the corporal. "But His Majesty's forces are also making this all possible. We will take a couple of these barrels for our efforts."

"I don't think that would be proper, sir" objected Jeremy, who had hoped for this kind of reaction, but didn't want to make it seem too easy. "They will not like their rum rations shortened."

"Tell them they are lucky we did not take all of it," replied the corporal, ordering his men to take one of the barrels. "Now off with you hooligans, and not another word."

The boys heaved a sigh of relief and started off, turning right toward Barton's Point at the last street before the river, where the boat was waiting. There was still the risk of being spotted by a British patrol on the river, but it was so shallow and marshy at this point that few ships ventured this far up.

"Look at all the campfires," whispered Samuel, looking out at the opposite shore as they approached the dock.

"There must be a thousand of them," observed Jeremy.

"More than that," said Nate. "I reckon the whole colony is out, from here to Maine and down to Connecticut. Ten thousand at least, and that's just what we can see over yonder."

Nate looked over the craft as he lugged in two half-barrels of powder under his arms. It was about forty feet long with a mast and sail, and a tiller in the back. There were also two heavy oars on each side. Carrying in the last of the gunpowder, along with the remainder of the rum, Nate, Jeremy, Peter, and Samuel jumped on board and shoved off. Timothy sat ready to grab the tiller once they reached deeper water.

It didn't seem that far to the opposite shore, but in the darkness, with the lights and the reflections and the thickening mist, it was hard to judge distances. It was tough going at first as they poled their way from the river bank. The barge was heavily laden and cumbersome, and the grass and weeds near the bank of the Back Bay clung to the sides of the boat like tentacles.

Once they reached deeper water toward the middle of the river, they took to the oars, but the tidal current and eddies were strong and made rowing the heavy craft difficult. Slowly but surely, they were being swept toward the bay at the mouth of the river.

"The tide is moving out," observed Jeremy. "And there is hardly any wind to aid us across. We will have to row hard boys or we will be swept into the harbor."

Nate pulled doubly hard on his oar, willing the vessel forward, but the tide was slowly overwhelming their efforts. Then the unthinkable happened.

Out of the mist from the river's mouth, loomed a British gunboat, a twelve-pounder sitting on her bow pointing in their direction. The boys were unnerved. All except Nate stopped rowing altogether, as their craft drifted silently toward the entrance to the harbor and the enemy ship.

"Don't worry, boys," said Jeremy calmly, as he began to row along with Nate. "They can't see us. And besides, that's not even a gunboat. That's nothing but an old scow they use to haul pig iron. The last one to Cambridge is a donkey. Row hard boys."

They started rowing with renewed vigor, but still they could not make any headway. Then the gunboat spotted them and gave chase.

Telling Sam to move aside, Nate grabbed his oar and began pulling strenuously on both of them, splashing them furiously into the water at an incredible pace. Slowly but surely, they started to move against the current toward the Cambridge shore. The tide began to turn as well, and the wind picked up. Soon they were moving swiftly away from the oncoming enemy vessel - but not fast enough.

The gunboat unleashed a shot from its bow-mounted cannon. The loud roar was followed by a spume of water not ten feet behind them.

"Faster boys!" yelled Jeremy, urging them on. "Row faster!"

A minute later another cannon shot boomed out. The ball dropped just to the left of them, less than four feet astern. A spray of water splashed the boat, as they all ducked instinctively. They were only forty feet from shore, but it seemed much further. Would they make it? The next shot, which was sure to come, was bound to hit them. The thought made them row even faster.

Suddenly, musket fire erupted up and down the western shore, as if every militiaman in Cambridge was firing on the British gunboat. It had strayed too far from the river's mouth and was in danger of running aground in the shallow, swampy water. It turned and headed for the safety of the bay.

Nate and the boys collapsed on their oars in exhaustion and let the Durham drift a little further up the river and away from the retreating gunboat, until they found a suitable spot to dock her. They were soon surrounded by armed men.

"Who goes there?" one of them, a sergeant, shouted. "State your intentions and be quick about it."

"We are here to help the army," yelled Nate. "Where is the general?"

"Who wants to know?" responded the man on the shore, as he tied the rope they threw him to the jetty.

"Who we are is not important, my good man," announced Jeremy stepping out of the boat. "We have something here that the general will be very interested in. If you would be so kind as to direct us to his presence so that we may present it to him, we would be much obliged."

"General Ward of the new Provincial Army is too important to talk to the likes of you, and old General Putnam is busy seeing to our defenses. You will have to tell me or no one what you have to say."

"We cannot trust such vital information to a mere militiaman. We must talk to someone with authority."

"I'll show you some authority," answered the man, growing angry and un-slinging his musket.

"What seems to be the problem here, Sergeant?" said a rider coming up on horseback. He was heavy-set with dark hair tied in a queue, and had on a vest with a tri-corner hat. Dismounting quickly, he examined the barge that was tied up on the riverbank with its crew of boys. "Well, what have we here?"

"Sir, these boys just rowed across from the city and almost got their heads blown off. They say they have something for the army. They want to talk to the general."

"So you are the cause of all the ruckus. The generals are busy. Will a lowly lieutenant colonel do? Hello, my name is Paul Revere. Perhaps I can be of some service."

Although Nate had not heard the name before, it was well-known to Jeremy and the others, whose fathers had spoken of him often, always in the highest terms.

"Yes, Mister Revere, sir," answered Jeremy. "That would do just fine. Boys, why don't you show the lieutenant colonel our cargo."

With that, Nate and the others pulled back the canvas tarp they had thrown over the crates and barrels of gunpowder.

"What's this?" Revere said in astonishment.

"Six hundred pounds of gunpowder," replied Jeremy. "Now you can attack the British."

"Good work, lads. Welcome to the Continental Army."

Chapter 11

Colonel Francis Smith's Brigade, Boston Commons

Corporal Charlie McBride was feeling claustrophobic. Firewood was scarce. You didn't have to be a quartermaster to know that with the city sealed off, food would soon be hard to come by as well. Charlie had been promoted for his heroic efforts during the retreat from Concord, as had most of the men in Smith's brigade, the few that had survived. It should have given him pride and honor, but it only made him bitter and resentful, considering the useless waste of men. The backbreaking and constant chores he and his companions had been forced to perform since their harrowing return to the city only made it worse.

Expecting an attack at any time, Gage had put his entire army on high alert. Pickets and patrols had been doubled. The men slept with their weapons, in full uniform. There was no rest for the weary. The most chilling rumors were about - the entire colony had come out to harass and murder them; tens of thousands of armed militiamen roamed the countryside in search of English blood. Only the previous day, hundreds of soldiers and loyalists had to be rescued from the South Shore where they were besieged by the bloodthirsty colonials. Charlie felt like a prisoner stuck in the middle of a hostile, foreign land, far from home and alone. The more than 8000 British regulars and German mercenaries did not seem enough to stem the on-coming flood, which some said was almost 15,000 hostiles.

"Why do we sit here like geese waiting for the slaughter while the rebels build up their forces to attack us?" complained Charlie to one of his friends, also from Smith's brigade.

"I do not know, but I am sick of digging ditches, tearing down houses, and piling up logs and bricks," said his friend. "I'd like to get some of those dirty scoundrels who did our mates in, especially that bloody coward with the tomahawk, the savages."

"We should not be back on our heels when we could be moving forward," observed Charlie. "These peasants would not stand a chance with our army in the open field. We would have their backs to us soon enough. They have no discipline and less leadership. We should attack."

"I agree with you, Charlie, but I also remember what these Yankees can do when riled, even if they are an ill-disciplined lot. They were led well enough on the road back from Concord. Many of them are fighters from the French and Indian wars. Some are even ex-British army officers, from what I hear, the traitors. These people have been mustering and drilling for a hundred years, and they are all good shots. But as you say, they cannot stand up to us in the open field. Not only that, they have little in the way of artillery. I agree, General Gage is making a mistake by sitting here. We should at least take the high ground on our north and south. Why does he not do something?"

"I'm afraid he is more interested in his entertainment and his love life to give the poor army much mind."

"Well, I think he is making another mistake letting those patriots leave the city. They would make good hostages to prevent their likeminded cousins from causing more trouble."

"Ah, let them go," replied Charley, "that many less mouths to feed. We will be on half rations soon enough."

"What about the fleet? They will be able to supply us."

"Not come winter, with those northeaster storms they have, with their sleet and snow. And anyway, they are too busy transporting more troops in to worry about the poor souls already here."

"I hope you are wrong, Charlie, but fear it may be so. Ah, it is an unjust fate that puts us here."

"It is a soldier's fate, just like marching and dying. We are the lucky ones. We have lived to fight another day."

Cambridge Commons

The Queen Street School boys wandered through Cambridge in a daze. General Artemis Ward had formed an army, as over 10,000 men came in from the surrounding provinces, Connecticut, Rhode Island, New Hampshire, and Maine. Men were still arriving. Soon there would be 15,000 of them, surrounding 9000 British regulars now trapped in Boston.

The yards and fields, the commons and greens, churchyards and potato patches were filled with men of all descriptions - farmers and dock men, tinkers and merchants, doctors and lawyers, all colors and creeds massed together in a chaotic carnival of voices, smells, and laughter. Nathan and the others had never seen so much excitement at one time, in one place, not even when the traveling circus came to town.

Jeremy had been right, their little gift was a precious windfall for the powder-strapped American army, an army that had materialized out of nowhere with just the clothes on their back. Revere had been ecstatic and treated the boys to a full course dinner. He even let them have some of the rum they had pilfered.

"You boys have done us a great service," he had told them over desert. "You will all be handsomely rewarded."

"Does that mean we can join the army?" asked Samuel.

"I do not know about that," answered Revere. "Some of you are a bit young, but I'm certain you can be of service."

"Do we get to fight redcoats?" asked Peter, who seemed to have a personal grudge against the British.

"Maybe, if you are old enough and have a musket, but my job is not fighting, my job is conveying information and orders from one place to another across this great province. It is a very important job. I could use a team of men like you to be my assistants, my errand boys."

"Swell," said Samuel. Jeremy seemed to like the idea as well, as did their smallest associate, thirteen year old Timothy Russell. Others, like Nate and Peter stood silent, not sure they liked being errand boys.

"Do we get a horse?" asked Nate, who was now sorry he no longer had his father's gun. His short time in Boston, where there were more British soldiers than citizens, and the treacherous actions of his uncle, had changed his perspective. The events of the other morning, the way the British responded to his prank, did much to feed his anger against them. He no longer wanted to see them come marching up the road, but he did not yet want to shoot them.

Most of all he wanted to tell everyone the truth. Then maybe they would all stop fighting. But the reaction of the few people he had told had only made things worse. How did Jedediah find out? He must have overheard him talking to his brother, John. Maybe he should have gone with the British soldiers and told the truth, but things had happened so fast he'd had no chance to make a decision. He was being whisked away before he knew it. In any case, he didn't like being arrested much. Once they had him, no telling what they'd do to him. Didn't they hang people for treason? He certainly didn't want to find out.

So far everyone he'd told had advised him not to tell anyone else. That was probably the best course of action. Then why did he feel the overwhelming urge to confess?

The next morning was raw and damp. The boys sat around a fire they had started to roast some walnuts and keep warm. Paul Revere had told them he needed their help, but so far he had yet to assign them any tasks. They were starting to get bored and were thinking of trying to get back into Boston, when he suddenly showed up.

"Hi, men," he said, riding up on a chestnut mare. "I see you are bivouacking with the rest of the troops. Good, I have a job for you."

"Great," said Peter. "I was starting to think you forgot about us."

"I will never forget you boys and what you have done for your country. But things sometimes move slowly in a big army like this. Peter and Samuel, I want you to go to Roxbury with this letter for General Thomas. You are to deliver it to the general himself. It is from his father. He will be very gratified to receive it. Go directly there. Do not stop anywhere on the way. Do you understand?"

"Yes, sir," saluted Peter and Samuel with a grin, running off with the letter.

"Jeremy and Nate, I want you take this note to Dr. Warren in Watertown, where the Provincial Council is convening. Do you know how to get there?"

"I was there the other night when I took my aunt to Boston," answered Nate.

"Good. As with Peter, you must talk to no one. Deliver it personally to the president of the council and bring back his response. Understand?"

"Yes, sir," answered Jeremy and Nate in unison.

"Timothy will come with me. We will be going to Framingham to pick-up some supplies. Ready? Good. Godspeed."

"I'm glad you are coming with me," said Jeremy, as he and Nate trudged west out of Cambridge and along the road to nearby Watertown. As they walked together down the path, Nate had an overpowering urge to tell his friend about that morning on the Lexington Green. He needed to confide in someone he could trust. See what *they* would say. He almost did bare his soul, but a rider came up on them suddenly from behind and scared them half to death.

"Where are you boys headed?" he asked.

The boys, mindful of their commander's orders to talk to no one, said nothing.

"Suit yourselves," said the man, "but if you are going to the council meeting, you better get a move on. It will start in a matter of minutes." With that, he spurred his horse and galloped off, riding west down the dusty road.

Although Revere would normally not have trusted a message carrying vital information to young boys, these youngsters had shown a high level of courage and ingenuity in pulling off their little operation. They had been bamboozling the English in the town for weeks. They would be less likely to attract attention, and through the zeal of their youth, they would be fearless in the carrying out of their duty. In any case, they wanted to be involved. The future of the American colonies could one day depend on the continuing ardor and love of these boys for their county. The more they were exposed to those ideals and to the great men that espoused them, the better it would be, or so thought Paul Revere.

Nate and Jeremy arrived at the council meeting twenty minutes later, well after it had started. A well-dressed man with a long face and a fancy haircut was talking. The boys stood in the back of the gallery, which was packed with men. It did not take them long to determine that the man who was talking was the one they had the message for, Dr. Joseph Warren.

"These are momentous times!" he thundered. "But also times fraught with danger. We must follow the great victory of yesterday with a peaceful demonstration of our resolve to resist tyranny in all its forms. The Crown must be informed, along with Parliament, of the behavior of His Majesty's troops on the 19th of April last. We must investigate what happened on that day in all its details, and send the results to England on a fast ship, before they hear the lies of General Gage. They must learn that not only did the regulars fire the first shot, but that they are now raging the most brutal and inhumane war against the innocent men, women, and children of New England."

The first shot, the first shot, those words kept echoing in Nate's ear, all other syllables lost in a haze of guilt and confusion. Why did life have to be so hard? Suddenly, he had an idea.

"I know who fired the first shot," he said, barely audibly over the noise of the crowd.

"What did you say?" asked his friend, Jeremy.

"Never mind. We need to talk to Dr. Warren."

84

After the meeting had been adjourned and the room cleared of most of the occupants, they showed their pass from Paul Revere and approached the knot of important men talking to the president of the Council to deliver their message.

"Mister Warren, sir," Jeremy stuttered. "Paul Revere sent us with a message for you. We are to deliver it only to you and are to wait for your reply."

"Ah, now Revere is sending boys to do his bidding for him, eh. Although you look big enough," he added after looking Nate over. "What is it you have for me?"

Jeremy handed him the letter, which the doctor read standing up.

"So, Gage wants to negotiate an exchange of citizens. Very generous of him. I wonder what he has up his sleeve."

"He doesn't want to feed them, I'll wager," replied the outgoing president, John Hancock, soon to be on his way to Philadelphia to join the Continental Congress. "He'll mix in a few Tory spies then probably change his mind when he discovers the whole city's being emptied."

"That may be, John, but we must go along. There are many patriots in Boston. It would be better if only British soldiers are locked up there."

"Aye," the other men agreed.

"Mister Warren, sir," said Nate, timidly interrupting the conversation. "I have some information for your investigation. I was there that morning on the Green. I saw the whole thing, sir."

"What?" exclaimed Warren. "You saw what happened on the Green? Who are you? What were you doing there? Were you with the group on the Green?"

"No, sir. I was sleeping behind a wall next to it. I got into trouble back home in Acton, sir, with the son of one of the big Tories in the village. I ran away from home, from my Uncle Jacob. He's a Tory, too. It was late and I was tired, so I laid down behind the wall and fell asleep. When I woke up in the morning, there were a hundred redcoats all lined up on the Green."

Warren held up his hand and said, "Wait. This is something for the Committee. It must be written down in private. Since I am the only committee member here today, I will conduct the interview with you alone. What is your name, son?"

"Nate, Nate Daniels from Acton."

"I will talk to Mister Daniels and report my findings though the committee at tomorrow's session," Warren said to those standing around him. "Thank you, gentlemen."

With that, the group dispersed and Nate and Jeremy were led to a side room where there was a pot of coffee brewing, with milk and cookies.

"You gentlemen must be hungry after your trek from Cambridge," said Warren. "I have some things prepared. Why don't you join me? Now we can talk in comfort and privacy. What you have to say may be very important."

"Thank you, sir," said Jeremy, as he picked up a sugar-coated treat. Nate was already stuffing his mouth and pockets, and could not speak.

Warren continued, "Mister Revere has mentioned in his correspondence how you and your friends have helped the army. That must have been quite a feat, smuggling 600 pounds of gunpowder out of Boston, right under the nose of the British. Sounds like you had quite an exciting time of it, getting away from the gunboat."

"Ah, it was nothing," answered Jeremy. "We do stuff like that all the time."

"Yes, so I've heard. Now, Mister Daniels, would you like to continue your testimony?"

"Heh?" mumbled Nate, his mouth full of cookies.

"Your tale, the story of what you saw on the morning of the 19th?"

"I don't know what date it was. It was last Wednesday, I suppose, around six in the morning. It was just getting light. I heard all this commotion and sat up. There were about 100 redcoats lined up facing a couple of dozen local men. They were all standing on the Green right in front of me, not more than fifty yards away."

"Did any of the British fire? Who shot first?" asked Warren.

"That's just it, sir, neither side did."

"What, what do you mean? Someone had to fire the first shot. I thought you said you saw what happened. What, did you miss it?"

Warren was becoming exasperated at the prospect of having his busy day interrupted by some boy trying to attract attention.

"Did you see it or not?"

"Yes, sir," Nate replied.

Now was the moment of truth. Of course, he couldn't tell this important patriot that it was his impulsive prank that had caused the whole thing, but he could claim he saw who did. Now all he had to do was make it sound real.

"I saw another boy across the way. He was behind a fence and had a gun. I saw him point it at an officer on a horse and saw a puff of smoke from where he was. At the same time the redcoat's hat flew off. Then the whole line of soldiers fired their guns. It was awful. Nothing seemed to happen at first, but the redcoats kept shooting, and soon a lot of our men at the other end of the field started falling. I could hear them screaming. That's when they fired back, but the redcoats kept up an awful fire. They were just mowing down our boys. It was terrible. After that I couldn't see much because of all the smoke and I ran away as fast as I could."

"And well you should, my boy, and well you should."

Warren was stunned by the revelation. The news was as unexpected as a kick from behind, but corresponded to what Captain Parker reported. He swore none of his men had fired before the British. This might change everything, for if the British did not fire first, much of their argument to the Crown would become irrelevant. He had to verify the truth.

"Are you sure?" he pressed. "This is very important. You must be certain. I know that place. The Common is quite large. Are you sure you saw someone shoot from behind a fence? Are you sure it was not a British soldier? There were more of them, from what I understand, standing away from your front, that you might not have seen."

"No, sir, I'm sure," answered Nate, trying to be as convincing as possible. "The redcoats were yelling and making a lot of noise, but none of them fired their guns. It was somebody from behind a fence. Maybe he was just trying to shut everyone up."

The last remark made Warren pause, but the story on a whole seemed to be truthful. He had to report this to the Committee.

"Thank you, young man. This is very important information and may avert a catastrophe of epic proportions. Perhaps there is a peaceful way to resolve this whole affair and reconcile our differences with our mother country. After all, we are all Englishmen."

Nate didn't know about that. He didn't think of himself as an Englishman, although he knew his Uncle Jacob did, but he agreed with Dr. Warren's sentiments.

"I hope so, sir. No one likes war."

"Yes, Nate, you can be quite sure of that."

Jeremy had been quiet through the whole interview, sitting in the background on a chair, but he had listened carefully, for Nate's story was of great interest. Being bright and inquisitive, and influenced by the leanings of his father, he was an ardent believer in the patriot cause. He believed the British had fired the first shot. Now he was not so sure, though he didn't quite believe Nathan either. His friend seemed to be holding something back. Things just didn't add up. Jeremy began to wonder if his new friend was telling the truth or just trying to make himself look important.

Chapter 12

Colonel Francis Smith's Brigade, Beacon Hill

Corporal Charlie McBride of Smith's Light Infantry felt like a chicken in a coop ready to be slaughtered. Most of the inhabitants of the city had left. Boston had become a ghost town, grass growing in the squares. Only die-hard Tories or those refusing to leave their business establishment were left. There was little reason for them to stay. All the shops and storehouses were shut up, their windows boarded, their doors locked. British transports full of reinforcements crowded the docks, unloading men and military stores, but little food, which was becoming harder to come by as the city was squeezed off by the surrounding forces.

Charley and his mates still slept in white tents lined up on the Commons, while the officers whiled away their time in the plush apartments of departed patriots. Regardless of where you bunked, you were shut up like a prisoner by a mob of hostile inhabitants, under perpetual alarm, expecting an attack any minute that never came. He would go mad if it didn't end soon.

He was struck by the contrast between the dismal decaying city they were trapped in and the surrounding countryside. Charlie was standing on the top of Beacon Hill doing sentry duty, manning one of the many barricades they had erected around the city. He looked out south, over the back of the bay. The gentle rolling hills, covered with green, disappeared into the hazy distance, while close at hand the water in the bay glistened in the sun amidst a dozen tree-dotted islands. The white sails of a few small ships flitted amidst the waves, while sea birds circled above. It looked so peaceful, yet he knew the calm was deceptive.

"Are we going to fight or what?" he asked his sergeant, an old hand that was new to the regiment.

"Oh, we will fight, all right. There is no doubt of that. It's just when, that's the question."

"Well, I for one wish it would be soon."

"Oh, and why is that, corporal? Are you so anxious to get a musket ball in the head?"

"It is I who will be filling someone with lead," growled Charlie.

"Very good, corporal. That is just the attitude we will want when we finally make our move."

"I don't know how much more of this waiting around I can stand. If I don't get off this stinking pile of sand soon I will go mad."

"That will not take you home, lad. We are here for the duration of this war. For that's what it is now. The general won't let us sit here for long. He's got something in mind, I assure you."

"I hope so."

"So you were there?"

"What, where? What do you mean?"

"You were there on the Green when the provincials fired on us, and at the bridge, out west, in that town."

"Concord?"

"Yes, that's it, Concord. It must have been pretty bad."

"You can't imagine. It was as vicious as I've heard tell about in the last wars. The bloody savages came out of the woods like animals. They waited behind trees and stone walls to ambush us, only to run away after discharging their firearms. They even tomahawked our wounded, and prisoners. This wasn't war. It was inhuman butchery."

"Wars are like that. They have a way of getting out of hand rather quick. That's why you have to be sure what you're about before you get into one. I'm afraid this one crept up on us. That's what happens when you are 3000 miles and six weeks away."

"It is foolish to keep us cooped up like this. An army needs to fight. Soon we will be fighting among ourselves."

"There's already been a little of that, but that is not necessarily a bad thing, as long as they don't start shooting each other. Don't worry. Soon those natural-born aggressions will be turned on the enemy. Then you will see what the British army can do."

Charlie hoped the sergeant was right, and prayed it would happen soon.

Cambridge Commons

Nate and Jeremy were back in Cambridge after delivering Paul Revere's message to Joseph Warren. They still hadn't seen Paul Revere, but were carrying the doctor's response in their pouch.

There was still a lot going on. If anything, there was even more excitement and activity than before, as militiamen from as far away as Rhode Island and Connecticut continued to pour into the town. Despite the crush of men, there was plenty of food - turkey, venison, beef, eggs, butter, milk, and bread. More troubling for those in charge was the abundant quantity of New England rum available, barrels and kegs of it, all coming in from the countryside and the abandoned houses of rich loyalists.

The first thing Nate noticed when they got back to town was the foul odor. It was a hot day, and there were obviously not enough latrines being dug. Men were relieving themselves wherever the urge took them - in the fields, the ditches, the gardens, and backyards around town. Nate had never smelt anything so foul, not even his uncle's manure patch.

Discipline was nowhere to be found. These were farm boys and young men from the surrounding towns, unused to following orders even from their own elected leaders. Left on their own, many for the first time in their lives, they acted on impulse and whim, and they all had muskets.

"I did not get any sleep last night," complained Peter. "Do they have to shoot their guns off all night?"

"It is the rum," observed Jeremy. "They drink that instead of sleeping. It makes them wild."

"If I had my father's gun," said Nate. "I wouldn't go shooting it in the air, wasting powder. We hardly have enough to go hunting with. They should not be wasting it so."

They all agreed and thought it stupid, but were buoyed by the numbers that had come out to defend the province, though to the boys it was just an adventure.

"What happened to it?" Jeremy asked. "Your gun, I mean?"

Nate hadn't expected the questions and was momentarily at a loss for words.

"I lost it in the river trying to get away from the redcoats."

"Is that when they shot our guys?" asked Peter.

"Yeah," said Nate, not wanting them to know he broke it himself or why. "I wish I had it now. I sure could use it."

"Especially since the British could attack at any time," said a voice from behind them.

They all turned at the sound to see that Paul Revere had ridden up unobserved.

"Hi, sir," said the boys, standing up suddenly and saluting.

"At ease, boys. How are you all doing? Did you deliver the messages?"

"Yes, sir," Jeremy replied. "We're good. We have Dr. Warren's reply."

"Ah, excellent. Let me see what the good doctor has to say."

Revere began to read Warren's letter.

"Good, the Council agrees to General Gage's offer. I will relay this immediately," he said after reading the first paragraph. "He also says he is worried about the state of the army. And well he should be. Never has a band of undisciplined men attempted what we are doing here."

He stopped and looked about him.

"It is a strange brew that we have here, men who fight and drink and gamble all afternoon and carouse all night, then attend prayer meetings twice in the mornings, hanging on the preacher's every word. But these are what we have. We must make due with them the best we can. The British could attack at any time. We must be ready. If only we knew what they were up to."

"We could tell you," offered Jeremy. "We used to spy on them all the time."

"Yes, I am sure you could, but it is much too dangerous. You lads were lucky to get out the way you did. It would be too risky to send you in again. And how would you communicate with us once inside? No, I appreciate you volunteering, but I would never forgive myself if anything happened to one of you."

He continued reading.

"Hmm, now, what have we here? It seems Dr. Warren has added a postscript concerning Mr. Daniels."

He stood and read the remainder of the message.

"Oh, this is bad news," said Paul Revere, after reading Joseph Warren's secret codicil. "This could change everything and ruin our chances of convincing Parliament to recall their troops. I must talk to Dr. Warren before tomorrow's meeting."

He looked at Nate with more than a little curiosity.

"It seems your observations have opened up a can of worms, Mister Daniels. We must leave immediately. You will come with me."

Nate was now having second thoughts concerning his idea. He thought it would be a good way of getting everyone to stop fighting and yet not get himself in trouble. Now he wasn't so sure. Things were getting complicated. He was confused as usual, his mind a jumble of conflicting thoughts. He would normally have relished the idea of riding out to Concord with the famous Paul Revere, but not if it involved telling the story he had made up. He was beginning to regret that he had opened his big mouth. He wasn't sure he could remember exactly what he had told the doctor and hoped he wouldn't have to repeat it all again. They had hardly left Cambridge on the road west when Revere asked him to recount what he had said.

"Are you sure you saw someone shoot from behind a fence? It seems that it would have been difficult to see from where you said you stood. I know that Green well. It is over 200 yards across from where you say you were. If someone was standing behind a fence as you say, they would have been difficult to spot from that distance."

"They were," said Nate, thinking fast. "I wasn't sure what I was seeing until the shot and I saw the puff of smoke. Then the redcoat's hat flew off. It took a while for me to figure out what happened, but after I was running away, I realized what it must have been."

"Everything must have occurred very fast," replied the militia colonel. "It must have been pretty confusing and scary."

"I wasn't scared," replied Nate, not wanting to admit how frightened he really was. "It sure happened fast, though. I ain't never seen anything like that, and I hope I never do again."

"So do I. So what do you suppose the person who fired that shot was trying to do, start a war?"

"No, I don't think he was really trying to shoot anyone. I think he was just doing it as a joke, shooting that officer's hat off and all. He probably just wanted to shut them up."

Revere noted that remark and continued on the road silently. Soon they were in Concord at the house where Dr. Warren was staying.

"Hi, Colonel," said Warren greeting them at the door. "Nice to see you, and you too, my boy. What brings you out this way?"

"Hi, Doctor. I needed to talk to you about the information you conveyed in your postscript as soon as possible. It is of the utmost importance that our response to the Crown be convincing or our cause will be lost."

"Why don't you come in for tea and we can talk about it."

Once inside Revere got right to the point.

"For the sake of our nascent rebellion, doctor, the revelations of this boy must be kept secret. Our only chance of convincing Parliament to recall their forces is to show that their army fired the first shot."

"But that would not be true," replied the Council president. "Our two sides can still be reconciled without more bloodshed or lies."

"I'm afraid the time for reconciliation has passed, Doctor," replied the militia lieutenant colonel. "It ended when the British shot down dozens of our people in cold blood, without provocation."

"But if what Nate said is true…"

"Nate," said Revere, looking at him sharply. "You say you saw something, but you are not sure what it was, a puff of smoke, you said. People's eyes can play tricks on them, especially when they've just woken up in the early light of dawn. You yourself said that you weren't sure what was happening until you were running away and thought about it afterward, but in the chaos of the moment, don't you think you could have made a mistake? Maybe it was actually one of the British marshaled on the other side of the Common, just out of your vision, that fired first. Perhaps that was the puff of smoke you saw. Could that not be?"

"Yes, I suppose so," answered Nate, not caring much at this point who fired first. "Like I said, it all happened kind of fast."

"See, Doctor, the boy was mistaken."

Warren was perplexed. He could see Paul Revere's point, but his honor did not permit him to lie to gain the advantage. Still, perhaps Revere was correct. The boy's story, although it sounded true enough, didn't quite fit, as if there was something missing, something left unsaid.

"Perhaps you are right, Paul. We will give this information to the Committee, as we have done with the rest of our findings, and let them sort it out, but we must not tarry. My sources tell me that Gage has already sent a ship out. I want to have something to send to England by the end of tomorrow."

"You shall, Mister President, and she will be a fast ship, I assure you. We will have our say."

"What about our army?" asked Warren. "Are they ready?"

"I do not know, Doctor, but it is a very dangerous group of men. If only they can be led."

94

"They can be led," said Warren. "And they will fight."

Chapter 13

The next morning at camp, Nate sat by the fire brooding. He was mad at everyone, especially Paul Revere. He thought they were all crazy, the Rebels *and* the British. They don't care who fired first, he realized, they just want to shoot each other.

"I'm going home," Nate announced to his startled friends. "I'm sick of this place. It smells worse than my uncle's manure dump. They don't need me. I don't want to be an errand boy anymore. I'm going home."

"You can't just desert like that," said Peter, who had become an ardent patriot.

"Why not?" replied Nate. "Everyone else is going. The men are leaving in droves."

"Nate's right," agreed Jeremy. "Colonel Revere said the same things. There's nothing he or the generals can do if the militiamen want to go home to their farms and things."

"Well, Nate doesn't have a farm," answered Peter.

"I'm going home," said Nate. "And no one can stop me."

"No one wants to stop you, Nate," said Jeremy. "But you don't want to miss all the excitement, do you?"

"What excitement? All we do is sit around and wait for something to happen. I'm sick of this. See you all later."

"At least tell us where you are going and when you'll be back, for we need good men like you."

"I'm going back to Acton, to my uncle's farm to make sure it's all right. Maybe I'll see my brother, John, let him know I'm safe. We have not spoken for some time. I will be back in awhile, I guess, if I have a mind."

"You had better come back," replied Peter. "You are part of our gang now."

"Yes, I promise. Maybe I'll bring you boys something good to eat, or some apple cider."

Soon after, Nate was heading west out of Cambridge. The further he got from the confines of the overcrowded town, the better he felt. Soon he was walking along well-worn trails through woodlands and fields, with broad pastures and cornfields on each side, and hills covered with blossoming apple trees in the near distance. He had forgotten how beautiful the countryside was in springtime, everything fresh and new. The burgeoning green of the budding trees was brilliant against the pale blue, burnished sky.

He stopped and ate lunch beneath a gnarled, thick old oak tree, resting his stick against the stone wall that stretched along the side of the road. A bird sang to him as he ate, a pretty melody repeated at different pitches. Nate almost fell asleep beneath the tree and woke with a start when a horse came thundering up the lane.

"Whoa, there," said the rider, a militiaman by the looks of him. "What are you doing, lying on the road, lad?"

"I am sorry, sir, but I'm not lying on the road. I am a good two feet off the highway on the grass."

"That may be, but to my horse, anything between the trees and the wall is a road. She is a wild filly with a mind of her own."

"Then I suggest you control your steed better. This is a public way."

"I am doing my best, but, as you point out, boy, it is a road, not a bed. Now get out of the way. I have news to deliver. The Council has declared a province-wide day of prayer and fasting."

With that he spurred his steed and galloped off at a good clip.

"What a rude man," Nate announced to no one in particular, as he proceeded on his way again. The last thing on his mind was prayer and fasting.

Making good time, he was at the village of Acton a few hours later. The place looked as if it had been forgotten by time. His uncle's farm was just as they left it when they hurriedly left a week ago, the furniture still sitting forlornly in the front yard. Many other houses looked the same. Bereft of people, like empty shells on a beach, they were slowly beginning to deteriorate. Weeds and grass grew in the walkways and roads, where cows and horses roamed freely.

Wandering around town he saw few signs of civilization - a lone wagon passing on the road, a rider on the hill, a face in a window - but no one spoke or tarried. Everyone rushed about their business with head down and eyes averted, as if the place was occupied by an enemy force, but it was only fear that held this village in bondage. Near the bridge across the creek close to the main part of town, he recognized a familiar face. It was Rebecca Adams, coming down the road in the opposite direction, carrying a pail of milk.

"Hi, Rebecca," he said shyly, as she approached. "How have you been?"

She didn't know him at first because of his unkempt appearance, but on a second nervous glance, she recognized him and smiled.

"Hi, Nathan. I am fine, and you?"

"Fair. I'm in the army now, working as a messenger for Paul Revere."

"Yes, everyone has gone off to fight in the war. It is just terrible. I was wondering what happened to you. You should not have hit Jedediah so hard."

"I didn't mean to. He shouldn't have hit me first without provocation." He knew that word would come in handy some day. "Thanks for not telling on me."

"It wasn't your fault. Jedediah can be mean sometimes."

"Yeah, try all the time. How have you been?"

"Not good," she admitted. "Dad has gone with his militia company to fight. I'm not sure where he is or when he'll be back. I am so worried. Now it is just Ma and me that have to do all the work. It has been hard."

"Maybe I can help you."

"I thought you said you were working for that Mister Paul Revere. He's famous, isn't he?"

"Yeah, I guess so. He knows the president of the Council and all the generals. He is a well-known patriot."

"Are you a patriot?" she asked.

"I guess so. I never really thought about it."

"If you work for Paul Revere you must be."

"Yeah, when you put it like that, I guess I am, but I bet you that Jedediah Weekes isn't. Have you seen him around?"

"Yes, he stayed after his family left for Boston. I saw him in town a few days ago, but he is gone now. Their house is boarded up, like a lot of them."

"Here, let me help you with that," he offered, taking the container of warm, fresh milk.

"But you are going in the opposite direction," she objected. "I don't want to take you out of your way."

"Naw, that's all right. I was just looking around. I'm not doing anything. It is nice to have a familiar person to talk to."

"Yes, it has been lonely around here."

As they walked back in the direction of Rebecca's home, they filled each other in on what had happened to them, Nate skipping the events of the morning of April 19th. He was in bliss. He had never walked alone with a girl before, and Rebecca was the one he had dreamed about when he imagined doing so. Here he was walking next to her in the flesh, so close he could touch her.

He spent the rest of the day helping her and her mother with some of the more difficult chores, and had dinner with them that evening. He lied when they invited him to stay, telling them he had to deliver a message and was staying at an inn in the next town. He left just after dark. He was sorry for lying, but could not bear hearing Becky's mother lament her woes any longer. It broke his heart and made him feel even worse than he had. He blamed himself for all their troubles.

Being dog-tired, he had planned to sleep on the ground under the stars, but a hard rain that started soon after he left Rebecca's house drove him into his uncle's barn. At some point during the night, it must have been around midnight by Nate's reckoning, he was awakened, when someone opened the barn door and came in. Hiding behind a stall in a pile of hay, he heard several voices talking in hushed whispers.

"No one will overhear us here in Daniels's barn, and knowing old Jacob, he would not object," said one of the men.

Peeking through a crack in the stable boards, Nate could see the speaker and three other men standing in a semi-circle before a lantern, which had been placed upon an upturned barrel.

"He has run to Boston like so many others," replied another man standing next to the first. "But what can he do for our cause there, shut up with the British army?"

"They were supposed to save us from these troublemakers," said another. "Instead they run to Boston like curs with their tail between their legs."

"No one can save us but ourselves," stated the first man. "*We* are the patriots. These rebels, who call themselves such and say they are for liberty, would deny us our freedom at the drop of a hat. We must fight now that they have declared war on our rightful government. What they would replace it with is the worst type of tyranny."

"What do you have in mind, Edward?"

"We can strike them where they least expect it, but where it will cause the most harm. Their leader, Dr. Warren from Salem, was just voted President of the State Executive Committee to replace that radical, John Jay. He has taken a lead in things and is this very night at an inn just outside of Concord."

"You seem well informed, Edward."

"I make it a point to be."

"What do you have in mind?"

"He is alone, without guard, out on one of his clandestine rendezvous with some young lady of dubious reputation."

"All these rebels are hot-blooded," interjected another man recently cuckolded by one of them.

"So much the better. He is making it easy for us. We can take him and hold him here for ransom."

"Even better," interjected one of them. "We could string him up by the neck like we should do to all of them until we drive every damned rebel out of the state."

"Your ardor is praiseworthy, Henry," said Ed Sikes, a blacksmith and loyalist. "But for the moment, Mister Warren might be worth more to us alive than dead, however desirable that may be."

"I'd really like to get my hands on that Samuel Adams," replied Henry. "There's a rabble-rousing radical if ever there was one."

Nate could hardly believe his ears. Were these men planning to kidnap Dr. Warren? It sure sounded like it. He had to warn him, but how?

He looked around the barn. One of the men's horses, which had been brought in out of the rain, was tied up next to the stall where he was hiding. He crawled over to it and was untying it when one of the men heard the noise and came to investigate, peeking into the stall.

"Who's there?" he yelled. The others, startled, started moving in their direction.

Suddenly, Nate burst out of the shadows, knocking the man standing at the gate backward into the others with a hard push. They fell against the barrel, knocking it over along with the lantern on top of it. The barn went black for an instant, before a small fire ignited in a patch of hay. In the confusion and darkness, Nate jumped on the back of the horse, unlatched the gate, and kicked the animal's sides sharply.

"Yah!" he yelled, wishing the horse to move.

The men started rising slowly from the floor, spooking the animal, which reared on its hind legs. Nate knew horses, however, and was able to stay on its back. Putting his arms around its neck, he whispered in her ear and kicked it in the sides, making her jump over the rising men and bolt for the half-open door. Nate ducked quickly, just avoiding the wall above the opening. As he did, a shot rang out, splintering the wood an inch above his head. The next instant, he was out of the barn, racing down the soggy, mud-covered road at full tilt.

He could hear men yelling as he galloped away, calling for their horses. His uncle's barn had begun to burn. Another shot echoed in the night. Where it landed Nate didn't know, only that they were shooting at him. He spurred the horse on.

A short distance up the road east out of town, where it rounded a hill, Nate darted off on a small side trail through the woods. It was a shortcut that he knew of, which went across country northeast directly toward Concord and the inn where Joseph Warren was staying. He had to get there before these traitors.

The night had turned stormy. Lightning cracked, thunder pealed, rain pelted him like hail, as he raced through the darkness, hardly able to see two feet in front of him. Arriving in Concord, he had trouble finding the inn in the inclement weather, and circled around town until he found his bearings. He hoped whoever was after him was still behind him.

Finally finding the house, he jumped off his horse and pounded on the door.

"Dr. Warren!" he yelled. "It's Nate. Dr. Warren, are you there?"

His frantic knocking and yells soon got a response. Someone with a candle came down the stairs to the door.

"Yes," he said, opening it. It was Joseph Warren. He was in his nightshirt.

"Quick, sir," yelled Nate. "We have no time to lose. They may be right behind me. They are coming to kidnap you. Hurry!"

With that he pushed the startled doctor back up the stairs and toward his room, where Warren was able to partially dress before they heard the sound of hooves and loud banging at the door.

"Back here," urged Nate. "I have a horse in back. Quick, out the window."

Warren climbed out the rear window onto the porch roof, where he let himself down to the ground. Nate's horse stood tied to a post. Without a backward glance, Warren spurred the animal and galloped into the stormy night heading east.

Nate, who had also climbed out onto the roof of the porch, watched the doctor ride off. He held his breath until he got away, then heaved a sigh of relief. Before he could climb down and make his own getaway, however, one of the loyalists, riding to the back of the house, spotted him.

"Here, here he is!" he yelled to the others, who came running out of the house and soon surrounded him. "It's the scoundrel from the barn."

"He heard everything," said another. "He must have warned the doctor. What are we going to do with him?"

"Hang the dirty rebel," yelled Henry, the man who wanted to hang Dr. Warren.

They held Nate hands behind him and manhandled him into the inn's stable, which was nearby and dry. One of them punched him in the face and blackened his eye.

"I've got a rope," yelled another, as he threw it over a ceiling beam.

"What have you got to say for yourself, boy?" asked the leader, Ed Sikes, a big man with a black beard.

"I haven't done anything. I work here," lied Nate.

"That can be determined soon enough."

"He's the one from the barn," insisted the one who had first spotted him. "I am sure of it."

"Were you the one eavesdropping on us?" asked the leader.

"No, I don't know what you're talking about," replied Nate, terrified.

"He's lying!" yelled Henry. "Hang him and be done with it."

"Find out who he is," Sikes ordered.

One of the men ran out to get the innkeeper. Nate was insulted and spit on as he waited. Two of them were holding his arms behind him. He knew what the verdict would be, but was being held tightly and could not get away, not that he would have gotten far. His captors were all armed.

The other man soon came back.

"He is not with the inn," he announced. "They say the boy is a messenger for the rebels. It was he who informed Warren we were coming."

"Hang him!" yelled Henry, seizing him and grabbing the rope to loop it around his neck.

"Don't kill me!" Nate screamed in anguish. "I have done nothing wrong."

"You are a traitor to your country. You will pay the price for your disloyalty. Roll that barrel over here," he ordered.

They held Nate tightly, but as Henry went to put the rope around his neck, Nate kicked him in the stomach, knocking him backward off his feet. As he did this, he stepped backward into one of the men holding him and hooked his leg behind him, making him fall backwards with Nate on top of him and free from the third man – an Indian trick his brother had taught him. Nate's elbow snapped back and smashed the man in the side of the head. Kicking out wildly at the third man, who was trying to grab him, Nate managed to break his nose, before Ed Sikes jumped on top of him and punched him between the eyes, knocking him senseless.

Suddenly, there was a shot.

"Hold it!" yelled Paul Revere, who held another pistol in his hand. "You are surrounded by Continental troops. Cease and desist or you will be shot."

All motion stopped as the loyalists looked around them. They were surrounded by several militiamen with muskets.

"Luckily we were nearby," said Revere jubilantly as he picked Nate up from the floor. "You had quite a close call there, Mister Daniels. Doctor Warren told us how you saved him and urged us to come to your aid, as he took note that you did not get away."

"You came just in time," Nate informed him, groggily, rubbing his forehead. "They were going to hang me."

"Were they now," said Revere. "We will see who dangles soon enough. For now, though, we will take these men back to Cambridge for interrogation. I'm afraid we will have to give you a medal, Mister Daniels. You are a hero, my boy."

Chapter 14

Things were not going well for the fledgling Continental Army. Sickness and disease decimated the once robust Yankee soldiers, and many had gone home to their farms and families. Things only got worse as spring turned to summer and the heat increased.

The British had not moved out of Boston since that fateful day in April, but General Gage had reneged on his promise to let people leave the city. He had instituted martial law, which only stiffened the resolve of the rebellious citizens. They were low on gunpowder and men, however, as they waited for the enemy to come out as many thought they would.

Nate was at the top of the world. Not only had he been presented with a new musket and powder horn, he had been promoted to the rank of corporal in Revere's messenger corps.

Earlier in the spring, old General Putnam, from New Hampshire, had marched his 2000 men into Charlestown to taunt the British, parading around the deserted peninsula and into the abandoned town right in the face of the guns of an enemy man-of-war. Nate and the boys were with them, jumping and whooping and having a grand old time. They were also observing the lay of the land and the ships in the harbor for their commander, Peter making especially good notes and drawings.

Putnam's exhibition was the talk of the colony, and stirred the patriotic zeal in people's breasts. Men came flooding back into the camp to rejoin or sign up. Many had only returned home for a short time, to help plant crops and tend their farms, some to visit wives and families not seen in weeks. Most intended to come back, but news of the old war veteran's sally made many hasten that return.

"How do you like your new gun," Revere asked Nate, a few days after the ceremony awarding it to him for saving the Council president.

"Swell, I like it fine. It shoots better than my dad's did, and that gun shot good and true. But this one's lighter and has more range. It sure is a wondrous thing, though I don't shoot it much cause of the shortage of powder."

"Good. We must conserve our powder for when it's needed. I hear you don't need much practice. The boys say you are a good shot."

"I guess so. I've been shooting since I was a kid. I used to hunt supper for my grandma. She loved turkey and things. I could always shoot her something."

"That boy you say you saw at Lexington that morning, he must have been a good shot, too?"

Revere had been wondering about Nate's story ever since he'd heard it. The import of what it implied was too huge to ignore, and left more questions than answers.

"I guess so," answered Nate, hesitantly, sensing a potential trap. "All I saw was a puff of smoke and the redcoat's hat fly off."

"Well, if the man on the horse was fifty yards from you, as you say, then that boy behind the far fence must have been a good 200 yards or more away, wouldn't you say? And he would have had trees and other soldiers standing in the way. It must have been quite a shot."

"No, he was standing closer than that," insisted Nate, not sure how far 200 yards was or how Paul Revere could know all that. "He had a clear shot, just like me."

"Oh, yes, I bet you had a nice clear shot. I am sure *you* could have shot the man's hat off. But that other lad, way across the field where the fence is, he must have been a dandy shot, even better than you."

"I guess so," Nate replied, not wanting to talk about it anymore.

"We will have to go up and take a look so you can show me how it was."

"What does it matter, anyway?" yelled Nate, making Revere start in surprise.

"It is a very important matter, Nate. We have to be sure that the report to the British Parliament, which governs the land and these colonies, is accurate. We must show that it was the British regulars who started this conflict, not the colonists."

"What does it matter who fired the first shot, if it wasn't them and it wasn't us? It was an accident. No one started it. We should be able to tell everyone and end the war."

"I'm afraid it is not as simple as that."

"Why not?" asked Nate, confused as usual.

"You wouldn't understand, my boy, but this could be the birth of something brand new, something never seen before. You wouldn't want it to be stillborn, would you?"

Corporal Charlie McBride, Colonel Francis Smith's Brigade, Copp's Hill

Corporal Charlie McBride marched up the steep, cobblestone street to the top of Copp's Hill, overlooking Hudson's Point and Charlestown peninsula beyond. The batteries setup by the British, all pointing north and east over the harbor and bay, were as impressive as any he had seen. The fortifications and redoubts constructed for defense of the city were also imposing. Every street and square had its own barricades and ramparts obstructing passage.

Looking out at the high ground across the channel to the north, he could not believe the army had not taken possession of it.

"Lord, I hate guard duty," complained his mate. "I'd rather have at it with the rebels than stand in the sun staring at the bay all day."

"Five minutes of their hot musket fire would change your mind well enough. Then you would dream of guard duty like a month long furlough."

"I'd of thought with the arrival of the new generals at the end of May that things would be different. General Burgoyne talks as if he would have at them, and Henry Clinton suggested taking the heights, but Howe, like Gage, is on the cautious side and willing to let the rebels make the first move. I say it is a mistake. Anything would be better than waiting like this."

"It was hoped they would make an attack on us," said Charlie.

"They have not the stomach for it, I'll wager. They would prefer shooting from behind trees and walls, the cowards. It seems Gage's defensive strategy is going to continue while they fight among themselves. Too many generals and not enough men."

"We have enough men, all right," replied Charlie. "They just don't know what to do with them."

"General Clinton wants to take the high ground to the north across the harbor," his mate told him, "and south near Roxbury. They say he has convinced the others, but I will believe it when I see it."

"Now there is a commander I would follow," announced Charlie. "He knows what he's about. If we are going to fight, at least fight with the advantage. We must take the initiative."

"Very good, Charlie, that's the spirit. Too bad nobody cares what lowly corporals like us think, even though we will have to bear the brunt of the fighting when it finally comes. What is wrong with giving us good advantage?"

"Ah, you know why, Bill, like every other soldier who ever marched for England, ours is not to reason why, but only to fight and die."

"Hello? What are those boys doing down there?" said Bill, pointing to two youths hiding behind a wall near Christ's Church further down the hill. One of them appeared to be sketching something.

"Looks like one of them is drawing a picture," replied Charlie.

"The lad must be a budding artist," observed his friend.

Charley peered in their direction more intently and said, "Or a spy, scouting out our gun placements. Let us take a closer look."

They left their post on Copp's Hill and walked toward the two boys, who were loitering near the church overlooking the North Battery. Charlestown stood not far away across the channel. As they got closer they un-slung their guns.

"What are you boys doing there?" yelled Charlie, approaching rapidly.

"Nothing," answered the boy with the pen turning around quickly. He was rather heavyset with shaggy hair and tattered clothes. "Just drawing a picture of the harbor."

"Let me take a look at that," Charlie demanded, grabbing the notebook and looking at the drawing. His partner stood behind him holding his gun in front of him. Charlie thumbed through the pages of sketches, all which showed the placement of the British fortresses and batteries.

"These appear to be drawings of our defenses," Charlie observed. "You wouldn't be spying on us, would you?"

"No, sir," replied the boy. "They're just pictures of the forts and things. I want to be an engineer someday like your fellows."

"Is that so?" said Charlie, looking at the drawings more closely. "I'm afraid you will have to come with us."

"What for?" objected the boy. "We haven't done anything."

"I think you are a spy. You will have to explain yourself to the Colonel."

The boy went silent and began to shake.

"Oh, let them be, Charlie," said his mate. "They're just kids. He wants to be an engineer like Captain Brisbane."

"Perhaps, but these pictures show all of our forts and batteries. It looks like he's been making note of all of our defenses in the North

End. I think these boys are spying on us. In any case, they can explain themselves to the colonel. He'll get the truth out of them."

Suddenly, the boy who had been doing the drawing grabbed his notebook and bolted around the corner.

"Hold that one," Charlie ordered his partner, running after the boy.

They ran down the street toward the Harbor and Freeman's Warf. The ground leveled out and the land opened up as they got nearer the water. There were only twenty-five or thirty yards separating them, but the boy was getting away. Charlie did not run well. He stopped and raised his gun.

"Stop or I'll shoot!" he bellowed. The youth kept going.

He fired and the boy fell. Charlie ran toward him. A few dock workers looked around in the direction of the noise but otherwise ignored him. As Charlie approached the boy, he saw that he had a neat hole in the middle of his back where the ball had entered. Charley turned him over gently and felt for a pulse. There was none.

He felt bad for the lad, who couldn't have been more than fifteen, but he was certain the boy had been spying on them. He picked up the drawings for evidence. The other youngster was taken to headquarters for interrogation by Charlie's commander.

"I knew the Yankees were scoundrels," said the Colonel as he perused the notebook. "But I did not think they would stoop to having children do their dirty work for them. There is no doubt of it. These are detailed sketches of our positions and gun placements. The boy was spying. It is too bad you had to shoot him. The lad had a good talent, but he was using it for the wrong cause."

"I had to," answered Charlie. "He would have gotten away with the drawing otherwise. Who knows what use would have been made of them. Perhaps the other boy will tell us."

"He will if he knows what's good for him," said the Colonel. "I will have him hanged otherwise."

British Prison, North End, Boston

Samuel was still reeling from the loss of his friend, Peter. He was terrified and shaken, ashamed he could not hold in his tears in front of the redcoats. Up until a half hour ago it had all been a game, a fun if dangerous adventure. Now it had become all too real.

They had wanted to do something big, like Nate had done. They knew how much the army needed information on the enemy positions across from Charlestown. It was easy for them to get a boat and row across the Back Bay at night to sneak into town. Drawing pictures of the forts and guns was Peter's idea. Samuel thought it was a good one and volunteered to go along as a lookout. Too bad he hadn't been looking out when the soldiers approached behind them, but he was having too much fun watching the boats in the harbor. If only he'd been more alert they would not have been caught. Now Peter was dead and he was sure to follow. They had told no one of their plan. Samuel wondered if his mates would ever know what happened to them.

Chapter 15

News of Peter's death and Samuel's capture cast a pall on what would have otherwise been a fine late spring day. Men were flooding back to camp and morale was high. For Nate and his friends, however, it couldn't have been a sadder occasion.

"What are they going to do with him?" asked Jeremy.

"They say they will hang him unless we give up all of our loyalists prisoners," replied Paul Revere, who had brought the bad news to the boys, "including the four men who tried to kidnap Dr. Warren and almost hung Nate here."

"I say it's a fair trade," replied Nate, who would have done anything to bring his friend back.

"Four treasonous collaborators, with information about our strength and numbers for one small boy is hardly a fair trade, but I suppose we have no choice. We have to do it. What possessed those foolish boys to try something like that? I expressly told them not to."

"Poor Peter," said Jeremy on the verge of tears. "He was only trying to help the army. He knew how much we need information. Poor Peter."

Nate was sad also, but was too familiar with loss to cry. Instead, he thought of his friend, Samuel, imprisoned in a British jail, and how to get him freed."

"Promise us you will do everything to bring Samuel back," he pleaded to the commander.

"Don't worry. Samuel will be back with us soon. We will not let them harm the boy, and if they do, they will be sorry."

After Paul Revere left to consult with the generals about their friend, the boys sat and talked about what happened, all except Nate. He wandered toward the river to think and mourn. He wondered about his brother, John, and hoped that he was all right. He had not seen him for so long, and he had been so agitated when they last met that Nate was worried for him. He had never known his brother to be so distraught and dejected.

He noticed a crowd of men by the river bank listening to someone preach. Nate had never been one for religion. The Reverend Smith was always spouting lines from the Bible, but none of them ever seemed to answer his simple question, no matter how hard the preacher tried to explain. He couldn't tell him why everyone who had loved him and cared for him had died and left him, why he was so alone in the world. Still, his curiosity drew him to the outside of the crowd where he could just hear the preacher's words.

"What you sow, so shall you reap, for the Day of Judgment is at hand. Only the righteous, those without sin, will gain heaven. What is it to have the world, only to lose your soul? Repent now and know the peace of His forgiveness. Turn your weapons into plowshares and walk in the path of the Lord. Forgive your enemies, as He above forgives you. Renounce violence and become a child of the Lord. Live in peace, peace will be done unto you."

Many of the men walked away in disgust. They sought solace and hope, and confirmation that they were fighting for the right cause, not the sentimental talk of a crackpot pacifist. Some started to call out insults. One even spit at the itinerate preacher.

"Aw, go on home," said a militiaman. "We don't need any of your sniveling talk. Just because you're afraid to fight, don't try to make others so."

Nate felt bad for the man, who wore threadbare clothes and obviously hadn't had a bath, haircut, or shave in weeks. He was emaciated and obviously troubled. Nate wanted to help him. He walked over as the audience dispersed. The man looked vaguely familiar.

"John?" Nate exclaimed. "Is that you?"

Despite the long, unkempt hair and beard, and the dirty clothes, Nate recognized his brother as he drew closer.

"Repent your sins," John told him. "It is the only way to peace. Renounce your sins to the Lord and pray His forgiveness."

"It's me, Nate, your brother."

"My brother is dead, dead to the Lord."

"No I'm not, I'm right here in front of you. It's Nate. I'm with the army, with Paul Revere's scouts."

"You have sinned against the Lord. You are condemned to eternal damnation. Get thee away from me, Satan!"

John pushed his brother away violently as he said these words.

Nate watched as John walked off. His brother was crazy and there was nothing he could do. Tears burning his eyes, he turned and trudged away, his heart crushed with the weight of his sorrow.

Like he always did when he was troubled, Nate walked. Leaving the Common, he hiked northeast to Spring Hill, then across country to Winter Hill overlooking the Mystic River. He then walked south toward the Bay and Cobble Hill. Everywhere he went men were building forts and constructing fortifications. There were redoubts and barricades in all directions, men all working together for a common purpose. He was struck by the size of everything and the strength it showed. He began to feel that he too was part of this immense and glorious undertaking. It felt good to belong to something, something bigger than himself. Those thoughts buoyed him.

Crossing a bridge over Willow Creek, he walked to Lechmere point, looking out over the bay at Boston beyond. It was getting late. The sun was sinking in the western mountains, casting an orange glow on the buildings of the city. The windows reflected it back in a thousand flashes, so that it seemed to shimmer in the air above the blue water.

He tried to envision his friend, Samuel, small and alone, imprisoned somewhere in its confines. His heart went out to him. He wished he could bring him home. If there had been a boat in sight, he might have actually tried, but he had never learned to swim and Boston seemed a long distance away across the water.

Not wanting to retrace his steps back to Cambridge, he cut across the marshes and almost got lost. It was well after dark, long past dinner time, when we got back to the camp.

"Where were you?" asked Jeremy when Nate crawled into the tent they shared. "We thought you had gone to Boston to get Sam."

"I almost did, but it is too far to swim. Have they any word?"

"No, but the Committee has agreed to the redcoats' demands. They are going to return the men they captured, plus a few others they have for Sam. He should be back here by tomorrow."

"That would be a good thing. Then I will be able to sleep. Do you think they are torturing him?"

"I hope not, though I'm sure they are questioning him roughly."

"He will not talk. I hope they go easy on him, but if they don't I will kill every one of them."

Jeremy looked at Nate probingly. "That is no way to talk, Nate. He will be all right."

"We shall see. In the meantime, I will stand watch. It will give me something to do, for I shall not rest until Sam is back. It is all my fault."

112

"Why do you say that?"

"It is because of me that Sam and Peter wanted to do something big. Now look what happened, Peter is dead."

"It was his choice. He knew the risks. Colonel Revere told him not to go, but he just wanted to be the big hero."

"Yeah, and look where it got him."

"Did you really see another boy shoot that redcoat's hat off?"

"What?" said Nate, not knowing at first what Jeremy was talking about.

"You know, the day the redcoats killed all those men out at Lexington? Did you really see someone else?"

"What are you talking about? Of course I did. Don't be stupid."

"It just sounded kind of strange, like you were making it up."

"Why would I do a stupid thing like? You're crazy."

"I don't know. It sounded kind of funny, that's all, like you were saying it so our people wouldn't be so mad at the redcoats."

"That is the stupidest thing I ever heard, Jeremy. I thought you were smart, but you are just plain dumb as an ox to think something like that. It is just as I said to Colonel Revere."

"I don't think he believed you either," continued Jeremy.

"Ah, shut up and go to sleep. I'll stand watch."

That was the end of the conversation, but Nate was more than a little concerned at Jeremy's questions. What would he and his friends do if they found out the truth?

The next day, when Jeremy awoke, Nate was still standing guard. They made a fire and brewed some coffee. Not long after, Lieutenant Colonel Revere rode by.

"Hi, men," he saluted. "Look's like it is going to be a warm day. How is everyone? You looked like you had little sleep last night, Mister Daniels."

"I am worried about Sam, sir. Any word?"

"Yes, he is being exchanged for the collaborators, the very men whose dastardly plot you thwarted. Now they will be free to do their dirty deeds again, but it cannot be helped. It is for a worthy cause. Sam will be with us soon. Then we can all relax and celebrate."

"How can we celebrate when Peter has been killed by the dirty redcoats?" said Nate.

"We can mourn Peter's loss and rejoice at Samuel's return, though I could scold him severely for his foolhardiness. In the meantime,

Mister Daniels, I am going out to Concord on business. I was wondering if you would accompany me. I thought we might stop and look at the Green in Lexington and reconstruct what happened. The report has already been sent to Parliament, but it would be good to confirm our story."

"I don't feel well," complained Nate, truthfully. His eyes felt like two heavy lead balls, his head as if it was split down the middle. Fierce pains shot out from his legs and back from sitting in one position all night. He was a mental and physical wreck. "I am in no condition to travel. I need to have some coffee and eat something."

"There is no hurry. We can leave later today. You have plenty of time to rest. We'll ride out and be back by dinner time."

Nate said nothing, planning on coming up with another excuse when the time came. Meanwhile, he could rest and think one up. He had no intention of going out to Lexington with Paul Revere and reliving that terrible morning.

Around noon the camp came alive with rumors there was to be a prisoner exchange. Several patriots were being allowed to leave Boston, along with a boy suspected of spying on the British. Some in the city wanted the boy punished severely as an example, and didn't think the trade was worth it. But the men being exchanged were important to the Crown, and local loyalists, on the whole, supported the trade.

Nate and the boys rushed to Roxbury to be there when their friend was released. Nate led the way. They approached the Neck, that broad strip of flatland connecting the Roxbury with Boston, with a mixture of trepidation and anger.

They walked down the road toward the British fortifications halfway across the causeway. There were sand dunes and fields of tuff grass on the left and right. The waters of the Harbor and the Back Bay lay just beyond.

A crowd had gathered at the gate before the British fortress and works that stretched across the Neck. The walls bristled with cannon. Columns of soldiers, all armed with muskets and bayonets, stood at attention within. As the boys approached they could hear the murmur of the crowd waiting for the release of the prisoners. The church spires and clock towers of the city towered beyond.

Nate noticed a knot of militiamen standing guard over a dejected group of prisoners, the men who had tried to hang him. Several of them looked at him with unabashed hatred, as if they'd still like to string him up. He glowered back at them with a sullen expression.

They had arrived just in time. A cart with the men to be exchanged had just driven up on the British side, and the authorities had finished signing the requisite papers. The regulars and Yankees looked at each other ominously. Nate could make out Samuel, looking small and forlorn, sitting at the rear of the cart, his feet dangling over the edge. He looked like he'd been beaten up. When he was finally brought over after being exchanged, they saw just how badly.

"Good God!" exclaimed Jeremy on greeting Samuel. "You look terrible. What did they do to you?"

"They tried to make me to tell them about the army and everything. They were going to hang me as a spy, but I wouldn't talk, so they beat me."

He had two black eyes and a gash across his cheek, as well as ugly dark purple bruises about his body. He walked stiffly and with a limp, and winced at any jarring movement.

"We need to take you to a doctor," said Jeremy.

"Those bastards," swore Nate.

The boys stayed with their friend as he was placed in a wagon and taken back to Cambridge and the army hospital. When he had been safely deposited in the surgeons' care, the boys regrouped at their camp to talk about events.

"They are not going to get away with this," vowed Nate.

"What do you aim to do?" asked Jeremy.

"I don't know, but I will surely think of something."

Chapter 16

Corporal Charlie McBride, Colonel Francis Smith's Brigade, Dock Square

Charlie McBride was beginning to think someone up there didn't like him. For the third weekend in a row he had pulled sentry duty. While the generals and officers were off enjoying entertaining shows and lavish balls, he had to stand guard all night in the street. It was beyond endurance, but what could he do? Instead of being promoted for thwarting the boy-spies, he was rewarded with extra sentry duty.

With no end to the siege in sight, and his commanders content to while away the days in dissipation and revelry, Charlie and the men were at their wit's end. When would this drudgery cease?

"They let that little guttersnipe we caught go today," said his partner.

"Just as well," replied Charlie. "I'd rather have him outside of the city than inside causing trouble. I hear they treated him roughly."

"Aye, he learned his lesson well enough, I think. He won't be troubling us for awhile."

"Ah, what have we here?"

An old horse pulled a wagon full of barrels up the hill. It halted at the guard post when Charlie stepped out in front of it and held up his hand.

"Who goes here? State your business," he said.

Two boys sat on the wagon, both around thirteen or fourteen years old.

"We are bringing some barrels of spirits to the wharf for our father, sir. It's for the navy."

"Is that so?" said Charlie. "There is martial law. No one is to be out on the road without proper permission."

"We have it, sir, signed only today by the admiral of the fleet."

"Oh, let me see that."

As Charlie dealt with the driver, his buddy jumped on the back of the wagon and started examining its contents. They were not going to be tricked by a bunch of boys.

"Bill, can you make out this writing?" Charlie asked his partner, who cut short his examination and joined his friend at the front of the cart.

The handwriting and signature were barely legible. Only the date and seal were clear enough to make out.

"No, we will have to get someone to verify it," his friend announced.

"In that case," said Charlie. "You boys will have to pull the wagon into that storehouse there." He pointed the way. The boys didn't object, but drove the wagon as instructed and followed Charley to the building. Once there, their horse was unhitched and they were allowed to take it back and report to their father.

"Come back in the morning when we can verify your papers," Charlie told them.

When the boys were gone, Charlie's friend opened one of the kegs.

"No sense letting the bleeding navy have all the fun," he said. "I think us army blokes should get a keg or two. They will never miss it."

Charlie didn't disagree.

They were sampling the rum when another wagon drove up. Charlie and his mate ran out to intercept it.

"Who goes?" he yelled as they came up, hats slightly ajar, their muskets held like farm implements.

"Who wants to know," answered a surly youth who appeared to be about eighteen or nineteen years old. He wore a slouch hat and had large features. A smaller boy sat beside him.

"I will have no guff from you," Charlie replied. "What is your business?"

"My business is my own, I reckon," answered the youth.

"I don't think I like your manner."

"I don't think I like your face."

"Now see here," replied Charlie, shifting his weight and swinging his musket up on guard. "Step down from that wagon. Now!" he ordered.

Suddenly, out of the darkness, something low and solid came zooming down an adjacent street, knocking Charlie off his feet. Before his friend could react, something swept his feet out from under him as well, and continued down the hillside toward the docks. The wagon and its occupants were gone by the time Charlie and the other sentry got to their feet, shaken and without their rifles. Charlie found his lying

117

nearby, while his partner limped across the street to retrieve the other. They were about to sound the alarm and give chase, when a loud explosion shook the night.

The shockwave from the warehouse as it blew up in a giant fireball knocked the two men off their feet again. As they went sprawling to the ground, another explosion rocked the night, followed by a series of others. The sky lit up, as warehouse after warehouse erupted in flames. Corporal Charlie McBride's world seemed to be falling on top of him, as he tried to determine what had just happened.

Nate and Jeremy rushed the heavy wagon down the hill toward the wharf, turning at the last street to head across to Hudson's Point, a haven for pirates, spies, and thieves. There, they had a boat waiting to take them and their precious cargo of gunpowder across the bay. They had borrowed the wagon from Nate's Uncle Jacob again. He wouldn't miss it until the following day, when he would report it stolen.

They hoped the exploding warehouses on Dock Square would be all the diversion they needed to get away, but a short distance from the turnoff to their destination, they were spotted by an officer on horseback, his company of foot soldiers right behind him. As he rode up to investigate, Nate whipped their horse and took off. The officer gave chases but had to halt periodically to wait for his men to catch up. Still, it was obvious to see where they were headed.

Nate pulled the wagon up to the jetty where Timothy was waiting for them in the boat. Although the wagon was filled with barrels of gunpowder, there was no time to unload it as they had planned. Still, Nate hesitated, thinking.

"Come on," urged Jeremy and the others as they ran for the boat. They could see the British coming up the road. "There's no time to spare."

"Go ahead," replied Nate, grabbing the lantern. "I'll catch up. Get that boat moving."

While the others jumped on the Durham and started poling it slowly through the shallow, weed-infested water, Nate waited patiently for the British to get closer. He could see the officer on his horse not far away, yelling for his men to join him. As they began to move in, Nate tossed the lantern into the wagon and headed for the water.

The boat was now a few yards offshore but still too close. Instead of swimming to it, Nate waded to a small dinghy that had been tied to the larger boat. He jumped in just as the wagon exploded behind him,

118

right in the face of several British infantrymen taking aim on the Durham, where his friends were frantically trying to row away. The explosion was just the distraction they needed to make their escape.

As the British made their way around the burning wagon, they began taking pot shots at Nate's friends, who were still within range. Seeing their predicament, Nate shot several of the regulars from the dinghy, drawing their fire.

A short time later, the boys made it to the deep channel and raised sail, making their getaway. Seeing Nate was in the dinghy tied behind them, they pulled him into the boat just in time to save him from drowning. He couldn't swim and the little craft was so shot to pieces by the redcoats that it was sinking.

When the boys reached the Cambridge shore, there were several hundred militiamen standing on the bank looking across the river at the firestorm, where almost thirty barracks and warehouses were burning. The conflagration lit up the night sky. Paul Revere was among the throng.

Noticing their boat coming to shore, he pointed across the Charles and asked, "Is that your doing?"

Jeremy, thinking fast and not wanting to admit what they had done, said no, but Revere suspected otherwise. He was torn between berating them for doing something so foolhardy, and giving them medals for bravery. Instead, he said nothing. It was probably better that no one knew.

The boys were elated at their victory, and celebrated long into the night. They didn't require any laurels or acknowledgement for their action. The look on Samuel's face when he heard the news was all the reward they needed.

The next morning, after giving out the assignments for the day and dismissing the boys, Revere asked Nate to remain.

"I'd like you to accompany me out to Lexington, if you are up to it," Revere told him.

"I'm tired of that," answered Nate. He was sick of people asking him questions, sorry he hadn't kept his mouth shut about the whole thing.

Revere pretended not to understand.

"Yes, you and your compatriots must be tired after last night. You probably didn't get much sleep. After you've rested a bit, perhaps. I'll come by later."

With that, Revere mounted his steed and trotted off.

Even though he felt good about their success the previous night, Nate still felt terrible at the loss of his friend, Peter. He couldn't shake the feeling that it was his fault - all the killing and all the hate, all the inhumanity man had shown to man - all his doing. It made him feel worse than low. It made him feel unworthy to be alive, especially when so many good, better people, like Peter, had died.

All he saw when he looked into the future was what he saw when he looked into the past, an empty solitude filled with loneliness. Everyone he had ever loved had died. Now people were shooting each other, stabbing each other, bashing each other's brains in, and it was all his fault.

Thinking of what Paul Revere had said, he had an idea. Without saying anything to anyone, he quietly left Cambridge and started hiking west. If Paul Revere was so all fired anxious to bring him to the scene of the crime again, Nate would visit it himself in hopes of building up his story. Perhaps if he was there and able to see how everything was, he'd be better able to construct the fabrication needed to prove his point without indicting himself. It was worth a try, and he picked up his pace as he approached the area of Lexington. It did not take him long to reach the Green.

Going to the spot where he had stood under a tree beside the stone wall not far from a stable, he studied the area in front of him. It was immediately obvious to him that the fence on the opposite side of the Green was too far away and set too far back. It would have been next to impossible for someone standing behind it to shoot the man on the horse.

Nate tried to remember where the soldiers were standing. There were lines of redcoats directly in front of him, perhaps not 100 yards away, and others formed up in columns further back on the road by the meeting house. Someone shooting from behind the fence would have been immediately apprehended. How was he going to explain that? Then he saw the tree. It was two-thirds across the green, and slightly in front of where the lines of soldiers were standing, shielded from the view of everyone. It would have been a perfect place to shoot from, with a clear shot to the man on the horse. All Nate had to do was change his story slightly, and he would have it, the perfect scene.

Elated at his realization, he retraced his steps and headed back to Cambridge. Let Revere take him here, he had his story. All he had to do was come up with a reasonable explanation of why he had changed it. He figured he could just say he was confused but remembered once he was showed the field again. He was sure it would work.

He made his way directly to the house where Paul Revere was staying, hoping to find his commander there and ready to take him to Lexington. Revere was there all right, but he had company. Nate froze in shock when he saw who it was.

Why would Paul Revere be talking to his brother, John? Even more importantly, what could John be telling him?

Chapter 17

Corporal Charlie McBride, Colonel Francis Smith's Brigade, Boston Commons

"Something is afoot, I tell you," said Charlie McBride. He had risen to the lofty rank of corporal only to be demoted back to private again after being on guard duty when Dock Square blew up.

"What makes you say that?" asked Bill, his partner from that night. "Have General Burgoyne and Howe finally put a pin under old General Gage?"

"I don't know about that, but something is up. There is talk that we will be moving out in a few days. Some say it is to take the high ground to the north and south of the city."

"It would be about time if it were true, but we have been inactive so long, it is hard to believe."

"Well, whatever the reason, we are being ordered to prepare for operations. Have you had any luck with that other little matter I asked you about?" McBride asked his friend.

"Yes, I have found out that there are others who have been attacked as we were that night. It seems there are boys in town who make it a practice to knock our men down. Up to now it was thought to be nothing but a little mischief making, but after that night it seems they have raised the stakes and joined the rebels."

"Then they will hang with them," said Charlie.

"It appears they have taken their winter sports and traded their sleds in for wagons of some sort. They come down the hilly streets, swoop in and do their mischief, then escape down the next hill, but we are planning to put an end to their games."

"Oh? And how is that?" asked Charlie.

"We are planning a little trap for them. We will catch them at their own game."

"Do they hate us that much?"

"Perhaps they are getting even for what happened to those two other boys, but they are all troublemakers, that is sure."

"Aye, and they will pay."

King Street Inn, Boston

Jacob Daniels, Nate's uncle, sat in his study with three other men. One of them was his friend from Acton, Joshua Weekes. Also present were two of the men, recently exchanged, who had almost hung his nephew. Jacob could hardly believe the news they brought. His misguided nephew had thwarted their plans and got them captured. After all he and his wife had done for that boy, he turns on them like this and brings this calamity down on their heads.

"That boy has been a problem from the first day we took him in when his grandmother died," Jacob complained. "God knows we've done everything we could to bring him up proper, but he has a wild streak. I'm afraid his older brother, John, has been a malevolent influence on him."

"Well, he has caused us much harm and must be dealt with," said Edward Sikes, the very one who had planned to kidnap Dr. Warren.

"I tried to tell General Gage about him, when he finally deigned to meet me," said Jacob, "but he just made light the idea. He would not believe a boy could have caused the fiasco on Lexington Green. As far as he is concerned it was the rebels that fired on his men first. He apparently believes in the iron-discipline of his troops, but I know better. I know that boy and what he is capable of."

"What are you going to do then?" asked Sikes.

"Joshua," said Jacob, turning to his friend. "Are you certain your boy heard correctly and is not making the story up? He does have a good reason for disliking my nephew. I don't want to offend you, but he might be just trying to get revenge. I would not blame him."

"Nor I," replied Weekes. "He treated my son very badly, but there is another boy who collaborates Jedediah's story. He is a very intelligent lad, not like my Jed, well-spoken and well-liked. The way he explained it, they overheard a conversation between your nephews, one who is a militiaman and admitted killing our men while they tried to make their peaceful way back to Boston."

"That would be John," Jacob informed them. "He is a bad influence on his brother."

Weekes went on.

123

"This boy explained that Nathan told his brother what he had done, insisting he had shot at the officer leading our vanguard that morning on the Green. It caused an argument between them. The older brother told him to tell no one and to deny it if asked. He even chastised the younger boy for doing such a dastardly thing. This hardly sounds like a made-up story. At least nothing my boy is capable of coming up with. It rings true."

"It sounds like treason to me," said Sikes. "Both of them should hang, guilty by their own admission."

Jacob shook his head.

"That's what I thought when I first heard of it," admitted Jacob. "But hanging may be a bit harsh, at least for the younger boy. He is only fifteen."

"Hanging is too good for them," said the other would-be kidnapper. "They should both be shot down like dogs, like they did our men."

Jacob thought that was a bit extreme as well, but was almost angry enough to shoot them himself. He had to be careful that he was not labeled a rebel by association. He was as loyal as any man and didn't want anyone to doubt it.

"We cannot count on the army," he informed them.

"Then we will have to do it ourselves," answered Sikes.

Cambridge Commons

When Nate saw Paul Revere and his brother talking, he had ducked into the crowd and tried to disappear. John being there did not bode well.

Could his brother have told the colonel what Nate had confessed to him? He wondered.

No one was at the camp, everyone having been assigned a mission, everyone but him. What could be going on? There was only one way to find out.

Gathering his nerve, he went to confront the colonel. Finding him alone at the stables, he asked him if he wanted to go to Lexington to reconstruct the events of the 19th. Revere looked at him sternly and did not answer for several moments.

"No, it is no longer of importance," he replied curtly, turning his back on him in dismissal. Nate knew then that something was wrong.

He returned to camp dejected. Jeremy showed up a short time later.

"Where have you been?" Nate asked.

"Nowhere, running some errands for Colonel Revere is all."

"I wonder why he didn't ask me to do anything," mused Nate.

"I don't know, probably because you weren't around. Why don't you ask him?"

"I did, but he seemed busy."

"I am not surprised. He has a lot on his mind."

"Like what?"

"It's rumored the British are going to make a move soon, maybe try to occupy Charlestown."

"Why don't we do it first," Nate suggested.

"Perhaps we will," answered Jeremy.

"Did the colonel say anything about me?" asked Nate.

"He asked where you were, and was upset to hear you had left. You just can't do that in the new Continental Army."

"I don't know nothing 'bout no Contnental Army," replied Nate. "But I'll come and go as I like. I'm a volunteer."

Nate decided to try out his new story on Jeremy before attempting it with the Commander.

"The Colonel was going to take me out to Lexington today to show him what happened, but when I asked him about it a little while ago he said it didn't matter. But it does matter. I think I figured out what must have happened out there that day."

"What happened? Tell me."

"I saw another boy standing behind a tree. He is the one who shot the redcoat's hat off."

"I thought you said the boy was standing behind a fence or wall or something."

"That was before I went out there to see it again. Everything was so confusing and happened so fast. But after seeing the green again, I remembered, he was standing behind a tree."

Jeremy looked at him dubiously.

"You told me he was behind a fence," he said finally. "Now you are changing your story. That's what happens when you try to lie."

"I am not lying," exclaimed Nate getting angry.

"Now you say you didn't remember right. I don't know what to believe. Maybe everyone is right."

"What? What does everybody say?"

"That you are just making it all up to make yourself important."

"Take that back!" hollered Nate, standing up from where he was sitting by the fire. "I am not lying. I told you what happened. Why don't you believe me?"

Jeremy, afraid of what Nate might do, backed away from him.

"Wait! Jeremy, wait!" Nate yelled as Jeremy turned and ran down the road.

Nate felt terrible. Now they were calling him a liar. He slunk away and found a lonely spot on the bank of the Charles River where he could sit unobserved and think things out.

Hasting House, Cambridge, MA

Joseph Warren paced back and forth across the wood floor of his office. Paul Revere sat watching him.

"Are you sure?" Warren asked finally.

"I am sure of nothing, but there is no reason for John Daniels to lie like that. He is under some kind of mental stress, perhaps from what happened on the road from Concord. There is no telling what he is thinking. His story was very disjointed, and too hard to follow to put much credit in, but still. He is trying to repent for something, trying to get something off his chest."

"What about the younger boy? Do you think he is lying?"

"I am not sure. That story about him seeing the other boy seems inconsistent, as if he's not sure what he saw. I don't know, perhaps he is just trying to make himself important."

"This is not a trivial matter, either way. The truth, whatever it is, could change things completely. We would have to send another report to Parliament. Maybe it is not too late for reconciliation."

"We cannot permit this to hang over our heads, Joseph. We must get to the truth of it immediately. Whatever the case, we must not let it interfere with this great moment in history. We have to stand firm and band together. The information we have reported to Parliament cannot be contradicted now. We must discredit General Gage and downplay his version of events. If what we suspect is true, we cannot let it be known. No one can know that it started this way."

Chapter 18

Nate returned to the camp after dark and sat alone under a tree, trying to figure things out. His attempt to tell his story and stop the war without admitting what he had done had backfired. Now everyone thought he was a liar, and the Colonel, who probably knew the real truth, would not talk to him. What was he to do? Even his mates were mad at him and shunned him. No one would even look at him.

He had not eaten since morning, but he was too upset to be hungry. Someone came up behind him. Nate turned sharply to see who it was.

"Hi, Nate," said Jeremy. "I'm sorry about what I said. I don't think you're a liar. It doesn't matter what you saw. I want you in the gang. We need you."

"I ain't going nowhere. I thought everyone was mad at me for what happened and everything."

"No, we've been talking about you to the new boy. He wants to meet you. No one saw you sneak in. Come on, I've got someone I want to introduce you to."

They walked back to the campfire, where the boys had a raging blaze going.

"Look's like the warehouses we burned in Boston," said Jeremy laughing as they approached.

Everyone greeted Nate joyfully as he joined the group. He immediately forgot his melancholy.

"Nate, I want you to meet Simon. He's from Boston. He just got out. He knows a lot about what's going on there. Colonel Revere has even talked to him. He's going to join the gang."

"That's nice," said Nate, suddenly jealous and on-guard. He immediately felt upstaged by the tall, slim stranger.

"I've heard a lot about you," said the new boy to Nate. "I'm glad to meet you."

"Me, too," said Nate, not knowing what to say. It sounded like the kid was giving him a compliment. Maybe he wasn't so bad after all.

"Simon knew Peter, and was in his class at the school," Samuel told him.

"Oh, how old are you?" Nate asked.

"Fifteen, like Peter," replied the new boy. "I was sorry to hear what happened to him. Did you really beat up those five Latin School boys?"

"There were six of them, and he sure did," exclaimed Jeremy.

"Yeah, I guess so," answered Nate. "I guess I got kind of riled when I saw what they were doing to Peter."

"Well, remind me not to get you riled."

Everyone laughed.

"That was really something what you boys did, blowing up their warehouses," Simon observed. "Everyone in town was talking about it. They thought it was the rebels in the city, but most of us knew it was the Queen Street boys. You guys are famous now."

"What's it like there," asked Jeremy, who like the others, hadn't seen his parents in over a month.

"Pretty bad," answered Simon. "The army is taking all the good houses, and tearing down most of the other ones for firewood. They've turned Faneuil Hall into a theater for their entertainment, and cut down the liberty tree. These are bad times indeed. They are punishing anyone who is not with them by taking their homes and depriving them of a livelihood. My parents would give anything to be able to leave. I am lucky to have gotten out."

"How did you do it?" asked another one of the boys.

"I stole a boat from the South End wharf and rowed to the heights south of the city. There are few patrols there."

"That might be a good way to sneak in," suggested Samuel, who was thirsting to take part in any action there might be, after what the British had done to him.

"I don't know," said Jeremy. "That's where all their ships are sitting?" He remembered seeing a map on Paul Revere's table. "That would be a difficult place to get to unseen.

"I know where they keep their gunpowder," Simon informed them. "I saw them loading it when I was leaving."

"How much?" asked Jeremy.

"A whole warehouse full of it," replied Simon. "If you wanted to, you could blow up the entire South End."

"Sounds kind of dangerous to me," said Nate.

"That's the Boston Latin boys' territory," observed Samuel, who was more afraid of them than the British.

"Who cares," replied Nate.

"That is not far from Fort Hill," said Jeremy. "There are batteries near there. Wouldn't it be famous if he could blow up some of them in the process."

"Now you're talking," said Simon, smiling.

Later that evening Nate and Jeremy sat by the fire. The rest of the company was having dinner at Paul Revere's house, along with Simon, the new boy, who was the guest of honor. Since Nate was persona non grata there and all alone, Jeremy had decided to join him in a simple fare of bacon and beans with some brown bread.

"What are you thinking?" asked Nate, concerned about what they had been talking about earlier that evening. "You're not going to try and blow up the South End, are you?"

"Why not? Sounds like the perfect opportunity," replied Jeremy.

"Sounds dangerous. I don't trust that guy. Who does he say he is?"

"Peter's friend from the school, Simon Sparks."

"Did you know him?"

"No, but I did not know everyone in Peter's class. He was a couple of grades ahead of me."

"Do any of the guys know him?"

"I don't know. I haven't asked. Why?"

"Oh, I don't know. I just don't trust him."

"Not everyone is a liar, you know." The tone with which his friend said this stung Nate. He turned red, but said nothing.

"I'm sorry," said Jeremy. "I know you must feel bad after the way the Colonel is treating you. But it will pass. Especially after he sees what we're about to do."

"I don't know. I don't think we should push our luck. We should not do anything like this without telling Colonel Revere and getting his permission. He would not tolerate it a second time, I wager."

"You don't have to go if you don't want to, but if what Simon says is true, it would be too good to pass up."

"That's just the problem. What if what he's saying isn't true?"

"Why would he lie to us? He's one of us. It is easy enough to check. Colonel Revere trusts him. He is having him to dinner tonight so he can learn more about what is going on in the City."

"Don't remind me," said Nate without humor. "This new fellow comes here from nowhere and takes over. I don't think we should do what he says. I don't trust him."

"You're just jealous," said Jeremy.

"Ah, jump in the river," replied Nate getting up and starting to walk away.

"Wait, Nate, don't take off. I didn't come out here tonight to argue with you. I didn't want you to be all alone while everyone is having dinner with the Colonel."

"It's all because of that newcomer," answered Nate. "He's ruining everything. I don't like him."

"You don't have to like him. Whatever we do, it will be because I say so. I'm still the head of this gang, remember that. I started it. You may be bigger and tougher, but you're not a leader. You have too many problems of your own to lead a team. You are too concerned with your troubles to think about the other men."

"I don't know about that," said Nate. "Anyway, I don't want to be the leader. I could care less about telling everyone what to do. I'll leave that to the blowhards, like you and your new friend."

"Well, from one blowhard to the other, let's agree on that.

They both laughed, and sat by the fire in silence.

Prancing Pony, King Street, Boston

Charley McBride and his partner from sentry duty on Dock Square were in the Prancing Pony, on King Street, sharing an ale. They sat with an elderly gentleman who called himself Jacob Daniels, an avowed loyalist, whose guests they were. They had been invited because of their knowledge and interactions with a certain gang of boys that very much interested the old man.

"Would you recognize the two boys on the wagon again?" Jacob asked, "the surly one you told us about?"

"Yes, I would not forget that churlish youngster and his accomplices," Charlie's friend, Bill, replied. "They are nothing but rebellious, seditious boys and should be taught a lesson."

"That is precisely what we have in mind. We will catch them at their own game, but we need a few stout lads who we can trust to help us. Your general is not so accommodating to volunteer your services, but I have reason to believe he will not object after what has happened at Dock Square. While you were on guard duty, I don't need to remind you. You can redeem yourselves by helping us."

"We should be happy to join you," answered Charlie, "but not without our commander's permission."

"My friend, Mr. Weekes, will be able to provide all the assurance you will need," Jacob promised them. "We will have Gage's signature, which Weekes is at this very moment procuring. Are you with us, lads?"

They raised their mugs.

"Aye," McBride responded. "We will see these troublemakers in chains, if I have my way."

"Or hung," added his partner.

Chapter 19

Despite their camaraderie of the night before, Nate was having trouble getting on board as Jeremy and the boys planned their big raid. In spite of what Jeremy had said, it looked like the new boy, Simon Sparks, was calling all the shots. Sparks knew the area. He could draw the map. He knew where the powder was. He knew too much as far as Nate was concerned, and talked too much to boot, but he had the ear of the group. They wanted Nate around when things got rough, but didn't much care what he had to say. They thought he was just being negative, jealous of the other boy. Maybe Jeremy was right, after all. Nate was no leader. And that suited him just fine. Maybe he'd just lead himself right on out of there.

Nate headed west out of Cambridge and kept walking up the turnpike until he reached Concord. Then he cut across the fields and side roads to his home in Acton. He wasn't sure where he was headed when he started, but by the time he had gone a mile his destination had become burned into his mind.

He had been thinking of Rebecca Adams ever since he had last seen her, just before the kidnapping incident. Despite all his trouble, he couldn't seem to get her out of his mind. Thinking about her made him feel better somehow, and he found himself walking faster and faster as he approached the village. He was almost sprinting by the time he arrived.

Heading in the general direction of the Adams' family farm, he again noticed the deserted, lonely look of the town, as if everyone had suddenly left. Although he saw a few people here and there, they were mostly women and old folks.

Her house was empty. He called through the opened door, but no one answered. The place looked like it had been ransacked. He walked through the first few rooms and called her name, but all remained silent. It didn't look like anyone had been there for some time.

Going back out to the yard, he noticed that the wagon was gone. There were no animals in the pen. The family must have left town like everyone else. Perhaps Becky and her mom were visiting relatives for the duration of the siege.

He walked across the dirt yard toward the barn. As he passed it, he heard a faint knock from within, like something had fallen over.

Thinking there might be a horse shut up inside, he opened a side door and poked his head in.

"Hello," he called out. "Anyone here?"

He looked around from the doorway until his eyes adjusted to the dim light. Then he went inside. The place was empty. He was about to leave when he heard something move in the loft above. Looking up, he caught a flash of white.

"Who's up there?" he demanded in his best parade-ground voice. "I've got a gun."

No one answered. He called out again.

"Who's there? You better tell me or else."

"Do not shoot," a small voice pleaded. "It is just me."

He looked up to see Becky Adams looking down at him.

"Nate!" she exclaimed, recognizing him instantly and climbing down. "Boy, am I glad to see you."

"Why? What happened? How come you're hiding in the barn?"

"Oh, it has been so horrible, ever since this stupid war broke out. My father went with the militia but was wounded on the road from Concord. He is at the hospital in Cambridge and is not doing well. He was only grazed, but he hurt himself something awful when he fell off his horse. He hit his head. He is not the man he used to be, poor father."

"That's terrible. I am sorry to hear it. I will ask about him and go see him when I'm back in camp."

"What are you doing here? I never expected to see you out here. I thought you were fighting with the army."

"Not exactly fighting, but I've been working as a messenger for Colonel Revere. I'm on a mission now," he lied. "But I wanted to come by and see you." This part was not a lie.

"I am so glad you did. I have been all alone here. My mom went to stay with her sister in Framingham after father was hurt. She did not want to stay here with just the two of us. Framingham will be further away if there is fighting."

"Why are you still here? Why didn't you go with your mom? Why are you in the barn like this?"

"I do not want those terrible boys to find me. I stayed to keep an eye on the place, and to be here when father came back. I did not think it would be this bad."

"Why, what boys? What are they doing? They haven't hurt you, have they?"

"No, not yet, but they have stolen everything, even our horse, and are very mean. I'm afraid of what they might do."

"You don't have to worry about them," he told her.

"They have guns."

"So do I," Nate said, hefting his musket and shaking it in the air.

"If I had our horse, I could go to stay with mother. There is no reason to stay here now. There is nothing left to steal. Thank goodness Mom took most of her good things with her in the wagon. Most everything she left was taken by those boys."

"Can't you tell the sheriff?"

"He has gone off to the war, but it would not matter. His boy is one of them causing all the trouble."

"I will get your possessions back for you."

"No, Nate, I do not want any trouble. They can have it. I just want the horse so I can leave."

He brought her back into the house where she made corn fritters with honey while they talked. Later that evening, just as it was getting dark, he went to get Becky's horse, promising her there wouldn't be any trouble.

Following her directions south of town, he hiked to the sheriff's farm, a few miles away. Peeking out of the trees, he noted there was no shortage of farm animals here like there was at most of the places he passed. The pens were full, the corral crowded. Luckily, there appeared to be no one around.

Making his way furtively to the pen, he noted a large, off-white mare that matched Becky's description.

"Molly, is that you? Come on, girl," he said, calling the horse's name softly as instructed by Becky. It didn't come to him, but it did perk up its ears. There was no other animal that matched the description, so he threw a bridle on it and led it out of the pen.

Molly followed without objection as he walked her off the property. Getting into the woods, Nate mounted her and headed back to Becky's house.

"Well, here she is," he announced ten minutes later as he presented the horse to her.

"Molly," she exclaimed. "I hope they were taking good care of you, old girl."

"I found her in the pen. She had plenty of company. It looks like they've stolen more than just your animal. They must have confiscated all the livestock in the area. They can't get away with that. Someone has to do something."

"They will get their just deserts when all this is ended and things get back to normal. I do not want any trouble. I just want to leave this place."

"I will take you to see your mom. We can leave tonight. I know the way to Framingham. It should not take more than half a day. We will stop somewhere tonight and camp, once we get away from here. We will be there by noon tomorrow."

"I am ready. I have packed a few things," she said, giving him a canvas bag to hold, while she used the fence to climb on the back of the horse. Nate tied the satchel to the animal's neck and jumped on in front of Becky. Before they made it out of the yard, however, four boys appeared from out of the darkness.

"Where do you think you're going?" demanded the largest one, dressed like a farmer in a wool hat and carrying a musket.

"None of your business," replied Nate moving the horse past him.

The boy stepped in front of them and grabbed the reins.

"Whoa there. Where are you going with my horse?"

"This is not your horse. It belongs to Mr. Adams. You stole it."

"Who says so?" objected the boy.

"I do," answered Becky. "This is our mare, Molly."

"It's mine, get off or I will pull you off," threatened the boy.

Nate slid off the horse and un-slung his gun in one fluid motion, startling the boy with his speed. He raised his gun before any of them knew what was happening, pointing it at the lead boy, with his feet braced and his strong legs apart. He seemed to grow in size as he stood there, a hard, determined glint in his eye.

One of the other delinquent boys un-slung his gun as well, while the two unarmed accomplices grabbed sticks and rocks from the ground.

"There are four of us," said the leader.

"I have seen men die, and I'm not afraid to die, too," answered Nate. "But I will take one or two of you with me." He pointed the musket at each of them in turn, back and forth. "Which one of you is it going to be?

The second boy with a gun gulped audibly.

"Let's not have any trouble here," said one of the unarmed youths dropping his rock. "Let them go, Larry. It's not worth it for one old hag."

Larry didn't want any part of the menacing giant with the big gun standing before him. He was about to back down when Nate said, "Put down your guns. Do it now!"

The lead boy hesitated, not wanting to give up his weapon.

"Do it!" Nate ordered in a deep, commanding voice, walking toward him with his gun raised. Both boys quickly laid down their muskets and backed way. Nate gathered them up and threw them in the well where they would be irretrievable.

"Colonel Revere will repay you for your guns, but you will have to explain why they had to be taken in the first place. You have been behaving very badly while everyone else is doing their duty, fighting the British. You are not collaborators, are you?"

"No," replied the leader, indignantly. "We are with the rebels. My father is a militiaman."

"Then you should all be ashamed. You should know better," answered Nate, riding off on Molly with Becky clinging to his back.

Later that night, after riding for several hours, Nate pulled the horse up at a nice spot just off the road near Marlborough. They built a small fire near a broad-limbed oak tree on a grassy hillside next to a spring. The water seemed to sing to him as he helped Becky down from her horse.

All the way from her home, she had clung to him like he was a lifeline in a raging torrent. He liked the feeling. He wanted to hug her in return, but kept his mind on moving the large mare forward in the darkness, watching the road ahead intently. Yet, the feel of her body pressing against him, holding him tightly with her head on the back of his neck, was the nicest sensation he had ever felt. The night seemed to sparkle in the half-light.

They pitched a simple camp, using blankets and their coats to protect them on the damp ground. Building a small fire, they sat before it close to each other.

"Here," said Becky, pulling a small object wrapped in wax-paper from the canvas bag. "I made this earlier, while you were out getting the horse. I wanted to thank you for all you have done."

"Aw, I haven't done anything, nothing a friend and neighbor wouldn't do. In times like these people have to stick together."

"Why do those other boys have to be so mean, and do those things?"

"I don't know. They are too young to join the militia. They want to feel important while their fathers are off fighting, I guess. They just don't know any better."

"Well, you sure took care of them, all right. I thought there was going to be shooting for sure, but you bluffed them real good."

"I wasn't bluffing," said Nate, unwrapping the package.

"I made that for you with the last of the corn meal and eggs. I did not have much milk or butter, but there was some molasses and a pinch of salt. I hope it is all right. We have a little honey, if you like."

"I haven't had a real corn muffin in ages," Nate said, viewing the contents of the package. "I love these, but I can't eat that big thing all by myself. I'll get fat like Jedediah." They laughed. "I'll share it with you."

"I was hoping you would say that," said Becky, taking the package from him. She broke the muffin in two and gave him the larger piece.

They shared the muffin in silence, listening to the brook and the night creatures, and looking out at the moonlit countryside. Nate put his arm around her as they sat by the fire, and kissed her cheek. She held it as if he had slapped her and almost came to tears. Nate, afraid he had done something wrong, pulled away embarrassedly.

"I'm sorry," he stammered. "I didn't mean to upset you."

"You did not upset me. That it is the nicest thing anyone has ever done. Can you do it again?"

He hugged her tight and kissed her on the mouth. She fell asleep in his arms in front of the fire. Nate watched the wood burn down to smoking embers, before he too, closed his eyes and went to sleep.

Chapter 20

"Where is Nate?" demanded Paul Revere. Jeremy stood at attention in front of their tent. "He has disappeared again, has he? Absent without leave, they call it. That boy is not dependable."

Jeremy, not wanting to divulge his own rapidly forming plans, said nothing.

In a way, Paul Revere would be just as happy to have Nate Daniels disappear. But he didn't like him just walking off whenever he wanted, and worried what he might say. If anyone got wind of his story it could mean the ruination of all their grand hopes. Parliament must hear that it was the British regulars who fired first. So he wanted the wayward boy under his observation.

"He will come back," Jeremy said finally. "He always does. I think he went home to check on his uncle's farm. He has a girl out that way."

"Well, I hope he is staying out of trouble." Revere looked at Jeremy, his head boy. "Has he said anything to you fellows about that morning on the Green, about there being a boy who fired on the British from behind a fence?"

Jeremy didn't want to talk about that. The whole thing had already caused enough trouble for him and his friend. No sense in bringing it up now. "I don't know," he replied finally.

"Well, if Mr. Daniels returns he will have to make up his mind whether he wants to be part of this outfit or not. We can't have our messenger boys running off whenever they feel like it. If one of you were ever captured by the British it would be hell to pay. You gentlemen have attracted their attention with your stunts. I would not be surprised if they were to try something. You'd all better be careful and stay close to camp."

"Yes, sir," answered Jeremy, thinking about his plans. He felt like he was about to explode with all the secrets he was keeping. Figuring the less he said the better, he stayed silent.

"You are dismissed, Jeremy. Take that message to the Council and return to camp. And Jeremy," he added as the boy turned to leave. "Tell Nate to report to me as soon as he returns. I don't care how late it is."

"Yes, sir," said Jeremy, leaving on his errand.

Framingham, MA

It took Nate and Becky, riding on the back of her old mare, most of the morning to get to Framingham. They arrived around noon and went right to Becky's aunt's residence where her mother was staying. It was a mixed reunion. The mother and daughter were happy to be together again, but sad that her father was in the hospital and their future uncertain. They thanked Nate profusely, but could not invite him to stay. He had lunch and took his leave, promising to look in on Becky's father and take him their letters. Afterward, he wandered around town taking in the sights.

There was more happening there than he would have expected - militiamen gathering from faraway colonies, mountains of stores being collected for the army in Boston. One thing in particular caught his eye – two large brass cannon sitting in the park. Just what they needed for the war, but not here where there were no British.

"What are these for?" he asked, approaching the militiaman standing guard.

"They're for the army in Boston," answered the sentry. "Paul Revere is supposed to be sending some men to take them back to Cambridge, but they don't have troops to spare right now, so here they sit. Everyone is busy building fortifications for the siege."

"That is just what we need these cannons for. I am with Paul Revere."

The sentry looked at him dubiously and said, "Oh, you are, are you. Do you have papers?"

"Papers?" snorted Nate. "No one has papers. We are lucky to have clothes on our backs. I was there at Lexington when the British attacked us. I was on the road from Concord when we got our revenge. Since then I have been working for Colonel Revere. Haven't had time for *papers*, but he gave me this gun here."

Nate showed it to the sentry, who noticed the small brass inscription on the stock with Paul Revere's name. He looked at Nate with newfound respect.

"How old are you, anyway?" asked the guard.

"That is not important. I report directly to the Colonel. I carry messages for him and do errands. Sometimes he sends us to get things, like these cannons here."

"Are you alone? Do you have horses? How are you going to take these cannons back to Boston with no horses or men?"

"Oh, I've got men," replied Nate, thinking fast, "and horses. They are on the road and will be here soon. In the meantime, you are doing a fine job guarding them. Keep up the good work."

The man saluted as Nate walked off. The first thing he did was return to Becky's aunt's house and negotiate the loan of her horse, which was not difficult, given the aid he had provided earlier. Then he went about getting some men. The only ones he could think of were the four boys that had caused Becky all the trouble. He would give them a chance to redeem themselves and help the army.

Taking Becky's horse, he rode all night, arriving in Acton around three in the morning. He slept in Becky's barn for a few hours until the sun came up. Then he ate some berries and drank some water from a stream. Making his way to the Sheriff's farm south of town, and making sure no one was awake, he crawled through a window into the house. Finding two boys sleeping on a bed, he woke them up.

"Shh," he whispered, shaking them gently and pointed his gun at them. "Don't make a sound. Get up."

The two boys did as they were told without making any noise.

"Where are the others?" Nate asked.

"In the next room," replied one of the boys, shaking. "What are you going to do to us?"

"Nothing. I have a job for you."

They woke the two other boys. Now that he had their attention, Nate told them what he had in mind.

"Not only will you redeem yourselves, but you will be helping the army and your fathers. Paul Revere will give you new muskets, like I've got here, to replace the ones you lost."

"Golly!" said one of the boys, seeing Nate's musket up close.

"What right have you to take those cannons?" asked their leader, the sheriff's son. "They won't give cannons to a bunch of boys like us."

"I work for Paul Revere. That's why I'm here. But he couldn't spare any other men to come with me. He told me to find patriots like you boys and get them to join. You will be working for him. The militiamen in Framingham will give us the field guns and help us take them to Cambridge. Are you with me?"

They all said aye.

The next day, Nate led the four boys back to Framingham. As he hoped, they were able to bring two more horses with them. Once there, Nate returned Molly and got the militiamen guarding the guns to help him find carriages and harnesses. Nate was also able to convince the wayward boys to return most of the items stolen from Becky and her mother. They even paid for the use of the Adams' horse. They were delighted to be actually contributing to the rebellion in a legitimate way. Wait 'til their fathers saw them!

The next day they headed northwest down the road to Cambridge with the cannons in tow.

Cambridge Commons

Simon Sparks showed his maps to Jeremy and the boys huddled around the fire.

"There are warehouses all along the shore," he told them pointing at the map, "from Griffens Wharf to the South Battery. If we distribute the powder along these buildings, most of which are deserted, we could burn the whole South End. They might even have to desert Fort Hill if the conflagration is large enough."

"It would be nice if we could get some of that powder for our troops," observed Jeremy.

"There is enough for that too," answered Sparks. "They've got over fifty barrels of it."

"Fifty barrels?" exclaimed Samuel. "Where did they get all of that?"

"It has been coming in all the time with the troops. They are stockpiling it for an attack. If we can get to it first we might prevent them from doing so."

Jeremy was impressed with Simon's knowledge and his understanding of military operations. He sounded like an adult when he talked. Even Paul Revere said he was an intelligent fellow. They were lucky to have him on their side. Too bad Nathan hadn't joined them. The two of them would make quite a formidable team. With these two on their side there's no telling what they could do. Still, Simon's plan sounded too ambitious.

"Why don't we just blow up the buildings on the wharf and take the rest of the powder? Why waste it blowing up deserted warehouses?"

"Because we can get the battery almost for free, it's so close, and that would be much better for our side."

"I don't know," Jeremy replied, looking at the map again. "How close did you say it was?"

"Not more than a quarter mile," replied Simon, using his thumb to gauge distance. He had his reasons for not divulging the true distance between the wharf and the battery, which was much further.

Their conversation was interrupted by a commotion in the distance to the west. They could hear cheers and clapping and a few gunshots, which seemed to move toward them at the speed of a slow horse. They wondered what the uproar was all about. Soon they could see movement on the road.

A group of boys on horses were coming down the dusty trail surrounded by a growing crowd of men. They were pulling something that Jeremy couldn't make out due to the throng around them. One of them was a big-boned boy with sandy hair, who looked like he had outgrown his clothes.

"Nate!" yelled Jeremy in excitement as he ran toward them. "It's Nate!"

"They got cannons!" added Samuel when he saw the guns.

The other boys cheered and followed, all except Simon, who looked on with a frown.

Nate pulled up the horses when his friends approached and slipped off.

"I told you I'd be back," he said.

"Where have you been?" asked Jeremy, pointing at the guns. "Where did you get those?"

"I took my friend, Becky, to Framingham to be with her mom. I found the guns there. They said they were for Paul Revere, so here they are."

"Wow," said the chorus of boys, inspecting the new 18-pounders.

"The colonel will be very happy to see these," said Jeremy. "You will be on his good side again. And we will get the powder for them. Then we'll really show those redcoats."

Nate introduced the new boys from Acton, who stood silent, in awe. Then he led them all to Paul Revere's headquarters.

Revere had intended to chastise Nate and cashier him out of his service, after giving him a good reprimand. Now he had to welcome him as a hero and express his gratitude. He had completely forgotten about the guns in the rush of competing responsibilities, which were all but overwhelming him. He couldn't believe this sixteen year old boy had accomplished this alone, with no supervision, on his own initiative.

It must have taken some ingenuity and not a little guts. He wondered what he was going to do with this youth, who he wanted to hug and berate all at the same time.

"We will have to celebrate," he announced. "I will arrange a ceremony for the formal handing over of the guns for tomorrow. You and your comrades here will be honored by the regiment. And yes, I think we can provide your accomplices with a few new muskets. I would like to hear more of this tale. Perhaps tomorrow over dinner."

Nate was back in his good graces. Still, Revere would have to be careful to not attract attention to the boy. The secrets he held were too important to leave to chance. He would have to be watched carefully, perhaps sent away or discredited. Whatever it took, he could not let the truth come out.

Later that night, as they lay in their blankets by the fire, Jeremy explained their plans to Nate, who hardly listened to him. He was so happy to be back with his friends, he would have marched on the British fort if they asked him to. Whatever they wanted to do was all right with him. He was in. He hardly looked at the map Jeremy was pointing to, or listened to the details. They were going to blow up some buildings and steal some gunpowder. Well, he knew how to do that well enough.

Chapter 21

The boys were ready to go the next morning. Only a few last minute details remained to be ironed out. Paul Revere had not been informed of their plans. In fact, they had been working hard to make sure he didn't know what they were up to.

"Can you get your boat around here?" Jeremy asked Timothy, pointing to the map.

"I don't think so," answered their boatman. "We usually come in by the Point here, from the Charles. There's no way I could take it past there into the Harbor without being challenged."

"Do not worry," Simon assured them. "We can use my boat. It is big enough. I hid it down on the South Shore. It will be ready, waiting for us when we need it."

"All right, then, everyone," announced Jeremy, gathering them all around him by the fire.

To Nate's surprise and chagrin, Simon interrupted Jeremy.

"Here's what I want you all to do. One by one, you are to make your way to Roxbury, where you will rendezvous on the road east of the town. From there the eight of you will move to the Neck in Dorchester where I will have the boat waiting. The rest of you will stay here to cover for us. You all know what you are to tell the Colonel.

"Once we row across the Channel to Windmill Point, we will make our way to the wharf and the warehouses where the gunpowder is being kept. There will only be two sentries on guard at the wharf. They are so sure of themselves that they think no one could come upon them from this direction. A couple of you will lure them away as usual.

"Then we will move to the deserted buildings between the wharf and batteries, laying the powder. Then back to the wharf to set it off and make our getaway, while the buildings explode one after the other."

Despite his euphoria of the previous night at being back with his friends, seeing Simon take over, and hearing his audacious, foolhardy plan, made Nate angry. He finally spoke up.

"I don't know," he said. "It all sounds kind of dangerous to me. It's too risky. What if there are other guards we don't know about? Or what if some of the boys can't get back to the wharf in time? And why waste all our time blowing up empty warehouses? Anyway, you can't do anything like that without telling the Colonel."

"Nate, we've been through all that while you were gallivanting around the countryside." To Nate's surprise, Jeremy was standing up for Simon. "Our information is good. Everything is set up on the other end with the Queen Street School boys in the city. We talked about this last night."

"Now, hearing it again in the light of day, from Simon's mouth, it doesn't sound so good." He looked directly at Simon when he said this. "It's downright stupid."

"You're downright stupid," said Jeremy. "We've got this all worked out. We don't need your permission, or the Colonel's. You are either with us or not. The voting is over."

All the other boys agreed and nodded their heads in approval. Nate had been outvoted.

"All right," he said. "If I can't talk you all out of it, the least I can do is come along to make sure you don't get into trouble."

Several of boys gathered around the campfire actually cheered.

"Ssssh," said Simon, putting his finger to his lips. "Keep it down. We don't want anyone to know what we're up to. And above all, say nothing to Mister Revere."

Even though Jeremy had not cheered and was still upset that Nate had tried to nix their plan, his big friend's presence did much to allay his own uncertainty. With Nate and Simon by their side they could do anything. They were invincible!

Corporal Charlie McBride, Colonel Francis Smith's Brigade, King's Commons

"It's happening tonight," Charley informed his partner. "Jacob Daniels notified me a short time ago. We are to meet them at the Old South Meeting House. It is but a short distance away. You know those boys we've been looking for?"

"Yes, I remember them only too well," replied his buddy, Bill. "I would be more than happy to meet them again."

"Well, now you will get the chance. We expect to catch them in the act, give them a little surprise."

Twenty minutes later they were at the Meeting House, where they met Jacob Daniels, Mr. Weekes, and Jedediah, along with Ed Sikes and one of the other would-be kidnappers. From there they moved to the wharf, where they boarded a whaleboat and rowed across the water toward Dorchester Neck. They were all armed.

"It's critical that we make our move before Gage's offensive begins," observed Jacob. "Once Dorchester is crowded with British troops, we would never be able to lure the culprits into our trap."

Jacob hoped they would not have to kill the boy, but he wasn't going to let him make a mockery of everything he stood for and attack all that he believed in. It was now all or nothing. Blood had been spilt, and it was all because of his troubled nephew's thoughtless actions. That this catastrophe could all be laid at his family's door was too much to bear. What had taken place in Lexington and Concord was nothing compared to what was about to happen when the British army went on the attack, which he hoped would be soon. This was unprovoked war, and treason of the highest order.

If he only had it to do over again, he never would have let Nathan live in his home. He loathed the day he ever set eyes on him. And this wasn't even the boy's only crime! For by all evidence, his nephew was responsible for the destruction of the warehouses around Dock Square. Nathan was a menace and deserved the inevitable consequences of his heinous actions, even if he was his brother's boy. The price he had put on his nephews' heads, 500 pounds apiece, ensured everyone's cooperation.

He instructed the men on what they were to do.

"It has to be quick and quiet. We don't want to attract the attention of the provincial forces gathered in Roxbury. If possible, we will capture my nephew and any other seditious boys we find with him and row back to the South End. If capture isn't possible, then we'll kill them. They are all traitors, including my nephew."

Jacob's friend, Joshua Weekes, and the others, would have preferred luring the boys to the South End, where they would be behind British lines, caught in the act and less able to get away. But Jacob feared Nate would for some reason not show up or come in by some other point. He wanted him badly, and argued strongly for preempting them on their own turf where they felt safe and secure. Although riskier, it made it more likely they would get their man, one way or the other. There would be no escape.

146

Dorchester Neck, Roxbury

That evening at dusk, one by one as chance allowed, the boys made their way to Roxbury and the rendezvous point on the road east of town. The area was covered by militiamen under General Thomas, part of the forces besieging the British in Boston. They were well-disciplined and busy building fortifications. They eyed the gathering boys suspiciously.

"What ye be doing there?" challenged one of them with a red ribbon on his arm and a musket in his hands.

The boys hadn't all gathered yet, but most of them were there, including Nate and Jeremy. Simon was bringing his boat up from the South Shore.

"We are part of Paul Revere's company from Cambridge," answered Jeremy. They had their alibi well prepared. "We are scouting the area for the colonel in the event the British decide to take the heights south of the city." He had a paper with Revere's stamp, pilfered from his office.

The militiaman read the forged document and looked up at the group of youngsters.

"Revere's boys, eh," he said, looking at Nate. "I thought I recognized you, Mister Daniels. It is your good friend, Sergeant Ford, but you can call me Captain, sir, now."

"Yes, Sergeant, I mean Captain, sir." Nate saluted, recognizing John Ford, his friend from the battle on the Concord Road. "What are you doing way down here?"

"I go where they need me," he replied. "Just like you, I suspect. Is there anything I can do to help?"

Nathan thought of a lot of things Captain Ford could do to help, none of which he hazarded asking. He wasn't the spokesman for the group. This wasn't his idea. He was just along for the ride, in case things went bad, which he was afraid would be the case. He certainly wasn't going to try and talk for them.

"No, sir," said Jeremy speaking up. "We are only going to scout the height and observe the Neck. Like I said, the colonel suspects the British will try to take it soon. The generals need information on how best to position the troops in such an event."

"Or take it first," replied the newly promoted militia Captain.

"Yes, sir, Captain," answered Jeremy with a grin.

Once everyone had gathered, Nate and the boys headed eastward across country toward Dorchester Neck and the water.

The night had grown cold and dark, with thick clouds overhead, perfect for a clandestine mission. As they got closer to the channel, the ground became sandy and windswept. Mounds of long grass and dunes rose on every side of them. They walked in silence, each locked in his private thoughts. The moment of truth had arrived.

Paul Revere's Headquarters, Cambridge

"We caught him trying to cross the bridge over the Charles," reported the lieutenant. "We believe he is a loyalist spy trying to leave the city."

Paul Revere stared at the man, but thought he looked a little portly to be spying, or hiking for that matter.

"What have you to say for yourself?" he asked the man.

"Nothing, sir," he replied. "I am just trying to make my way to Lincoln to see my ailing father. He is old and may not be long with us."

"You know there is a siege on, don't you?" said Revere. "You need papers to enter or leave the city. Where are yours?"

"I'm afraid things are getting lax," answered the man. "No one asked me for papers. I had no indication it was required."

"Our men would not be so slack, I assure you. You must have evaded the sentries to get this far with no authorization. Only the Committee can grant such permission. You must be a spy or a crook, but in either case, I will not have you walking around at your will. You will be detained this evening and brought back to Boston in the morning. You can explain to the British how you left the city without authorization. You will be lucky if they don't shoot you. Martial law has been declared. There is a war brewing."

"I am not in the British army but a civilian. Free to go where I wish. I am guilty only of being trapped in the city against my will. My business has been ruined. I only want to get out of there. I have no affiliations. I believe in live and let live. I have no opinion either way. I would just like to get on with my life. I am trying to get as far away from here as possible. The world has gone crazy, everybody with their opinions, inflaming people and causing trouble."

"I'm afraid you cannot get away from this," answered Revere, happy to have a chance to espouse his beliefs. Maybe the man could take the message abroad with him when they finally let him go. "It is everywhere men are denied that freedom that is their God given right. The government or Parliament or the King himself, cannot send troops to the colonies and invade our homes with impunity. You are either with us or against us, Mister Tanner. There is no middle ground. You can get away from it as little as you can get away from your own skin. We are either free men or we are dead men. There is no denying it. By firing upon our peaceful citizens, they have broken all ties to civilized humanity. What are these troops doing here, marching through our free colony?"

Revere looked at the lieutenant.

"Keep him under guard tonight and take him to the Neck in the morning. If the British don't take him, shoot him."

He would rescind the last command once the prisoner had been taken out, but he hoped the lesson would make an impression. There could be no more sitting on the fence. You were either with the rebellion or you were a traitor to your species.

While John Daniels walked around in a distracted state, seemingly lost to the world, he had slowly but surely regained his sanity. Recovered, somewhat, he continued to wander about the area surrounding Boston, getting odd jobs working on the fortifications. He appeared to be every part the shell-shocked victim he pretended to be. No one bothered him, but he was observing things, watching, taking note. He did not have to answer to anyone, but everyone knew him.

The militias were being mustered into General Ward's Continental Army, and John, still coming to terms with his experiences in Concord, and on the road from there to Lexington, wanted no part of it. However, he had never lost his love of his country.

The cruel, vengeful things he had done in the past did not negate all that they were fighting for. It was an aberration, due to fear and anger, the result of lack of training and supervision. He still believed in the dream, what they were striving for. It was much bigger than them and their flaws, yet they were part of it. He repented his misdeeds, and resolved never to do such things again, but it did not diminish what this started out to be - a fight for liberty, for their natural rights as men, with all possibilities before them. They had been born independent and they would die that way. Like a plant bursting through the broken pavement, freedom would win out.

Only Paul Revere knew of John's recovery, and he encouraged him to continue his surreptitious meanderings. People basically ignored him. He was unseen but saw and heard everything. He knew their uncle had put a price on their heads, and suspected something was afoot, but other than that knew little. Because of this, he kept vigilant.

John had been the one who alerted Paul Revere about the latest Bostonian fleeing the city. Like the Colonel, he did not consider the man a threat, but contrived to be in the stable where they were keeping the prisoner for the night. Even though the man seemed harmless, John thought he might know something of interest.

"I see they have caught you too, the bastards," he said when the man was brought in. "They have the gall to cry liberty yet take our freedoms from us who are just trying to survive. They are all crazy, I tell you, these dirty rabble-rousers."

"I agree with you, friend," said the prisoner, who was just who he said he was, an unfortunate merchant caught in the middle of a catastrophe. "I am just trying to see my dying father in Lincoln."

"I know, there are a lot of boys who are also separated from their fathers. It is a hard thing when families are kept apart like that, and these bastards are the cause of it."

"Yes, it is a hard thing," agreed the man. "I know of several such men in town, whose boys are all trapped outside of the city. None of the good families, mind you, but some of the lesser classes. It is a pity to hear their mother's lament."

"When will this madness cease?" said John, in earnest.

"It is probably a good thing these boys are not still in the city. They are all a pack of hooligans, a real menace in the winter with their sleds. I saw them out by the river sitting around a bonfire like Indians. I know those boys. They are all rebels, as are their parents, all except one of them."

"Oh, perhaps I know the lad."

"I do not know his name, but I would recognize him anywhere, and know his parents. The lad is hard to miss in a crowd, a tall, good-looking boy. His father is an ardent king's man, like us."

"I hope he is not in danger, running with such a dangerous crowd," said John, his instincts aroused.

"I would not worry over much, sir. I hear they have a surprise in store for these boys, if they be the ones talked about."

"Oh, is that so?" replied John.

The man became quiet after noting John's interest.

"I am sorry, sir, but I do not want to be involved with any of this business. I do not know what the future may bring. Things are so uncertain. I just want to get to my old father's home. They have threatened to shoot me, these terrible people. Oh, what am I to do?"

"Do not worry, good sir," replied John. "All will turn out. And thank you for all your valuable information."

With that, John knocked on the stable door and was let out.

A short time later, he was announced to Paul Revere.

"I had an interesting conversation with the prisoner you were just interrogating," said John, on entering the room. "He said something I thought you should hear."

"Please continue, Mister Daniels. I am pleased to see you so recovered and am all ears."

"He said he knew many of the parents of the boys camped by the river. He called them all a bunch of rebels, except for one of them, who he said was the son of an ardent loyalist, a noble voice against the rebels."

"What do you think this means?" asked Revere.

"I think he was talking about that new boy, Simon. I think my Uncle Jacob could be up to something. He put a bounty on our heads. It is funny how this boy, the son of an ardent loyalist, just showed up out of the blue."

"Ah, Simon. He certainly is a talker, a fountain of information. He has even drawn maps of the British fortifications. The boys love him."

"I do not think he is who he says he is," replied John. "They might be trying to lure Nate and the boys into a trap."

"Where are they now?" Revere asked with concern.

No one knew.

"We must find them!" shouted John, running out of the room.

.

Chapter 22

The boys peeked over the last grass-covered sand dune before the water, a hundred yards away. A boat was pulled up on the beach. Someone stood by it with a lantern in his hand. They assumed it was Simon. There was nothing but sand between them and the water. Dunes marched away to the left and right into the darkness. All else was empty and quiet. They lay still and watched.

"Looks like a trap," observed Nate. "How do we know it's Simon? Why don't we check it out first? Jeremy and I will go talk to him and signal if it's all right."

Jeremy agreed, but said that Nate should stay back with the others in case something went wrong. Samuel volunteered eagerly to take his place, and Nate reluctantly agreed. Only he and the sheriff's boy, who'd helped him with the cannon, had muskets. If everything went to plan, they wouldn't need them, but they might be the difference between escape and capture, or worse.

The two boys sprinted across the intervening ground and approached the boat. They soon signaled that everything was all right. It was Simon.

"It's all clear," said the Sheriff's boy, starting to get up and move across the beach.

"No!" ordered Nate, grabbing his arm. "I still don't trust that fellow. Larry, you stay here with the others while I check it out for myself. Stay put until I tell you otherwise. If there is any trouble, I want the six of you to head back into the dunes and get out of here. Don't worry about us. You understand?"

"Yes," answered Larry, "but shouldn't we stay and cover you if something goes wrong?"

"No," Nate answered. "It's better only a few of us get captured, than all of us. If we have to use our muskets, we've already failed. Get back to our lines if there's trouble and alert them of a possible attack."

Nathan had effectively taken command. He started across the sand. It was as if he had been born on a battlefield.

As Nate reached the halfway point across the wide expanse of beach, several figures rose from the ground to his right. At the same time, two more got up from behind the beached whaleboat. One of the two boys standing next to the boat - it looked like Samuel - called out a warning, and was hit on the head by Simon. He went down silently.

At that moment, a man on a horse rushed up the beach from the dunes.

"It's a trap!" the rider yelled. "It's a trap!"

A shot rang out and the horse and rider fell.

Instinctively, Nate fired back at the flash. A man yelled and fell to the ground. Another shot was discharged near the boat where Jeremy and Sam were.

The men to the right of Nate started running toward him. He turned and fled back to the dunes as someone shot at him from behind. Another yelled out and fired from Nate's left, very close at hand, but the shot went high.

Nate ducked and continued running.

"Run, run! Get out of here!" he yelled to the others as he dashed back to safety.

The six boys behind the dunes did as ordered and disappeared into the night, heading off the neck to report the gunfire.

Nate made it to the dunes, but was pinned down as several mini-balls threw up the sand around him. Rapidly reloading, he blasted a man who rushed at him out of the night. The other attackers fell back as he followed up with several more quick shots.

Nate was thinking fast. He was loath to leave Jeremy and Sam. Instead of running back into the dunes and safety, he stayed where he was to see if he could somehow help them. He knew that Simon had stayed by the shore with his friends and probably had them covered. If only he could get to them, but there was no way he could cover the intervening flat, open space without being riddled with bullets. He could see the horseman lying in the sand only a few dozen feet away and wondered who he was. His assailants were also nearby, lying in the darkness.

Suddenly, the shooting picked up and two men ran at him from the right, their guns blazing. Nate shot one of them who was almost upon him, at point-blank range, killing him instantly. The other attacker screamed and fired, but Nate twisted his body away at the last minute and the shot went wide. The man fled back into the night.

The two men who had been hiding behind the whaleboat moved up toward the action, but another couple of shots from Nate sent them scurrying back toward the boat again for cover. Nate fired a third shot so fast his assailants thought they were facing two opponents instead of one.

While Nate crouched behind the sand dune reloading, the enemy's fire intensified, pinging the sand all around him. Something slammed into his shoulder. He dropped his musket and fell to the ground. He had been hit. He rolled back and forth in the sand in agony and shock, until he realized he wasn't dead. Then he sat up holding his shoulder, and was about to rise, when someone tackled him and knocked him over, landing on top of him. Nate reached out just in time to catch a knife plunged at his heart. The searing pain in his shoulder left him momentarily as adrenaline flooded his body.

There on top of him, his face inches from Nate's, was his nemesis, Jedediah Weekes. No longer having his mouth wired shut, he leered at Nathan.

"I am going to kill you, you rebel bastard!" he cried.

With a quick explosion of strength, Nate spun Jedediah around and threw him off, jumping on him as he tried to rise. Grabbing his arm, Nate used all his weight and strength, and despite the pain in his shoulder, pushed the knife back onto his attacker. Jedediah grunted and gasped, then said no more, as the blade pierced his heart.

Nate rolled off him and crawled to the prone horseman. He wanted to see who had saved him. Turning the man over, Nate peered at him closely and was shocked to see his brother, John. His handsome face stared, opened-eyed, back at him. Nate tried to rise, but collapsed on his back instead, where he lay staring at the sky. He vaguely sensed men in red running at him up the beach, and musket fire, then all went black.

Private Charlie McBride, General Howell's Light-Infantry Regiment, South End

Twenty minutes after their aborted mission, Charlie McBride was trying to come to grips with what had just happened. He had been in battles before, but this covert type of operation unnerved him. Now he was retreating across the channel back to Windmill Point and the South End with his mate, Bill. Three of their companions, Ed Sikes, Henry Fry, his associate, and the Weekes boy lay dead on the beach where they fell. The leader of their party, Jacob Daniels, lay dying in the bottom of the boat. It was a total disaster.

Charlie wondered what he was going to tell his superiors. Despite Jacob Daniel's assurances, Charlie had not seen any sort of written approval, and the arch-loyalist, who had promised them so much, was in no shape to answer his questions now. How could a bunch of boys be so deadly?

It was supposed to be an easy capture. It turned out to be a bloodbath. Musket balls came at them like hail. It was as if the intended victims had been warned and were expecting trouble, instead of just walking into a trap. They must have been well-trained and well-led. The shooting sure was hot. No one told them the boys would have muskets and be able to shoot like that. He would be lucky if he was not court-martialed and shot for his part in the affair. He might never see his home again. The thought stung Charlie to tears.

He kept replaying the battle in his head. He and his partner, Bill, had moved up from the beached boat, keeping up a hot fire, while the others ran in from the left. He saw several of them rush the rebels only to be shot down and killed, but Charlie and his mate got off a few goods shots, one of which hit its target. When they moved in for the kill, they saw the two boys fighting, the lone rebel killing the Weekes boy with a knife. They were about to dispatch the culprit, when they saw enemy soldiers coming up the beach. They were shooting at them, so Charlie and his partner ran back to the boat, taking the old man, Daniels, with them.

Jacob Daniel lay mortally wounded. He had been the first one shot and the only one they had brought back. As he lay in agony, a lead ball in his gut, the only thing that flashed before his mind was his dismal failure. Things had not gone as planned.

As soon as Jacob recognized his nephew crossing the beach alone, he had signaled for his men to move in. But someone on horseback came riding up shouting out the alarm. Jacob had shot him, but was shot by his nephew in turn. Worse, it was all for naught. He was going to die and Nathan had gotten away scot-free.

Joshua Weekes, who was waiting at the dock, was inconsolable when he learned about the death of his son, and berated Charlie and Bill unmercifully for not bringing his body back. The sight and pitiful condition of his friend, Jacob, however, stopped his tirade and sobered him up. He had sacrificed his son for their cause. His friend, Jacob, had given his life. For it was obvious from his wound he would not live out the night. His suffering was grievous.

155

Simon Sparks, who had also escaped in the boat, guided their prisoner to a wagon tied up near the dock. He was still in a state of shock. Not only did he witness the carnage on the beach first hand, he actually had to kill somebody, the boy Jeremy. It happened when the fool had tried to attack him after he hit Samuel.

Samuel, who they had taken back with them, was just coming to and groggy. Simon was relieved that he had not killed him. The thirteen-year-old looked small and helpless in the back of the empty cart, where they also laid Jacob Daniels. Their single captive was little reward for the effort and the deaths. Simon had not signed up for this, and was sorry he had taken part.

It was all supposed to be so simple. Old man Daniels and Mr. Weekes had convinced him of the plan. They assured him no one would get hurt. He had done his part and fooled them all, all except for that Nathan character. Things just got out of hand so fast that they could never recover. Nathan had beaten them. Simon was sure that all the shooting came from him, no matter how many it seemed. It was a good thing, thought Simon, that he had stayed by the boat. Everyone who came near Nate Daniels had died violently.

Chapter 23

"That was a close call, Mr. Daniels," said Paul Revere, when Nate finally opened his eyes. Nate lay on a cot in a tent in the new army's hospital. When he looked about him, he noticed his arm was in a sling and a large bandage covered his shoulder.

"What happened?" he croaked, still groggy from the operation.

"They had to take a mini-ball out of your shoulder," answered the militia lieutenant colonel. "You lost a lot of blood and passed out on the beach. I do not know what you boys were doing, but if it hadn't been for your brother, John, you would not be here right now."

"John," croaked Nate. "He was shot!"

"I'm afraid your brave brother is gone. He saved your life. I am very sorry."

"Oh, no," cried Nate in anguish, wincing in pain as he jerked his shoulder forward trying to rise.

"Whoa, there," said Revere, restraining him. "It is best you rest and recover. Try not to get upset. I should not have mentioned it. There is much we must talk about, but for now try to rest."

The doctor gave Nate some tincture of laudanum and he went into a hazy delirium, feeling no pain.

Paul Revere could not believe what had happened. It was the worst kind of disaster. If it wasn't so heartbreaking he would have been furious. Nate's brother had been killed. A boy, Samuel, had been captured, and was believed to be hurt. He was now languishing in a British prison. Even worse, another boy, Nate's best friend, Jeremy, had been killed, shot during a struggle at the whaleboat.

"The scoundrels paid dearly for their reprehensible act," Revere informed the doctor. "Three loyalists were killed outright, all by Nathan here. He also mortally wounded his Uncle Jacob, who is reported to be dying in a Boston hospital. Mercifully, he is not expected to suffer much longer. Apparently he was the one who put a price on his nephew's head and planned the kidnapping. One of the dead was a youth named Jedediah Weekes, from Acton, who had a knife in his chest. We believe Nathan killed him after he had himself been shot."

"This is quite an extraordinary lad," observed the doctor, looking down on the patient.

"We believe the boy Simon Sparks, the son of an ardent loyalist in Boston, lured the boys to the ambush. He and two of the remaining attackers escaped to a boat and back to Boston, taking their prisoner with them."

"You should give the boy a medal," suggested the doctor.

"He will be lucky if I don't court martial him," replied Revere.

Despite his admiration for Nate's ability under duress, the Colonel couldn't help blaming him for the debacle. The worst thing was they had done it behind his back, purposely keeping it from him through ruse and lies. He was furious.

After John Daniels realized the youngster calling himself Simon was the son of a rabid loyalist, and the boys were all in Roxbury, he had taken a horse and ridden south to warn them of a possible trap. No one could stop him. Revere gathered a company and followed hoping they would arrive in time. When he encountered the boys returning from the aborted mission, he followed them back to the location with his men, arriving just in time. The remaining attackers, two British regulars, were approaching Nate to shoot him, when Revere's men chased them off and rescued the boy. Securing the area, they took note of the carnage. He still couldn't believe all that damage could have been done by a single sixteen-year-old. He must have reloaded and fired at an incredible rate.

The Colonel had to admit that Nate had conducted the mission with great skill, preventing the whole group from being captured, but he should have known better. He was older than most of the others, and a natural leader. He should have stopped it. Instead, he went along and led them into a trap. Too bad Nate couldn't be trusted. The last thing he needed was for the boy to tell his story. As far as he was concerned, Nate was a liability as much as he was an asset.

A few days later, Nate was up and recovering from his ordeal, but having problems dealing with the aftermath. His brother and his best friend were dead. He was shocked that his own Uncle had actually lured him into a trap and was now dead himself, along with Jedediah. He tried to tell the colonel it wasn't his fault, but he didn't believe that himself. He felt responsible for the whole thing. He had ended up leading them into an ambush. He couldn't believe it had been set up just to get *him*.

None of the other boys had visited him. As a matter of fact, he had no visitors except for Paul Revere during his convalescence, and the colonel had been cold and remote, although concerned for his well-being. His commander hadn't come right out and blamed him, but had made him feel guilty just the same.

Now that he was feeling better, he had been told not to leave the camp. The colonel said it was for his own good, but had posted someone to watch him. It felt like house-arrest, although he was able to roam around the hospital grounds.

In the process, he remembered that Becky's father was in the clinic and looked him up. To his delight, Becky was with him.

"Becky," he exclaimed. "What are you doing here?"

"I came to bring father home. He is well enough to leave the hospital. We are going back to the farm." She looked at his sling.

"What happened to you? Have you been hurt?"

"Oh, it is nothing. I was wounded on a mission. The British ambushed us."

"Oh, that must have been terrible. I hope you are all right."

"Yes, I will be fine. Another boy was killed," he told her, thinking sadly of his friend.

"You still don't look so good. You have lost your color and a lot of weight. You must take better care of yourself."

"I try, but I can't wait to get out of here and back with the boys. How is your father?" he asked, trying to change to subject away from himself.

"Not good, I'm afraid. He was hurt in the head and can't really take care of himself. We will have to keep an eye on him so he doesn't hurt himself, but there is nothing more they can do here. He will be better at home where I can take care of him."

"That's too bad," said Nate, sorry to hear of Becky's problem. "Maybe I can help take him home."

"That would be nice, but you must take care of yourself first."

"I'm almost mended. They are going to take this sling off in a few days. I'll be as good as new. Anyway, you can't take your father all the way back to Acton by yourself. You will need someone to drive the wagon while you tend to him. It would be difficult for you. Even with this sling I should be able to do that with no problem. I would like to help."

"That would be nice. I have the horse and buggy. I was wondering what I was going to do. The road is terribly bumpy and father needs to be watched."

"Let me arrange a few things and we can go," said Nate, liking the idea of spending more time with Becky. Leaving the noisy, overcrowded city would be a blessing. He hoped the Colonel would agree.

He went to see Paul Revere and got a rude awakening.

"I'm sorry, Nate, but under the circumstances I cannot allow you to leave. There is too much to account for. You must stay and explain what happened. There will have to be an inquiry, you know."

"What can *I* tell you? You know more than I do. It wasn't my idea in the first place. I didn't think it was a good plan. I didn't trust that guy, Simon, but no one wanted to listen to me, so I went home and brought you back those cannons. It's not my fault and now you're trying to blame the whole thing on me. They were going to do it anyway, without me, no matter what I said, so I went along in case something went wrong. And it did."

"We are not blaming you, Nate, but you have to understand, you and the boys staged an unauthorized military action against the enemy. That kind of thing cannot be condoned."

"You didn't complain when we blew up those warehouses for you," replied Nate in a vain attempt to defend himself.

"I ordered you to never do anything like that again, once I found out. You all promised. You and the boys disobeyed direct orders and lied to me."

"I tried to tell them," said Nate. "But I wasn't going to be a snitch."

"You should have told me, Nate."

"Aw, you were so in love with that new guy, just like everyone else. You were already mad at me for what I said earlier. You wouldn't have listened to me. You didn't even want to see me."

"This has nothing to do with that."

"Becky needs help. I promise I'll come back, but I have to do this. She is all alone and her father has been grievously wounded."

"I'm sorry, Nate, but I cannot allow you go. I will get a couple of the other boys to help her. A few of the fellows who assisted you with the cannon are going back home. They can do it."

Nate was even more upset when he heard the colonel was going to assign the very boys who had robbed and terrified Becky, to help her. He objected, but Revere was adamant. He could not leave the camp. Later that evening he informed her.

160

"I am sorry, but I will not be able to help you with your father. I am needed here to explain to the Committee what happened. We were bushwhacked and there was shooting, people got killed. Those of us who survived need to testify."

"I can wait and be with you," said Becky.

"I don't know how long it might be," Nate replied. "The colonel said he would send some boys back with you to help, two of the ones that were bothering you, but I think they will be all right now. They have learned their lesson."

As he said this he realized that they, too, would be needed to testify. Why could they go and not him? The question haunted him that night as he tried to sleep. The pain in his shoulder that he thought was subsiding came back with a vengeance to plague him, along with the feelings of guilt.

Joseph Warren's Headquarters, Hasting House, Cambridge

Revere and Warren sat together in the doctor's room as Revere explained what had happened. The general, trying to understand, repeated what his friend just told him.

"So Nathan's uncle put a price on his head, and tried to lure him into a trap and kidnap him? That *is* quite a dastardly plot."

"I am furious the boys would do something like this without telling me," confessed Revere. "But I am deeply saddened by the loss of John Daniels and the young boy, Jeremy. Although I do not hold Nate completely responsible, he should have known better, he should have told me."

"So this new boy, Simon, was planted in their midst by loyalist collaborators with the sole intent of luring Nate into a trap."

"It makes me angry that Samuel is now languishing in prison and might be injured," said Revere. "And there is nothing we can do about it. How could the boys be so foolish?"

"Don't blame yourself, Paul. It is not your fault."

"Aye, but I am partly to blame. If I hadn't treated Nate so harshly, if I had been a little more understanding, perhaps he would have confided in me, but I shut him out."

"Well, from the sound of it, the young Daniels boy is downright lethal. Three killed outright, one with a knife, and his uncle languishing on his death bed in a British hospital for days. I would say they got their just deserts."

"Nathan has attracted a lot of attention to himself," observed Paul Revere. "This is not a good thing."

"What do you want to do?"

"I don't know, but whatever it is it must be done quickly and quietly. We will have to be careful."

"Remember, Paul, he is just a boy, a volunteer at that. We must go easy with him."

"We are all volunteers," replied the Colonel. "To turn these patriots into an army we will have to enforce military discipline."

"Yes, I agree. Some kind of formal inquiry is required to come to the truth of the matter and learn whatever lessons might come out of it, whatever that may be."

"But that's a problem, don't you see?" replied Revere. "If others learn Nate's secret they could turn it against us. That could ruin everything we are fighting for. We can't have this come out. We must convince Parliament that we were fired on first. You know Gage's report, which should be arriving in London at the same time as ours, will insist that it was us. We can't now say, yes, excuse us, the general is right."

"I understand what you are saying, Paul," replied Warren. "But we have to do something about this most recent incident. Your boys got out of hand. A boy got killed and another has been captured. He is in a British jail at this very moment. They want the return of all prisoners we have captured in skirmishes with their grenadiers, and an apology for the unprovoked attack on Dorchester Neck. It is a very delicate situation. I and the Commission cannot interfere with military protocol and discipline, but I can talk for the Committee. You and I should be able to determine the truth of what happened on the Green in Lexington. No one else need know. Then we can formally inquire into what happened out there on the Neck, and who was involved. Nathan's secret should never come up. It could be that everyone who knows about it is dead. Only Nathan can tell us what really happened that morning on the Common. He is not a bad boy and has done some heroic things. We should have more such youths."

"God forbid," replied Revere. "It would be the ruin of us. They don't follow orders. Each one is their own commander. They are like a bunch of Indians."

"That is not necessarily a bad thing," answered Warren. "We might do well with such tactics."

"Nate is a liability," said Revere. "Like too many in our new army, he cannot be trusted."

"Ah, who knows," said the doctor, become President, become General. "These may be the very men we can trust to bring us liberty."

The next morning, Nate was summoned to Paul Revere's headquarters. To his dismay, Joseph Warren, the President of the Council, was there as well.

"Ah, Mister Daniels," said Paul Revere when Nate was ushered into the room. "We have need to talk to you."

"I told you, it wasn't my fault," insisted Nate defensively.

"No, not that. We can discuss that some other time. This is about the morning of April 19th and what you saw."

"I told you what I saw."

"Please tell us again," said Revere, sitting in a chair next to Warren's desk.

Nate hesitated, trying to get his thoughts together.

"You can tell us the truth, Nate," coaxed Warren. "We will not blame you for what happened, but it is very important that you tell us."

"I saw a boy standing behind a tree on the other side of the Common. He shot the redcoat's hat off."

"I thought you said the boy was behind the fence," objected Revere, finding the opening he was looking for.

"I was confused, but now that you made me think about it so hard, I realized he was behind the tree. I went out there the other day and was able to reconstruct things."

"If you were mistaken about that, you might have been mistaken about a lot of things," said Revere. "Admit it, there was no other boy. You are making that up."

Nate was going to deny it, but said nothing instead.

"Could you not have been mistaken, Nathan?" asked Warren, in a kind voice. "Maybe it *was* the English who fired first. Perhaps not someone standing right in front of you, but one of the soldiers on the road, on the other side of the Green."

Now it was Nate's turn to be confused. Again he said nothing.

The doctor continued. "It would be very easy to be confused. After all, you had never seen an actual battle before. Things happen fast. It is a rather shocking thing to witness. Maybe your senses were playing tricks on you and your eyes deceived you."

"Nate," Revere said suddenly. "There was no other boy, was there?"

"No," Nate admitted quietly. "It was me. I shot the redcoat's hat off. It was just a joke, to shut him up."

Revere and Warren looked at the sixteen-year-old as if he were a sphinx, something unfathomable.

"How could you?" Revere said despite himself. What John told them was true, as he suspected, but the realization that this boy had actually caused the war stunned him nonetheless.

"You must tell no one," Warren ordered. "No one must know. Do you understand, Mister Daniels? No one must ever know."

"Under pain of death," added Revere ominously.

After Nate left, Revere and Warren discussed his fate.

"Do you think he will keep quiet about this matter during a formal inquiry into the Dorchester incident?" asked Warren.

"I do not know," replied the lieutenant colonel. "It would depend who interrogates him, under what circumstances, but now that you have been made general over our forces, you should be able to control this thing. We need to make sure only people who are his friends, who can be trusted, are involved. Whatever we do, it must be kept quiet. We can't have him attracting attention."

"I will conduct the proceedings," stated Warren, "and find a suitable prosecutor and defense that will help us protect the boy and his secret. We don't want to ruin so fine a lad. I will talk to General Ward and the Committee and explain things. No one has to know about Lexington except you and me. We must handle it so that nothing comes out, and make sure he is not prosecuted for this other unfortunate incident. The whole thing will be kept secret. Nate just went along like the other boys. His punishment should be no more than theirs. The lad would get a medal if I had my way."

As they sat discussing Nate's future, a sentry came in with a message for the newly commissioned general. Warren opened the dispatch and read.

"What is it?" asked Revere as Warren read it a second time.

"An informer has just told us that the British are planning to take Dorchester Heights and Bunker Hill."

"Are you sure?"

"Yes, the informant is a person of great veracity and is well placed. I know him well. I'm afraid it is true."

"Then I must ride," said Revere. "There is no time to lose. We must alert the troops."

Nate wandered the vast camp like a lost child. His sling was gone as was his girlfriend, Becky. His heart felt heavy and empty, but that didn't feel half as bad as the knot in his stomach from his impending court martial. He had been notified by Paul Revere who read him the formal charges. He had been accused of disobeying orders and leading an unauthorized attack, endangering the lives of his friends. He had also been told by Dr. Warren that he could save his skin by keeping his mouth shut about what had happened in Lexington.

Nate thought they were all crazy, the redcoats, the patriots, the loyalists, the militiamen. They *wanted* a war. They didn't want to stop and be friends again like it had been. They didn't even care that it was his fault, just like they didn't care that Becky had to go home with boys that had terrorized her. He felt like a firecracker had just blown up in his hand. How could he have been so stupid to start all this?

Eventually ending up at camp again, the warm bonfire drew him to where the others were sitting. No one greeted him when he came up. Several stood and walked away.

"Where you going?" he asked.

"We have things to do, not like some people who can't be trusted," one of the original Queen Street School boys replied.

"What do they mean by that?" Nate asked. No one answered immediately.

Then another of his mates said, "Jeremy is dead and Samuel is in prison because of you. He's hurt and no one knows if we will be able to get him back."

"That was Jeremy and that creep, Simon's, idea," replied Nate. "I tried to tell them not to try it."

"Ah, don't blame it all on poor, Jeremy. He's dead."

The rest got up and left.

Nate sat alone. It seemed like everyone, even the Colonel, was against him.

As he sat there forlornly two militiamen walked up.

"There he is," said one of them. "Hey, mister big-shot, you have to come with us."

"Leave me alone," yelled Nate, throwing a stick into the fire, and standing up.

"We can't do that," said the other one coming forward. "But it is good that you are standing, for you have to come with us."

"I'm not going anywhere with you."

"You had better, the colonel's orders. You either come with us or we will hog-tie you and carry you."

With little alternative, Nate followed the two men. Neither would tell him what it was about, but he had a good idea. He just didn't think they would hold his trial so late at night.

Chapter 24

Nate's court martial was conducted in Joseph Warren's Concord residence, where Nate was brought that evening on horseback.

On reaching the army's headquarters Nate noticed that only a few people were present. Two soldiers stood at attention at the entrance with their muskets. He thought there would be more people, other witnesses and things, but at this time in the evening it was quiet and all but deserted. Why weren't the other boys here? Surely they would need to talk to them, too.

Newly-appointed General Warren sat behind a long table next to Lieutenant Colonel Revere. Two other men were seated behind small desks on each side of the room. One of them was Captain John Ford, Nate's friend from the Concord road. Nate did not know the other man, who appeared to be an officer of some sort. A third man - this one a general - sat in a chair at the front of the room.

"Command the defendant to stand before the court," ordered Warren.

Nate gulped at the term 'defendant' and blanched as he was led to the front of the room to stand before Warren and Revere.

"General Heath," Warren said, addressing the man sitting at the front of the room. "The defendant's name is Nathanael Daniels. He is accused of disobeying orders and leading an unauthorized clandestine attack on the British lines. They were ambushed by a company of soldiers and loyalists. One boy was captured and one killed. You have read the dispositions of the other boys involved. You know the advocate for the defense, Captain John Ford, and the prosecuting officer for the army, Major Lewis."

General Heath nodded his head in the affirmative.

"Captain Ford," continued Warren. "How does your client plead?"

"Not guilty," answered Ford.

"Let the court martial begin," said Warren.

Nate stood speechless in front of the court. Everything was happening so fast. They had told him it would be all right, but he didn't really know what that meant. It probably meant that they wouldn't shoot him or put him in jail, but there were a lot of other things they could do to him. He had heard of men being whipped for disobeying orders, but that was in the British army. They wouldn't do that here, would they? He would have liked to ask the lawyer, but the captain and he had not even talked.

Ford objected that he had not had time to consult with his client, and that it was late and he hadn't yet supped. The court agreed to adjourn so that he and Nate could eat and confer. It turned out to be the best food - roasted venison and crisp potatoes - Nate had ever tasted. They talked while they ate. Nate told the whole story to Ford, who seemed to know most of it already. The captain asked questions and ended up ordering desert, a peach cobbler that had Nate thinking he'd already been shot and gone to heaven. He almost forgot about the court martial.

"I would not worry, lad," said his advocate. "You are obviously innocent. We will just tell your story to the court and you will be fine."

When the proceedings continued a few minutes later, the prosecutor read the testimony recorded from the six surviving boys, those who had not been captured or killed. All of them stated that Nate led the mission on the British with the intent of blowing up the warehouses on the South End, telling everybody what to do.

One of the boys testified that Nate had ordered them to stay behind the dune and retreat. "Nate gave the orders," the boy had said.

Another witness told them that Nate started telling Jeremy what to do as soon as they got to the dunes.

"The defendant shot four of the attackers, killing three outright," the prosecutor informed the court. "The forth died later of his wounds. We have reason to believe the plot was aimed at Nate and the boys because of what they did on Dock Square. They were lured to the spot and ambushed. Nathan Daniels led them there."

Paul Revere was called as a witness for the prosecution. He testified that after the Dock Square affair, which he discovered they had been involved in, he had ordered Nate and the boys not to do anything like that again.

"They all promised to do so," he stated. "They lied to me and misled me, and disobeyed my direct orders. Nathan is the natural leader of the group."

Finally, John Ford was allowed to speak in Nate's defense.

"Your honors, Mister Daniels tried to dissuade the boys from this mission. They all admit that he was not too keen on the idea and had said it was too dangerous. They thought that he was jealous of the new boy, Simon, who's the one who lured them into the trap. He did not trust the new boy and told them so. This treacherous youth escaped

168

with one of the boys as his prisoner. Mister Daniels had actually left the camp in protest, but Simon was able to persuade Jeremy - who was the real leader of the group - and the others to carry out the plan. Nate went along reluctantly at the last moment only to protect his friends, which he did. Much of their survival is the result of Nate's actions. Mister Daniels should be given a medal, not a court martial."

The court adjourned until the next day. To Nate's embarrassment and over his attorney's protests, he had to stay in the stables behind Warren's residence under guard. Captain Ford brought him a blanket.

"I am sorry, young Daniels," he said. "We must keep up appearances for the General. We will have you out of here by tomorrow and on your way home."

Ford's words sounded ominous to Nate, who turned them over in his mind as he lay in the straw under his thin blanket. He wasn't sure he wanted to go home, not like this.

Next morning Nate was brought before the same group he had stood in front of the previous evening. After a short consultation, Joseph Warren announced their verdict.

"The court finds Mister Nathan Daniels guilty of disobeying orders, and not informing his commanding officer of his intentions to attack the British. He is hereby discharged from Paul Revere's service. He must leave the encampment and surrounding area. He is not to undertake any military service in the militia or the Continental Army until he comes of age on his eighteenth birthday. He is not to mention, write, or talk about his actions during his time of service. He will also be relieved of his musket, which is already in the court's possession. Thank you, gentlemen." Warren bowed to the three men sitting before him. "The court is now adjourned."

Everyone shuffled their papers and left the room without looking at Nate. Even his friend, John Ford did not linger. Things were stirring back in Boston and everyone expected action soon. Paul Revere was one of the first to leave the building.

"Take heart, my friend," said Ford, on his way out. "This will pass. I have a feeling the army will be needing you soon enough. Go home and wait for the call. It will come. You are sixteen, are you not? Two years is but a short time to wait. If this thing is for earnest, which I think it is, it will be going for quite some time."

"Two years! Why am I being kicked out? What about the other fellows? I have no place to go. My mates are my family. It's not fair."

Nate was on the verge of tears. He would rather have been whipped than kicked out of the army.

"The other boys who were involved are also being sent home, those who can go home. Mister Revere has other responsibilities now. His errand boys are being disbanded, so you are not being singled out or blamed. It is for the best that you boys go back to your families."

"I have no family," insisted Nate. "The other boys' families are in Boston. We need each other. You can't disband us like that."

"I'm afraid I have nothing to say about the matter. I follow orders, just like you. This is all for the best. Your involvement in this whole affair must be kept from coming out. It would not look good for our new army. I'm afraid the ransom for your young friend will be very high."

Those words left Nate with nothing more to say.

"Take heart, we will meet again, in one world or the other," said the captain as he patted Nate on the shoulder and left the room.

Nate sat in the deserted chamber wondering what to do, feeling empty and alone. He was thinking of visiting Becky to see if she needed any help. Another part of him was drawn back to Cambridge where his mates were. They probably needed him more now than ever, even if they didn't know it. He was pondering these things, when Joseph Warren entered the room.

"Oh, there you are, Nathan," he said. "I was hoping I'd find you here. I need your assistance."

Warren had waited until everyone left, telling them he had to go to Roxbury on Committee business. However, he had a delicate matter to attend to that required privacy, a hard thing to find in the hustle-bustle of his public life. The way things were rapidly developing, he knew he might not have another chance, even though he did not feel quite up to it. He needed someone to assist him, but his aides and apprentices were all on other errands. He had to make sure the recent proceedings were kept secret. He had one more secret to keep, just like Nathan.

He admired the boy, as he did all these New England patriots, for their exuberance and fortitude, their courage and passion. He wanted to help Nathan deal with the terrible burden he carried.

"Yes, sir," stammered Nate, taken off guard and embarrassed. "What can I do for you, sir?"

"I have to go to Dedham to see a patient," answered Warren. "I am not feeling well tonight. I need someone to accompany me. Think of it as one more assignment before you leave our service."

"Yes, sir, I will be happy to go with you. I think I know the way."

"As do I, young Daniels. We shall have a pleasant trip. I will tell you what I believe is going to take place in the next few days. This could be the turning point."

A half hour later, after procuring two horses, Nate and Warren were riding south on the road to Wayland. From there they would ride across country southeastward toward Needham, which Warren expected to reach a couple of hours after leaving Concord.

As they traveled, Warren tried to explain things to his young friend.

"I am sorry if it seemed we were all blaming you. We are doing something here that has never been done before. It doesn't matter how it started, what accident of fate led us all to this point. The important thing is that we are here, at this very moment in time. Now we must act. It will take bravery and discipline, and a lot more. I know you understand. You boys have attracted too much attention. The British put a price on your heads and tried to capture you. So your company had to be disbanded for the sake of all.

"We are about to enter another phase of the struggle. There will be no more sitting and waiting. The time for action has come, and it will come soon. There will be blood, and many men may die, but it can no longer be denied. We will be a free nation. I want to be part of it. That is if this damned headache will let me be."

He told Nate all the dreams he had for his country, but never told him why they were going to Dedham. Nate supposed it was for one of his patients, as he said. The man sure did have a lot of responsibilities, as well as stamina. Nate was too excited being with the new general to be tired. Still, the verdict of the court laid heavy on him.

"I still don't see why you're all blaming me. The other boys didn't get court-martialed, just me. Everyone will think I'm the troublemaker."

"No they won't," replied Warren. "The proceedings were secret and no record of it was kept. It will be as if it had never happened."

A short time later, they pulled their horses up to a tavern on the west end of the town. Warren went in, while Nate attended to the horses. He rested in the barn until the doctor woke him up several hours later. It was still dark.

"Hey, Mister Daniels, we have to go, but I don't think I will be able to ride. I am terribly fatigued and I feel one of my headaches coming on."

171

"What do you want me to do, sir?"

"The tavern keeper, Mister Ames, has lent us his wagon. We can tie the horses behind. I want you to take us back to Cambridge. I will rest in the back."

A short time later Nate was driving the wagon north to Cambridge, his future coming at him just as fast as the earth could turn.

Chapter 25

Private Charlie McBride, General Howell's Light-Infantry Regiment, Long Wharf

Charlie's and his friend's participation in the debacle on Dorchester shore had become known. If they had expected medals, they were sorely disappointed. They were lucky not to be in chains. Their co-conspirator, Simon Sparks, was not so fortunate.

The fact that four loyalists were killed, two of them prominent men, caused an uproar. Questions were asked, suspicions voiced. It was odd that the rebel boys seemed to have been forewarned of the trap. Who could have told them? Perhaps it was the loyalists who had been led into a trap – by Simon. His solicitation and concern for the captured boy also spoke to the same conclusion. Simon was working with the rebels.

Of course, such preposterous accusations were refuted by Simon's father and his lawyers, but Jason Weekes, who had lost his son in the affair, had some incriminating information on Simon in the form of his reported meetings with Paul Revere, in which he described the British defenses. This prejudiced the court, which found Simon guilty of spying, and aiding and abetting the enemy. He was currently in a prison ship, in a dark, dank hold, bereft of sunlight, on a bread and water diet sure to kill him before he reached an English jail.

Charlie and his mate did not escape unscathed. They were treated like criminals and court-martialed for insubordination and desertion, although Charlie insisted that he had been assured the operation was authorized. When asked if he had ever seen such a document, however, he was forced on oath to answer in the negative. It did not go well. He heard the wrath of his superiors in every word; saw the condemnation of his peers in every look. He and his mate were found guilty. The only reason they were not in a dungeon was that General Howe - that splendid commander - liked their spunk. After reprimanding them for their naivety and recklessness, he commended them for their spirit. He was going to give them a chance to redeem themselves and die for their country.

"I will need men like this where I am going," Howe told the court.

Now Charlie was being mustered, along with 1600 other regulars, on Long Wharf near the North Battery, which was at this very moment raining a firestorm of lead and iron at the enemy defenses across the bay. He hoped it was softening up whatever force was arrayed there, for he knew that's where he was headed.

General Howe was to lead them himself. Despite all McBride's troubles and worries, to be led by such a man was a great privilege. Now there was a commander not afraid to lose a few men! Charlie would have followed him anywhere, even hell, which was probably where they were going. As he boarded the small sailing ship assigned to take them to the peninsula across the bay, he thought of nothing but honor and death. Finally, the British army was on the offensive.

Hasting House, Cambridge, June 17, 1775

It was early in the morning when Nate crossed the bridge into Cambridge, a clear day. The sun was beginning to spread its fingers over the bay to the east. Warren was lying in the back of the wagon in a state of severe distress. Nate drove directly across the Green to the Hasting House, where the Committee of Safety met. The general, completely incapacitated with pain, went directly to his room to lie down. Nate sat below in the kitchen and talked to the servants.

"Something big is up," one of them said. "General Ward is in a fine fiddle waiting for word from his generals out in Charlestown. We've been hearing cannon fire all morning. General Prescott led about 1000 men from this very spot out there late last night. We have been waiting for word ever since."

This was all news to Nate, who had been so caught up in his own problems he hardly noticed there was a war going on. The siege had turned into a battle.

He fell asleep at the kitchen table when the servants left for their appointed rounds. Warren still slept in an upstairs room. All hell was about to break out in Charlestown, as Prescott and Putnam were creating a perfect storm of a disaster, but all was peaceful in Cambridge.

Nate woke around noon. He had never heard it so quiet. For a minute he wondered if he had lost his hearing. He rose from the table and stumbled outside. It was a clear hot day and the sun momentarily

174

blinded him. The Common looked deserted, as if a carnival had just left, with paper and empty bottles littering the grass. He wondered where everyone was and if it had anything to do with the fighting in the north. He went back inside to ask someone, but the house was deserted. Going upstairs a short time later to check on the general, Nate found him sleeping soundly. On the way back down, he heard a commotion on the Green and ran outside.

Suddenly, all around him men were gathering and rushing to the Common. One minute everything was still, the next, pandemonium. The sound of drums and church bells resounded through the city calling men to arms.

"The British are storming the defenses on Charlestown!" someone yelled.

Nate wanted to join the mad rush as militiamen mustered from all directions to come to the defense of the beleaguered city, but couldn't leave without permission from Dr. Warren, who was still resting upstairs. Nate had learned what it meant to obey orders and wasn't about to disobey them now.

A short time later, one of the doctor's apprentices arrived.

"Where is the General?" he asked.

Nate knew the young man by sight, but had never really met or talked to him.

"He is resting," replied Nate. "He is not feeling well. Who is asking?"

"I am David Townsend. The British are attacking the fortifications on Bunker Hill. He would want to know."

"He told me that no one was to disturb him," said Nate.

"That is all right," answered the aide. "He would want to know this."

Without asking Nate's permission, the man rushed up the stairs to the General's room. Nate was about to object, but knew he was on the lowest rung in the important man's staff. Instead, he held his tongue and waited for orders.

A short time later, both men came down the stairs.

"Mister Daniels," said Warren. "I am glad to see you are still here. I was in a bad way last night. I'm afraid I did not give you much company, just the opposite. Thank you for helping. I could not have accomplished what I needed to do without you. Your aid is highly appreciated."

175

"It wasn't nothing," muttered Nate, embarrassed and tongue-tied.

"Your assistance was well received. Now, there is one more thing you can do for us. I am feeling much better after my rest and on hearing the great news. There is only one thing I need for a full recovering. If you would be so kind as to brew us a pot of chamomile tea, I think I will be as good as new. It is the only cure I know for my oppressive headaches. Mister Townsend has brought us some. I'm afraid the normal staff has all gone to Charlestown. We must hurry or we may miss it, but we must have some tea first."

Nate took the tin of leaves and brought it to the kitchen, where he found what he needed to carry out his orders. He had never seen anyone dressed as fancy as the general. He had a coat with silver buckles, and his hair was all done up with curls and pins like an actor on the stage. Nate thought it was a funny way to go to war, but that's all Warren and his aide talked about as they sipped the hot tea Nate brought them. The general seemed to be in a buoyant mood.

"This is a great day, David," he said to his aide, "a day that will go down in history. I must be part of it."

"You must lead it," said the apprentice. "You outrank everyone on the peninsula. Both Putnam and Prescott are below you in standing."

"They are generals to you. Call them by their proper names," Warren admonished him. "They have more real experience in battle than any two people in the army, as much as Howe and Gates. I would not presume to tell them how to fight one."

"They do not know how to work together," said his young but astute assistant. "They can't stand each other. We need someone like you, someone they will both listen to, to get them to fight as a team. Our defense must be well coordinated. That's something only you can do. If you go, go as the commander of our forces."

"You are overly imprudent in your ardor, my young friend," said the doctor. "War is not as you might imagine it. It is a terrible, blood-covered thing. I would not presume to lead anyone into that. Let us go and see what is happening before we jump to conclusions."

As they talked, the British unleashed a deafening barrage from their batteries on Copp's Hill and North Point.

"They are firing on our redoubts!" exclaimed Townsend.

"Unbelievable," replied Warren. "I would never have thought such a thing possible. Things have indeed come to pass that can never be taken back. They seem intent in denying us our liberty."

"We must hurry," said his aide. "We can take the horses. It is over three miles from here."

"The Charlestown Neck is no place for a horse. No, we will walk with the other men who are going there. The defenders will need reinforcements, for those men have been out there all night building the forts. They must be exhausted, but there is plenty of time. The British won't attack until they've thrown some cannonballs at them for awhile."

Warren had forgotten all about Nate as he talked of leading men into battle, although he was standing by the door waiting to be told what to do. For now that he was obeying orders, no one was giving any. He had no will of his own.

After drinking the tea, the general appeared to feel much better. Despite the threat of an impending battle, he seemed to be in high spirits.

"It's a good day for a stroll," Warren said, getting up and walking out of the building with just his cane. Nate followed not knowing what else to do.

They headed east along the road that led to Charlestown. Nate thought it was strange that neither of them had powder or a musket. What a funny way to go to war. Maybe generals didn't need muskets, but he certainly did. He felt bad that his piece had been taken away, but even sorrier he had broken his father's gun. It was the only thing he had to remember him by, a priceless family heirloom, and he had wantonly destroyed it. He had so many regrets. They mounted like a black tide before him. If only he could take back the things he had done, then none of this would have happened. Now he was going into what looked like the greatest battle that had ever been fought, and it was all his doing. But there still might be a way to atone. Nate hoped that if he stayed with the general, he would find it.

As they approached Willis Creek overlooking the bay, another barrage was unleashed by the British ships standing opposite the town of Charlestown itself, close at hand.

"They are firing on the town," observed Townsend. They could easily see across the river to the east where flames were beginning to erupt among the buildings. Soon the whole town was engulfed.

"It is going to get hot for those poor men on the hill above," observed Warren looking on. "They will need reinforcements. We must not tarry."

Private Charlie McBride, General Howe's Light-Infantry Regiment, Charlestown Peninsula

Charlie McBride followed his general up the hill toward a long rail fence next to the river. The battle raged around him, a hurricane of ball and iron, as 1600 men in red marched in lines across a broad field of deep grass. They climbed over fences and leaped across gullies in the face of a galling fire. There were dozens of unseen obstacles that barred their way and broke their advance, but still they marched on. Everywhere they turned, over every knoll and hill, there were rebels. They crouched behind every hedge and fence, laid in every ditch and trench on the peninsula, dug in and well-armed.

The cannons appeared to have done little damage to their rag-tag army. Many of their barricades seemed to have never been fired on at all due to the timidity of Admiral Graves and his boats. Although it may have made sense from a naval perspective, it did little for the poor souls who had to march over this cursed ground into the teeth of the enemy's guns.

The rebels were all pure devils, shooting the officers like criminals as they tried to urge their men forward and coordinate the attack. Soon it was a mad dash with every man for himself and with one objective - take the barricades directly in front of them.

The very presence of the provincials on the hill had been a blatant provocation, as good as spitting on His Majesty's flag. That thought fueled the heart of Private Charlie McBride, as it did many others, including their commander.

General Howe led the attack. He was magnificent in his scarlet coat, his sword in his hand. He had no fear and read the battlefield like an expert chess player. It was only a matter of time and they would prevail. But at what price?

Charlie was seeing his mates fall all around him as they moved in lines toward the rail fence, trying to get close enough to unleash a bayonet attack. But *these* foes would wait until the last minute, and hit them with such a devastating, rapid, accurate fire, it made any thought of attack impossible. Again and again, they were repulsed with heavy losses. It was not only surprising. It was maddening.

No matter what vantage point they gained, whether on left flank or right, the same thing occurred. Whatever subtle flaw Howe saw in the defense, he found it had been covered for when he tried to exploit it. His men were being cut down like hay by a sickle, by the hundreds.

It was a constant, continuous fire that defied all expectation, as the rebels stood three-deep taking turns shooting. They were all marksmen and usually hit what they shot at, which more than not was an officer. Many men, without someone to urge them on, stopped and fired, and before long the whole advance was halted as lines got entangled. Discipline broke down. McBride knew enough to keep moving. If you stopped to fire and reload, you were dead. He urged on the men around him.

"Attack! Attack!" he yelled, but to no avail.

With no choice but to retreat, Charlie ran back down the hill fearing for his life. It seemed that every rebel gun was shooting at him. He darted and dodged every which way, keeping his head down. Somehow he made it back to safety, halting where the lines were being reformed, about 250 yards away from the enemy. He turned and looked back in mortification.

There was Howe, standing alone by the rail fence, resplendent in his scarlet and gold uniform. All his staff and aides-de-camp lay dead or wounded around him. Realizing his predicament and his tremendous loss, he slowly staggered back to his troops, unharmed but devastated just the same.

McBride gasped in shock and burst into tears when he saw his commander walking unsteadily alone down the hill, and urged the men around him to rush to their general's defense, but no one moved. They did not have to. As deadly as the colonial muskets were, none found Howe that day.

As he reached his lines and called for what officers were still alive to gather around him, Charlie heard the general say, "We are going to have to change our tactics if we are going to win the battle this day."

179

At that moment, despite their humiliating and costly retreat, Charlie McBride took heart. All was not lost. They were commanded by an inspiring leader - or a madman. In either case, they would prevail!

Chapter 26

Nate, David Townsend, and Joseph Warren approached the Neck, the doctor with only his cane. He had been talking animatedly about the great opportunity before them, the great experiment, he called it, of free men governing themselves. As they got closer to the area they noticed a commotion taking place in the street. Some wounded men were being taken to a nearby building and a woman was shrieking for help.

"Some of our men appear to have been wounded," Warren told them after going to investigate. "You must stay, David, and help these poor people. They need medical assistance, and there are some ladies under distress. I cannot be delayed."

His young apprentice, unable to get his general to assume command, did not mind staying behind. He was just as happy not to go if his hero was not going to take over the leadership of the defenses. His patron seemed more than happy to go as a volunteer, a lowly private, just like the men manning the barricades out on Breed's Hill.

Townsend obeyed Warren's orders with no objection, although none of this made any sense to the well-educated young man. He knew someone had to take overall command to get everyone to fight together. It was the only way to defeat the well-led British regulars. Anything less meant certain destruction. That was something he did not want to witness. In any case, his duty as a medical apprentice was to stay in the rear and tend the wounded, so that's what he did.

Nate was under no such obligation. He had not had an instruction or an order since making the tea. Warren seemed to have forgotten all about him, so Nate followed, as the doctor headed across the Neck.

They could hear the constant barrage of a dozen gunboats and gondolas pounding the narrow stretch of land between Mill Pond and the Mystic River. As they approached, they saw a knot of men blocking the way, all of them too timid to cross the iron gauntlet.

"Move aside you men," bellowed Warren. "If you are too afraid to cross, do not block those of us who are not. Stand aside."

He raised his cane like a broad-sword and shook it in the air. Those he didn't intimidate recognized him and moved aside respectfully.

As he crossed over the strip of land separating the mainland from the peninsula, Nate could see the ships lined up on his right like at a shooting gallery. Cannon balls and shot tore up the ground around them as they passed, amidst a deafening and continuous roar.

Warren seemed to be unafraid, but walked slowly across as if on a stroll in the park, seeming oblivious of the danger. He looked out of place among the men around him. Although there were some dressed in their Sunday best, most wore simple homespun every-day clothing, as people wore in the country. Many, like Nate, wore old dirty attire, torn and tattered from months of living outdoors digging fortifications, patched together as well as possible. The general appeared like he was going to his own wedding – or perhaps his funeral, Nate wasn't sure which. He feared for his life the whole distance across as cannonballs whizzed by his head, but felt it was inevitable, only fitting that the one who started this madness would be at the finish of it. For nothing could survive this holocaust.

As harrowing an ordeal as crossing the Neck was, Nate suspected that what they were headed for was much worse.

On the other side of the land-bridge they found a makeshift hospital, where the injured were being treated. Others milled about aimlessly as if lost. Although Warren was unaware of it, Nate's fate was tied to his, for the boy had no will of his own.

Nate looked around in horror when he realized he was surrounded by wounded and dying men. Some were bleeding from the head, some from the legs and arms. Some lay still with holes in the bodies. One man had been cut clean in two by a cannonball. The men milling about, on closer inspection, were shell-shocked victims from the battle raging just a short distance away. Nate had never expected to see anything like this in his life. It was even worse than the things he had seen on the road from Concord.

"Hello, Doctor," said Warren, recognizing a friend of his, who was tending a wounded man.

"Hello, Dr. Warren. Or should I say, General?"

"Neither," replied the newly commissioned major general. "I am just a simple volunteer today, just like the rest of you."

"We need more than volunteers, Dr. Warren. We need a leader."

"In that case, Doctor, would you be so kind as to lend me your musket, lying yonder there? You will not be needing it here tending our gallant wounded. But I will have use of it where I am headed."

"Good! Take it then, sir, and go with God. Old Putnam and General Prescott will listen to you. We must coordinate our defenses or all will be lost."

"Thank you, Doctor. I will relay your recommendations."

Nate was relieved when they left the medical area with its dying and dead. They moved straight ahead toward Bunker Hill. Warren no longer had his cane, but carried a musket and had a powder pouch over his shoulder.

As they passed by the evacuated British fortifications to the base of Bunker Hill, they noticed a general standing there yelling at the militiamen around him, trying to get them to join the battle at Breed's Hill.

"You men, those of you standing about there," he shouted. "Form up in front of me. We are going to the relief of the redoubt."

No one seemed to hear him. Many were rushing away west toward the Neck.

"General!" shouted Warren, making his presence known. "What can we do to assist you?"

Prescott noticed Warren standing there.

"Oh, hello, General. Are you here to take command?" Prescott had been expecting as much, and was surprised when Warren replied.

"No, General. I am here as a volunteer, as are all these brave men. What can I do to help?"

"We need men to relieve the force down at the redoubt. You must help me rally the troops and lead them there."

As they talked, a murderous fire erupted along the peninsula to the east and down the hill, and from ships anchored in the bay, all of it directed at the fort. Nate stood transfixed, unnoticed in the shadows behind Warren.

"They need me," announced Warren on hearing the barrage. "I must go."

He started walking up Bunker Hill. Nate followed.

At the top they could see the eastern part of the peninsula about 100 feet below them down a long, broad hill. To the right was the burning city of Charlestown. Forward of them and lower was the smaller height of Breed's Hill, where a tremendous battle was taking place.

"Here is General Putnam," observed Warren. "He appears to be out of sorts."

Putnam could be seen riding back and forth on his horse. He seemed to be agitated and confused, yelling orders at the top of his lungs, then countermanding them with equal vehemence. He fumed at the men around him who were fleeing their posts on the redoubt on Breed's Hill. As with Prescott earlier, they paid him little heed. There was nothing to make them turn back and fight, no discipline except the strength of each man's heart. There were some, however, who ran toward the fighting.

Warren headed down the hill toward the redoubt.

"We've got to relieve those poor men," he yelled over his shoulder to no one in particular. "Follow me, boys."

He did not look back, but if he had he would have seen there was no one behind him. There should have been legions, but he was all alone. Perhaps if he had looked someone in the eye, or asked them personally, or given a rousing speech, they would have followed. But he did none of these things. Perhaps he didn't care. He would gain glory whether anyone followed him or not.

Nate hesitated. He could plainly see the horror of the fighting below, the fire from the guns; the flashes of a thousand muskets; the black smoke and dust thrown up by the struggle. It was the most terrible thing he could think of. No wonder no one wanted to go there. No wonder they were running away. When he thought about it, however, it again seemed fitting. Of course he would go. It was destined, inevitable. He deserved no less for having caused it all. He had seldom prayed, but he stood there alone and did so now.

"I'm sorry, Lord, for causing so much trouble. I never meant to do it. It was all a joke, but it turned out so bad, I never could have imagined. I'm so sorry. Please forgive me, Lord. I will make up for it. Let it end with me, Lord. Let the war end when I die, as I surely will. That's why I go willingly. Please, take my life and end the war."

With that, Nate followed his general down the hill toward battle and certain death, unnoticed and unsung.

Captain John Ford had rushed back to Cambridge from the secret trial in Concord, and was one of the first to come to the defense of the peninsula when the British began their bombardment. He had lingered by the neck for some time, waiting for orders that never came, trying to organize things. Having no luck with either, he pushed on over the Neck to Bunker Hill. Chaos reigned around him.

General Putnam was there, railing at two artillerymen that had deserted their cannons in the fort. He noticed Ford.

"Captain," he said. "Can you help me? This cannon will do us no good up here on Bunker Hill. Here, help me bring it down to the redoubt. We will give those redcoats what for."

Ford thought that was a good idea. Finally, someone had given him an order. He helped the old war veteran drag the cannon down the hill to the redoubt. The British lines stretched the entire width of the peninsula in front of them. Putnam pulled the fieldpiece to an embrasure on the battlement on Breed's Hill and aimed it at a knot of regulars forming in the open directly in front of him. Ladling in the powder from an open cartridge, he stuffed it down the barrel of the gun. Then he pulled the lanyard and fired it off with a loud explosion and a cloud of smoke.

"That will give them something to think about," said Putnam

"That did it!" yelled one of the men. "You mowed them down good."

Their exuberance would be short-lived. They had attracted Howe's full attention.

"That was a foolish thing to do, General," Prescott said to Putnam. "We are short of powder. The cannons are ineffective."

"To hell they are!" replied Putnam, his dander up. "I killed an even dozen with that shot."

"You have attracted their attention, General. They are about to attack us with their full force. We can't waste any more powder."

Prescott raised his voice. "Don't fire until the last minute, men. Conserve your powder."

A few militiamen ignored him and fired their guns at the enemy who were standing in the field in front of them.

"Cease fire!" he ordered, knocking the muzzles of guns down of the men nearby. "We must make every shot count!"

Captain Ford noted Nate standing not far from him.

"Mister Daniels, what brings you to this spot? I thought you'd be home by now. What are you doing here?"

"I have come with General Warren," Nate replied.

"He is a brave or foolish man to lead you here. This is no place for a young lad like yourself. You should leave."

"I will not run," answered Nate. "I have come here to fight and die."

At that moment, the British launched their attack.

185

Private Charlie McBride, General Howell's Light-Infantry Regiment, Charlestown Peninsula

Charlie was facing a small hill covered with fortifications that bristled with muskets. His company had been reformed and moved to the left of the redoubt on the right flank, where Howe had decided to focus his attack. General Pigot's Grenadiers were on the far left.

Up to a few minutes ago, the fort had been spitting out lead like venom from a thousand guns. Now all was quite. Had the Rebels evacuated the fort? It would certainly be like them to shoot and run. No force of provincials could stand against the concentrated formations of this many of His Majesty's troops.

Suddenly, from out of nowhere, a lone cannon fired from the barricade, smashing through a group of Grenadiers forming up to McBride's left. Charlie and his men ducked for cover, expecting more such cannonading, but none came. Half a dozen men had been cut down. Several lay dead.

A few minutes later, Howe's entire force, which completely surrounded the small fort, rushed it with bayonets lowered, shouting in unison. No order had been given.

Neither side fired as the space between them shortened. It was odd, how quiet things had become. Had the rebels fled? Charlie hoped they hadn't.

Closer and closer they charged. Still no one fired. Then, when Howe and his men were almost on the stronghold, their bayonets ready, only fifteen yards away, a withering volley erupted from the barricades.

This time they were ready for it.

Where before they had attacked in long, straight lines and had been cut down and their ranks broken, this time they moved in columns, eight-by-eight deep, with their whole force focused on the redoubt and breast-work. In this formation, nothing could stop them.

McBride, impatient to reach the parapets and use his bayonet, yelled with the others, "Push on! Victory or death!"

Again, Howe led the attack, a conspicuous figure in his great scarlet coat.

They were unstoppable. Stepping over the bodies of their fallen comrades, they kept coming no matter how many in front of them were shot, and there were many.

"Conquer or die!" they cried with mad fury, as the bodies of the fallen piled like driftwood on the beach. The living used the dead as a wall for protection.

Without warning, Howe's artillery fired a heavy salvo into the left flank of the enemy, killing many. McBride yelled with glee to see the destruction.

"Give them more of that," he encouraged. "The guns will change the tide of things!" The provincials began to abandon the breastworks and run back into the fort. Still, McBride and his comrades were stymied. They could make no headway against the blistering fire. Charlie hugged the ground face first as the turf was torn up around him.

"Into the trenches, quickly!" he yelled. Others started following his lead. The burning houses of the town below, the terrible heat of the day, the relentless hot firing from the enemy, was as close to hell as you can get on earth. It made the harrowing day on the road from Concord look like a mere schoolyard scuffle. If he lived through this, he vowed, he would dedicate his life to good.

The men lay on the ground, behind piles of the dead, firing at the enemy, who fired back from within the fort, pinning them down. They were half mad with fear and frustration, their officers all dead or dying.

Charlie had had enough. He wanted to get to the foe or die trying.

"Stop shooting!" he shouted standing up. "We'll use the bayonets, boys. Prepare to charge."

Others followed. They started moving forward again at a quick pace. As they rushed up the dirt parapet atop the wall, they were met by a tremendous barrage. Three mini-balls ripped into the chest of the man next to Charlie, a major. He fell backward down the pit. Charlie stepped over another corpse and continued up the dirt barrier, only to be forced back down again by the rebel guns. Three times they tried before they broke through.

Charlie, like many, was surprised that the provincials had not yet begun to retreat, but stood there facing them toe-to-toe on the opposite wall, fighting for every inch of ground, firing hot and heavy. Who would have thought that a few shots on a Green in Lexington would come to this?

.

187

Chapter 27

Out of powder, exhausted by the long constant stress of battle, the firing from the redoubt sputtered out like a spent fuse. Many started throwing stones at the approaching British. A few waved swords in the air. Some clutched their empty muskets across their chests. Only a smattering had bayonets.

Nate stood in the middle of the fort amidst the chaos of fighting men. He had followed Warren to Breed's Hill and was now standing not far from the general, who was firing over the wall at the British regulars swarming into the fort. Nate had no gun, and had no intention of partaking in the killing. Then one of the enemy came onto the berm, between the ditch and the rampart, and almost upon them, was about to bayonet the general. Nate grabbed the musket and pulled it from his hands, bayoneting the man instead. He fell withering to the ground.

After that, it all became a wild, chaotic, horrendous struggle for survival. Despite his feelings of guilt and self-sacrifice, the urge for self-preservation was strong. Men were slashing, stabbing, choking, and bashing each other in frenzied, tumbling hand-to-hand combat, tearing up the dirt floor of the fort. The raging fury of the attackers was terrible to behold. Nate shot another man charging at him with his gun lowered. Then he grabbed the still-warm barrel of the musket and swung it back and forth, battering down anyone who came near him.

Most of the defenders had fled or were fleeing, but Nate held his ground. As did his general, Dr. Joseph Warren, who stayed behind to help others get out. The dust and smoke made it impossible to see more than a few feet in front of them. Nate sweated so much his eyes stung, almost blinding him. He squinted and wiped it away. When he could see again, he watched in horror as the general was killed right before his eyes by a cowardly little man who ran up from behind and shot him in the face, killing him instantly. Nate rushed at the murderer and struck him down with the hard stock of his gun. As he did, several regulars fired their muskets at him and he went down.

Nate lay in a daze, blood streaming down his face, the dead strewn all about him. The world grew dim and unusually quiet. Slowly losing consciousness, he muttered, "Thank you, Lord. Let it end here."

Then all was darkness.

Private Charlie McBride, General Howell's Light-Infantry Regiment, Charlestown Peninsula

Charlie and his men had reached the top of the ramparts and flooded into the fort, where it became a desperate close-quarter struggle. He had still not fired his weapon, but used it as a battering-ram and a sword, to bash and stab the enemy, who swarmed all around him. Minutes turned into hours as the battle raged. Then finally, first one, then two, then six, then a dozen, the defenders began to leave the fort and run toward the rear to escape. Still, a few diehard rebels fought on.

One man in particular caught Charlie's eye. He wore a coat with silver buttons and had a sword in his hand, which he used to keep his attackers at bay. From his appearance and demeanor, he had to be someone of importance, a general perhaps. He was surrounded by regulars, who appeared to be standing off due to respect or curiosity. It was like he wanted to die, the way he taunted and baited the soldiers around him. Then someone – it appeared to be the servant of one of the officers – darted up and shot him in the face. Although the man who was shot was an enemy, by the looks of him, a high-ranking officer, Charlie was shocked at the act. The rebel could have easily been captured, which would have given the British much more advantage. However, when one of the defenders, a large youth, battered the killer to the ground, Charlie, like several others, raised his gun instinctively and fired. He was sure he had hit the culprit, who he had to admire. Then he was himself hit from behind and knocked unconscious.

When he came to, the colonials were in full retreat and Howe's men were spreading out over the peninsula, securing the forts. They had won, but no one celebrated. Charlie stood where he was amidst the slaughter and the dead, in a daze, unable to move or even think. He sank down on a stone outcropping and rested his head in his hands in anguish. He never felt so far away from home. The look in his commander's face said it all.

Charlie had a feeling they would be leaving soon, for there was nothing for them here but death and privation. This would be a long, hard, bitter battle, a revolution, a civil war. He realized then and there - and Howe realized it, too - there is nothing worse then fighting men who are fighting for their freedom, for then you are not only fighting the enemy, you are fighting yourself.

Hasting House, Cambridge, After the Battle

After the secret court martial of Nathaniel Daniels, Paul Revere had ridden to Framingham and Worchester to relay the news of the impending British attack. He returned to Cambridge late, where he reported to General Ward. The general was incensed at both Prescott and Putnam for turning a simple order to fortify the heights into a full scale battle.

The British had driven his men from the peninsula and now had possession of the forts on Bunker Hill, but it had cost them dearly. The defenders had formed up again on Prospect Hill to the west, while Putnam and Prescott flung recriminations and insults at each other over the mismanagement of the affair. There had been a total lack of coordination, not to mention reinforcements that never came.

"It is a shame that Dr. Warren was killed" observed Paul Revere. "Who knows how far he could have gone in the new government or what aid he could have given."

"What a waste," Ward agreed, "to die as a common soldier instead of a general commanding our troops. Are you sure he is dead, that it was he that was killed on Breed's Hill?"

"Yes, sir," answered Revere. "They say he stayed to help others escape. He was one of the last to go."

"Are they certain he was not taken by the British?" persisted Ward. "I would not put it past them."

"No, sir. He was identified by his brother and a fellow doctor, who recognized him by his false tooth. His clothing had been taken."

"The cads," swore the general.

"They paid dearly for the effrontery," said Revere. "We estimate they lost, killed or wounded, over 1000 men, almost half their force. Our losses amounted to 115 killed and 305 wounded. We lost the battle, but with a few more such victories, they will lose the war. Their losses were staggering. This news will echo in the halls of Parliament and bring down the British government."

"Yes, and our poor brave men will never be forgotten," added Ward. "Their lives were dearly spent. The sad thing is, Dr. Warren's life was worth 500 others."

Paul Revere agreed and left the General's presence with a heavy heart. On the way out he met Captain Ford, who was coming to report on the latest developments.

"Hi, Captain," said Revere. "I have not had the pleasure of seeing you these past days. I hope all is well. I hear you were at the redoubt when the British attacked."

"Aye, sir," answered the veteran militiaman. "I went down with General Putnam and helped him fire his fieldpiece. If only there were more men with his spirit."

"Yes, and if only the old general were a better field commander. I hear he was pretty much useless."

"You wouldn't say that if you saw all the regulars he killed."

"He left when the walls were breached, along with Prescott?"

"Yes, sir, and I went with them. It was pretty much over by then. The British were flooding into the fort. It was a mad scramble. We covered our retreat. Then fell back. It was an orderly withdrawal."

"Did you see Warren?"

"Yes, he was conspicuous in his bravery and composure. He was helping men get out of the fort."

"Did you see him get shot?"

"No, sir, he was hale and alive when I last saw him."

Revere hung his head and sighed. Ford continued, as if he had something important to add.

"Colonel, I saw someone else in the redoubt."

"Yes, who was that?"

"As I was leaving I saw that lad, Nathan Daniels, the one we supposedly drummed out of the army."

"What, Nathan! Why? What was he doing there?"

"He was with General Warren. Warren led him there."

"Why would he have done such a thing? The boy was to be sent home. He should not have been there. Did you see him leave?"

"No," said Ford sadly. "Last time I saw him, he was bashing in the heads of the British with the butt of his gun. I stood on the hill as long as I could, waiting for him. Men were streaming out of there, running up the slope, but Nate never appeared. I don't think he made it. I think he died with General Warren. They were close when I last saw them."

"Perhaps it is for the best," said Revere, sighing. "Perhaps Dr. Warren, in his wisdom, did the right thing for his county, taking Nathan and his secret with him.

Epilogue

Charles Street, Boston, May, 1818

Paul Revere lay on his bed alone in his room. The doctors didn't think he would last the night. The family was close by, and had all said their good-byes. They would be there at the end. His breathing had become so labored at times that they were in constant alarm. The medicine helped, however, and he had been resting peaceably. Someone knocked on the door. It was his son, Joseph.

"Father, you have a visitor," he said poking his head in the room. "He said he was one of your messengers during the siege. He wanted to pay his respects."

"One of my messengers? One of those marvelous boys? I wonder who it could be."

The news seemed to give the old man an added boost of energy.

"It wouldn't be Samuel, now would it?" he guessed, conjuring a name from his past. "We had to ransom him back from the British, twice. He cost us a pretty penny. I've told you about those boys."

"Yes, father, and it was a very good story. I did not get his name. I wasn't sure you'd be up to seeing anyone. Should I let him in? He seems to have an old war injury. His left arm doesn't quite work properly."

"War injury?" muttered Revere, his thoughts flying to that place and time in search of who it might be. One person came to mind. Could it be? He dismissed the thought as too absurd.

He waited impatiently as the visitor mounted the stairs, his footsteps slowly shuffling up the steps. There was a light knock on the door. It opened slowly.

"Hi, Colonel," said the man, bowing. He was big with thick gray hair, broad shoulders, and a bull neck. Revere noticed that one of his arms dangled limp at his side. Despite his age - perhaps not more than ten years younger than Revere – and his handicap, the man moved fluidly and seemed to be quite fit.

"I am sorry to disturb you, sir, but I wanted to pay my respects. They say you are ailing. I hope that is not so."

"I am dying, my friend," replied Revere, "but I have had a good life."

"As have I. I wanted you to know."

"You were one of my boys during the siege? There is only one you could be," he added, his heart racing. "You are not…"

"Yes, sir, I am Nathan."

"Nate!" stammered Revere, sitting up suddenly. "But you were killed in the redoubt, on Breed's Hill. How could you have survived? Where have you been? Why did you not tell us?"

"I was on the battlement with General Warren when he was killed. It was a cowardly act, for he was surrounded and could do no harm. I tried to go to him, but was shot down by the Brits. One hit me in the shoulder, in the same place I was shot before."

They both laughed.

"I was also grazed in the head. It kind of knocked me out. I was laying there for most of the night. The Brits must have thought I was dead and left me for the morning, but I was only wounded."

"You must have been in a great deal of pain and weak from loss of blood."

"I patched up my shoulder as well as I could, and stopped most of the bleeding. The worst blood was from my head. I had to wrap part of my shirt around it, but it turned out to be only a flesh wound. I crawled away in the early morning when they started to bury the dead. It was still dark. I crawled by the British sentries and off the peninsula. I crossed at the pond on a piece of driftwood. Most of our men were on the hill west of there, but I stayed near the water the whole time heading home. Everyone was too busy to notice me."

"How did you make it on your own like that, with such a grievous wound?"

"I guess it must not have been so bad. It didn't hit a bone or anything, went clean through. When I finally saw a doctor, a few weeks later, he said whatever could heal was healing fine. Only thing is the nerves were damaged. After I got away, I walked back to Acton. I guess I was in a bad way with fever, 'cause I don't remember much of what happened next. I must have made it to Becky's house and collapsed.

"I stayed there for awhile. Her pa had died not long after being brought home. He ran out of the house one night. They found him in a pond the next day. He had fallen in and drowned. It was sad, but it was

193

probably for the best, because it freed them to start a new life. The three of us made plans to head out west to Pennsylvania or Ohio.

"Then I heard that my Aunt Margaret was in trouble. She stayed in Boston after the British left, but was being persecuted by the radicals for being married to a loyalist. She was being blamed for all the trouble even though it wasn't her fault. Her husband was dead and she was alone in the world. She sent me a note asking me to help her. I could not leave without coming to her assistance.

"I borrowed a buggy and rode into Boston. They were holding her prisoner in her own house, after stripping it of every piece of furniture, porcelain, and silver. They didn't want to let me have her at first, and were even starting to doubt my loyalties, but I recognized one of them. It was Samuel. Things became easier after that."

"Ah, dear Samuel," said Revere fondly. "So the lad came out all right in all this. He had gumption, that one. But what of you, Nathan? What did you do? Where have you been?"

"The four of us, Becky and her Mom, and Aunt Margaret headed out west to Pennsylvania, trying to get as far away from the war as possible. As you can see, since I went so long without setting my arm properly, I kind of messed it up. It ain't good for nothing these days except for swatting flies, but I managed to build a log cabin good enough so we survived the winter. Her mom died on the way out, my aunt in the spring. We fought the Indians and the weather and the wilderness. Becky had a baby girl that first year, and another, a boy, the year after. They're all gown up now with their own children. Becky, my dearest wife, died a few years ago. We had a good life together. She helped me conquer my guilt and my anger.

"I ended up going further west, out to Ohio, did some trapping and guided other pioneers. The last few years were lonely, but, that's how I wanted it. I had a lot of time to think about things."

Revere looked at the man as if he had come out of a cloud. Of all the people to show up at his death-bed this was the most unexpected, but the most fortunate as well. He had so much to say to him.

"Nate, I am so happy you have come. I have often thought about you and those times, and about what happened to you. There was so much I wanted to say to you, to tell you."

"I know. I did a terrible thing. I have spent my life atoning for it."

"That is not what I wanted to say, just the opposite. I want to tell you what a *wonderful* thing you did. You have done your country a great service. Some might even argue that if you hadn't done what you did

ISBN-10: 0-9976333-7-5

Peacock Deceiving a Suitcase
www.PeacockDeceivingASuitcase.com